continued ...

A STIFF CRITIQUE

When the most egotistical author in her writing group is murdered, it's up to Kate to find the killer—before he can plot a sequel . . .

"Very funny and entertaining . . . essential reading."
—*Mystery Week*

TEA-TOTALLY DEAD

Kate attends a dysfunctional family reunion—and someone turns the homecoming into a homicide . . .

"Another winner . . . a delightful sleuth . . . fiendish fun."
—*Margaret Lucke, author of A Relative Stranger*

FAT-FREE AND FATAL

Kate takes a vegetarian cooking class where a student is found murdered—and she must find the killer before she's dead meat herself!

"Jaqueline Girdner triumphs again."
—*Mystery Readers Journal*

MURDER MOST MELLOW

Kate teams up with a psychic to solve a murder—and the message channeled through is crystal clear: Butt out or die . . .

"It's about time someone mined the murderous minds of mellow Marin."
—*Julie Smith, Edgar Award–winning author of*
New Orleans Mourning

THE LAST RESORT

Kate muscles her way into a ritzy health club to investigate a murder—and finds that detective work may be hazardous to her life . . .

"Fresh, vivid, and off-the-wall original."
—*Carolyn G. Hart, author of Love & Death*

ADJUSTED TO DEATH

A visit to the chiropractor—who has a corpse on the examining table—teaches Kate that a pain in the neck may be pure murder . . .

"A wonderful talent."
—*Painted Rock Reviews*

A SENSITIVE KIND OF MURDER

✤

JAQUELINE
GIRDNER

BERKLEY PRIME CRIME, NEW YORK

This is a work of fiction. Names, characters, places, and incidents either are the product of the author's imagination or are used fictitiously, and any resemblance to actual persons, living or dead, business establishments, events, or locales is entirely coincidental.

A SENSITIVE KIND OF MURDER

A Berkley Prime Crime Book / published by arrangement with the author

PRINTING HISTORY
Berkley Prime Crime mass-market edition / January 2002

Visit our website at
www.penguinputnam.com

ISBN: 0-425-18315-7

Berkley Prime Crime Books are published
by The Berkley Publishing Group,
a division of Penguin Putnam Inc.,
375 Hudson Street, New York, New York 10014.
The name BERKLEY PRIME CRIME and the BERKLEY PRIME CRIME
design are trademarks belonging to Penguin Putnam Inc.

PRINTED IN THE UNITED STATES OF AMERICA

10 9 8 7 6 5 4 3 2 1

To my parents,
Audrie and Bill Girdner,
then, now, and always.

ACKNOWLEDGMENTS

Often, readers ask me where I get my ideas. In answer, I'd like to thank:

Stan Feldman for his information on men's groups;

Dorie Gores for the resurrectionist idea;

Elaine Yamaguchi for the gossip on governmental shenanigans;

Alexander Bingham for the clue that started me off;

Barbara Landis for the MAADwomen newsletter layout;

And Lynne Murray for alerting me to the possibility of super-cool spirit guides, and most especially for her unparalleled support in the department of telephonic whine and gee's parties.

Thanks, guys!

Cast of Characters

✣

Members of the Heartlink Men's Group
(and their Significant Others)

Wayne Caruso: Restauranteur and charter member of the Heartlink Group. He'll have a severe case of heartburn soon.

Kate Jasper: Wayne's wife, the "Typhoid Mary of Murder." She shares his heart; she'll probably share the burn.

Steve Summers: Journalist and professional husband. He joined Heartlink to get away from publicity's glare.

Laura Summers: Steve's wife and an honorable Member of the California State Assembly. She approves of Steve's sensitivity.

Isaac Herrick: Former professor of education and human development. He's retired to alcohol . . . and Heartlink.

HELEN HERRICK: Educator in her own right, she's retiring from her marriage to Isaac . . . by divorce.

VAN EISNER: Computer genius and full-time amorist. He hopes the men of Heartlink will steer him away from his addiction to women.

GARRETT PETERSON: African-American, gay, and worried about his partner's health. Being a psychiatrist doesn't mean he can't use the support of Heartlink.

JERRY URBAN: Garrett's partner, who has diabetes and a hot new robotic golf caddie that ought to make a fortune.

TED KIMMOCHI: Successful but unfulfilled financial advisor. He hopes Heartlink will provide him with the meaning his life has failed to deliver.

JANET MCKINNON-KIMMOCHI: Ted's wife, she's a financial advisor, too, but she isn't worried about the quality of her life.

NIKI AND ZORA KIMMOCHI: Ted and Janet's daughters, eight and thirteen . . . and a handful.

CARL RUSSO: Accountant and single father. He needs all the fatherhood help he can get from Heartlink.

MIKE RUSSO: Carl's son. He's sixteen and makes Niki and Zora Kimmochi look like angels.

THE CORTADURA POLICE DEPARTMENT

CAPTAIN YALE WOOSTER: Divorcing and bitter.

SERGEANT MARGE ABBOTT: She laughs a lot, but not around the captain.

OFFICERS ORR AND QUESADA: Nervous but loyal members of the force.

THE REMAINING PLAYERS

BARBARA CHU: Kate's friend, a psychic when it suits her.

FELIX BYRNE: Barbara's sweetie, pit bull reporter, and recent spiritual convert.

ANN RIVERA: Another friend of Kate's, uncursed by psychic powers.

GRACE KOFFENBURGER: Kate's mother.

DOROTHY KOFFENBURGER: Kate's aunt and uninvited wedding consultant.

Family, assistants, co-workers, employees, food servers, strangers, bureaucrats, and, of course, the media.

PROLOGUE

༚

The living room of the house that Garrett Peterson and Jerry Urban shared was a study in achromatism. White walls and black furnishings made the room, along with the stark black-and-white photos on the walls.

But it didn't smell achromatic. Not with the Heartlink Men's Group potluck being held there. It smelled of wine and beer and apple juice, bolstered by the mixed scents of garlic, aftershave, chocolate, deodorant, and strawberries, not to mention sweat. All the members of the Heartlink group and their significant others were boisterously contributing to the mix.

It didn't sound achromatic, either. Voices bounced off the pale walls, drowning out the Enya track playing softly from multiple speakers.

"Watch this!" Carl Russo's son ordered, and then stepped carefully, like a tightrope walker, onto the humped back of the pristine black leather couch, traversing the back with an invisible pole in his hands and a chocolate-covered strawberry sticking out of his mouth. Kate Jasper chuckled along with Carl and the Kimmochi girls. It was easy to spot the children in the crowd, whatever their ages. Who else would find Mike Russo's antics funny? Ted Kimmochi and Janet McKinnon-Kimmochi spoke loudly and earnestly to Helen Herrick and Wayne Caruso, hands waving, while Jerry Urban simultaneously munched on the last ginger snap and laughed heartily at the punch line of one of Isaac Herrick's endless series of bad jokes. Steve Summers smiled privately at his wife over Isaac's shoulder. Laura Summers smiled back. Isaac may have been older, but he certainly wasn't wiser. Garrett Peterson made the rounds, ensuring that everyone had plenty to drink. Van Eisner stuck out a wineglass and downed his measure of good merlot in a gulp once it was poured, then stuck out the wineglass again.

"A toast!" Isaac proclaimed.

"To Heartlink," Jerry finished for him.

Glasses of apple juice, beer, and wine were raised with a cheer.

Not long after the cheer had echoed off the white rafters, one of the partyers slipped away to the darkened bedroom where the beds were heaped with coats and purses. *I can do it*, the absentee thought, quickly feeling through the purses, feeling for the right one and finding it. A tingle passed though the hand that pulled the key from the ring. And through the mind that thought triumphantly, *Kate will never miss it*.

ONE

✾

I was minding my own business on that warm Wednesday in July. Honestly. It was almost noon, and I was sweating and designing gag gifts for music teachers when the phone rang.

"Kate, this is your mother," the voice on the telephone told me.

Her announcement didn't help my perspiration problem, especially once my heart began to race.

"Are you all right, Mom?" I asked, wiping my sodden face with the back of my hand.

"I'd be better if you had a real wedding," she answered and paused. My brain began to play tag with my heart. "So I'm sending out your Aunt Dorothy. She's a certified wedding coordinator—"

"But—"

"She'll be arriving on the four o'clock, afternoon flight into San Francisco tomorrow. I told her you'd pick her up—"

"But—"

"You wouldn't just leave her at the airport, would you, Kate? She's in her eighties now."

"Of course I wouldn't leave her at the airport, Mom," I said, thinking that maybe air-conditioning might help. Or an antiperspirant. "But—"

"She's made reservations at the Best Western nearest to you."

"But—"

"I know you don't really have room for her in your house." Her voice lowered. "Your brother, Kevin, told me about the state of your house."

I decided to kill my little brother later. And what was wrong with my house, anyway? I looked across the entryway that separated my home office from the living room, seeing all the loveliness of overflowing bookshelves, clutter, towering houseplants, pinball machines, and swinging chairs suspended from the ceiling. And the handmade wood-and-denim couch. Who could ask for anything more? *My mother*, a sane voice in my head answered.

And it wasn't just my house that was bugging my mother. In her opinion, a gag-gift business was no business for a woman in her forties, especially for a woman who was her daughter. And then there was my marital status. Mom had almost forgiven me for divorcing my first husband, Craig. Almost. Until she'd learned that I was living with Wayne Caruso. Then she'd thrown a ladylike and thoroughly guilt-inducing hissy fit. And finally, the marriage march had begun in her head. *Wayne and Kate, thump, Wayne and Kate, thump, Wayne and . . .* And if that wasn't bad enough, Wayne wanted to get married, too. So Wayne and I had compromised, agreeing on a brief civil ceremony that was supposed to have remained secret until the perfect time to let our loved ones know. But, of course, it hadn't. Once the shock had worn off, my mother threw another fit, this one less ladylike but just as guilt-inducing.

A brief civil ceremony wasn't enough for my mother. My mother wanted formality. Wedding dresses, bridesmaids, color coordination, guests, invitations, music, and food floated through her mind and into mine, via her mouth. Now came Aunt Dorothy. Mom couldn't have strategized her attack any more effectively. She should have been a general. She probably had been in a past life. I liked my Aunt Dorothy. How could I tell her I wasn't a willing party to my mother's plans?

Twenty minutes of phone hell later, I put the key in the ignition of my elderly Toyota, reflecting on my inability to utter the word "no" when my mother was involved. Even my keys felt strange in my hand. They felt lighter, for one thing, and they seemed to jingle differently. I attributed the difference to the effect of talking to my mother. Everything always felt weird after talking to Mom. I turned the key, applied my hands to the oven-hot steering wheel, and backed out of my driveway, popping gravel as I went. I was going to be late for my twelve o'clock lunch date with Wayne. How had it happened that I had not managed to make clear to my mother that I didn't want a formal wedding? That I'd *hate* a formal wedding?

I tore my brain away from Mom and forced myself to think about something else. Wayne's Heartlink Men's Group was always good for extended speculation, I decided as I urged my Toyota onto the highway entrance. My car was of an age at which it needed a reassuring—"you can make it"— every once in a while, not to mention the reassurance *I* needed.

Wayne and Steve Summers had started the Heartlink Men's Sensitivity Group some years back, along with a couple of other guys who'd eventually dropped out. Over the years, sensitivity had given way to support, but the group still lived on, and Wayne still attended the group meetings, from ten to twelve, two Wednesdays a month. And I met him for an after-meeting lunch whenever I could.

Excepting Wayne, of course, the members of Heartlink were as weird as . . . well, as my home county of Marin, in my opinion. Steve was too quiet for a journalist, Garrett too sad for a psychiatrist, Ted too flighty for a financial advisor, Isaac too childish for an elder statesman of education, Mike Russo too emotional for an accountant, and Van Eisner was too irresponsible for anything, much less his own successful business. These were my own observations, however. Wayne had certainly never expressed those opinions.

Wayne was a man who took the concept of "confidentiality" seriously. He never told me what was said at the meetings. And it drove me crazy, as much as I admired his scrupulous nature. But I had eyes, not to mention ears. And every second month, the Heartlink Group allowed its members and significant others to mingle at a potluck at one lucky member's house. Garrett had hosted the most recent one a week before. I'd heard the jokes, complaints, and significant silences of the members. They were weird, all right, no matter what Wayne did or didn't say.

Despite my feelings about the members of the group, I had to admit they had staying power. The seven met faithfully, no member missing a group without good reason. And they did seem to be a support for Wayne. He certainly didn't need any more sensitivity—any more sensitivity and he'd be out saving the whales with his own outstretched arms.

Two exits down, and I was on my way into Cortadura. I could feel the temperature cool as I headed down Main Street. Ah, heaven. Cortadura was on the beach. At least the tourist part was.

Cortadura was a town with a split personality. The beach-front was lined with T-shirt shops, poster shops, over-priced restaurants, and every kind of novelty outlet that you could think of, from crystals to puppets to Native American artifacts. But Main Street led to the old downtown section. This part of Cortadura was inland by ten or so blocks, still solidly small-town, with brick buildings, civic pride, and less-traveled streets.

The library in Cortadura was big enough to offer a meeting place for the Heartlink group. Theirs was one library that hadn't downsized in space or availability. The taxes generated by the tourist trade probably helped. And nothing much ever changed in downtown Cortadura, unlike the tourist section, which sported a new shop or restaurant every week. Still, the ocean's coolness filtered all through the town, indiscriminate of nouveau tourism or downtown traditions.

I was enjoying the rush of air coming through my open front window when two of the dreaded tourist species jay-walked in front of my car. I could tell they were tourists by their shorts, cameras, and the merry smiles they flashed my way as I screeched around them, missing them by a good yard.

"Go that way!" I yelled, pointing my finger out the window, back toward the beach.

They smiled again and kept walking in the wrong direction.

I took a deep breath and told my car to calm down. And I reminded myself that I was also a tourist when not in my home county. But even so, I didn't dart in front of old cars. Cool air or not, I was sweating again. That encounter had been too close for me.

Now I had two things not to think about: my mother and the possibility of accidentally hitting someone with my car.

I let my mind drift back to Heartlink, wondering for the hundredth time why each of the members of the Heartlink group *did* stay.

I thought about Garrett Peterson. He was a psychiatrist and a genuinely nice man. His dance card had to be filled with friends. And his lover, Jerry Urban, was a laugh-a-minute kind of guy despite his recent diagnosis of diabetes. What did Garrett need with the group? It didn't seem to make him any happier.

Mind you, I'd asked Wayne these questions, but of course he hadn't answered.

And what did Isaac Herrick need with the group? I used to think he'd been using them as an alternative to Alcoholics Anonymous, but he'd never stopped drinking, not even after his wife, Helen, had left him because of the alcohol. She was currently filing for divorce, though they claimed they were still friends. And I believed that they really were still friends; they had come to the last potluck together. Neither of them could have been younger than eighty. Somehow, I didn't think they'd just go their separate ways completely after the years they must have spent together.

And then there were Ted Kimmochi and his wife, Janet McKinnon-Kimmochi. Ted had two little girls, Niki and Zora, as well as a successful financial consulting firm. But the way he slunk around, sighing melodramatically, you'd think his life was tragic. Maybe it was. How would I know? Wayne wasn't about to tell me.

Still, I could almost see why Steve Summers came to the

group. His wife, Laura, was a member of the state assembly.
The group was probably the one place he could be himself,
out of the glare of the spotlight. But as a journalist, he'd
certainly done his share of shining the spotlight. There was
irony there somewhere.

Come to think of it, Carl Russo needed the group, too,
being a single father of a teenager, and a goofy teenager at
that. And Van Eisner needed all the help he could get, with
his string of women, and, I suspected, drugs. Not that Wayne
would confirm my suspicion of drugs, of course. I felt a little
growl start in the back of my throat, surprising me. Was I
mad at my own sweetie? I couldn't be, could I?

Wayne's continued attendance at Heartlink was really
what I didn't understand. What was it that he got out of the
group? Something that he didn't get from me? That little
growl burbled up again and, for a moment, I glimpsed the
jealousy that fueled my hostility toward the Heartlink Group.
Even my car seemed to feel it, delicately coughing as it continued forward. I shook my head. Other women had to worry
about other women, and I was jealous about Wayne's support
group. I chuckled, glad again that I was married to my loyal,
if occasionally frustrating, sweetheart.

Still, I knew something had gone wrong with the last
Heartlink group meeting. I knew it from the way Wayne had
shut down when he'd come home afterward. I knew it from
the faint distance members had put between themselves at
the last potluck. Even the wives and children and lovers had
seemed different at the potluck. Of course, *their* significant
others had probably told *them* what had happened, unlike my
own confidence-honoring Wayne. I shook my head again,
hard this time. My obsession with his group was definitely
getting unhealthy. I was going to overheat before my Toyota
did.

Was it jealousy that had made me feel such an urgent need
to have lunch with Wayne after today's group? Because I
had felt an urgent need. My pulse quickened again, just
thinking about the feelings I'd experienced when Wayne had
left for the group this morning. Dread, anxiety . . . forebod-
ing? I told myself I'd been friends with a psychic too long.

I just wanted to see Wayne for lunch. That was all. Just in case. But just in case of what?

I shook off the shiver that settled on my shoulders just as I spotted a parking space in front of the Cortadura Library. I slid my Toyota into the space carefully, turning off the engine and saying a "thank you" to my car for getting me there.

And then I saw Wayne, walking out of the library with Steve Summers. I smiled upon seeing him, his battered face serious under his low brows. My Wayne, always so serious. But Steve's slender, lined face looked serious, too. He squinted through his wire-rimmed glasses and said something to Wayne. I stopped smiling. I wondered what they were talking about. Wayne nodded and touched Steve's shoulder, the male equivalent of a hug.

The two men parted company at the sidewalk and Steve made his way across the road in the crosswalk, turning to wave at Wayne once more. No jay-walking for him—Steve Summers was a straight arrow.

I opened my car door, already imagining myself hugging Wayne hello. But I never got that far.

A car came screaming down the road, a car that looked familiar.

When the car hit Steve, he was flung into the air as if in slow motion, but he landed with a definite crunch—a crunch that would make me sick later, but that was too surreal now. And then the car backed up and ran over him.

My body was immobilized. Then I figured it out.

It had to be a dream.

Because the car that had hit Steve Summers and was now speeding away was Wayne's own Jaguar.

Two

I stared at the back of the bottle-green Jaguar racing down the road for less than the time it took to let out my indrawn breath. I couldn't read the license plate; it was obscured by something like mud. But even in the time it took me to exhale, I saw the dent I'd put in the car three years ago, backing up into a concrete stanchion. There was no question left in my mind. The fleeing car was Wayne's vintage Jaguar.

As I stared for that ever-so-brief moment in time, I wondered if I'd just seen an accident. *No*, I told myself. When I'd almost hit the tourists, that had been an accident. But I'd swerved to go around them. And I hadn't backed up over them. And I most certainly hadn't been driving Wayne's car.

Wayne's car? The thought galvanized me, finally. I wasn't immobile anymore. Someone had run over Steve Summers with Wayne's car. Whatever had just happened, it was likely that Wayne would be blamed. My limbs began to move again. And my mouth.

"You take care of Steve," I yelled at Wayne, who was already running toward Steve's body. "I'll follow the car!"

And then I began chasing the Jaguar on foot. It never even occurred to me to get back into my own car, which was probably just as well—considering my car's age, I could probably outrun it.

But I couldn't outrun Wayne's Jaguar. As I ran, I watched

the car get further and further away, until it was out of sight. My legs were strong, but my lungs ached and I couldn't get enough air. For once, I wished I'd taken up jogging instead of tai chi sixteen years earlier. The car disappeared altogether as it turned onto one of the side streets that led to the beachfront.

Still, I kept running. It seemed endless. I couldn't even guess how long my legs had been pumping. And then, in that endless time, I turned onto the same street the Jaguar had taken and saw the car again, parked at the end of the street, blocks away, by the water.

I ran even faster then, or maybe I only imagined that I did. Finally, I reached the Jaguar. I couldn't see the driver inside. I leaned up against the door, panting and sweating like a summer storm. Then I peeked in the window. No one lurked inside the Jaguar. It was empty, absolutely empty.

I jerked my head to the side, surveying the scene, hoping to spot the driver. But all I saw was a collage of tourists, milling around, looking murky though my sweat-obscured eyeballs. I reached for the handle on the Jaguar's door, then thought better of it. I wasn't exactly sure what had happened back at the library. In fact, I wasn't sure I even wanted to know what had happened. But whatever I had witnessed, I was sure the police wouldn't want me touching the car.

With that thought, I collapsed, letting my bottom hit the pavement. There was nothing more I could do. I had run, but I had lost. So I sat there, feeling the ocean breeze cool my wet body, still searching the faces around me to no avail as my breathing began to slow to a series of controlled gasps.

"You okay?" a man in madras shorts yelled.

"Fine," I tried to call out. My voice squeaked. I waved to show my okay-ness, and then the man was gone.

I tried not to think as I sat there regaining my breath. But of course that didn't work any better than chasing the car had. Steve Summers had been hit by Wayne's Jaguar and run over. The breeze felt too cold now. Steve Summers had to be dead. And I had left Wayne there alone with him.

I wish I could say that I had run all the way back to Wayne, but I just wasn't able to do it. Whatever adrenaline had buoyed me to the beach was all gone. I was shaky and my feet hurt. Still, I pulled myself up to a standing position and limped my way back to the Cortadura Library.

Wayne was out front when I got there, standing guard over Steve's body.

As I walked the last few yards to Wayne, he said, "Steve's dead. I've called the police."

I closed my eyes for a moment. Until he'd said it, I'd hoped I'd seen something incorrectly. But I'd seen it all too clearly. And now Wayne's friend was dead.

"What's taking the police so long?" I asked. "I must have been gone for at least twenty minutes, maybe more."

"I didn't call them right away," Wayne explained. "I sat with Steve. I . . ."

"Oh, Wayne," I whispered and held him. He was shaking like he'd been the one doing the running. Then I realized that standing with Steve's body had probably been the harder task.

"What can I do?" I asked him. "Can I—"

And then we heard the sirens.

The first members of the Cortadura Police Department had arrived.

The police car screeched up to the curb and a uniformed man and woman jumped out, their guns drawn. Wayne and I parted from our embrace in record time.

"Get away from the body," the woman yelled.

Wayne and I walked slowly away from the crosswalk where Steve Summers lay.

Wayne cleared his throat. "I called in the incident, officers," he informed them quietly.

"Name?" asked the male officer.

"Wayne Caruso."

"Who's she?" the officer continued, swiveling his head toward me.

"Kate Jasper, my wife."

The guns were holstered. Both the man and the woman looked disappointed. I wondered how much excitement the CPD usually offered them.

Before I could answer my own question, an ambulance

skidded to the curb, an unmarked car screeching in right behind it.

As paramedics hopped out of the ambulance, a new uniformed man and woman stepped from the unmarked car. The uniformed man was young, with a long, brown face and dark eyes under a buzzcut; the woman could have been his twin, but with blue eyes and pink skin under a blond perm.

And then an older man pushed himself out of the back seat of the unmarked car. He was a man who would have looked better with a beard, I thought uncharitably, but he probably wasn't allowed that much facial hair as a policeman. Still, he had a jaw you could hang a hat off of, a long nose with overdefined nostrils like a horse's, and the meanest eyes I'd seen since my high school algebra teacher's.

"Where the hell is Marge?" he asked.

"Marge?" I repeated.

"I wasn't asking you," he growled. "Samson's hair! Are you one of the witnesses?"

I nodded. "Kate Jasper. And you?" I asked. Sometimes my mouth works without permission.

"Captain Yale Wooster of the Cortadura Police Department," he answered me, with a long glare to top off his introduction. I didn't offer to shake hands.

Minutes later, the paramedics were gone. They had agreed with Wayne: Steve Summers was dead. Three of the uniformed officers, Captain Wooster, and Wayne and I were seated in the meeting room of the Cortadura Library where the Heartlink groups were held. The chairs were old, comfortable, and well-padded. The table was real wood. The ceilings were high, and light streamed into the windows. The room smelled of age and books. It should have been a place to be content. But the other officer was out with Steve Summers' body. And someone from the county was setting up a tent to shield the scene. They'd arrived and started that process before the rest of us had even walked into the library.

"Okay," Captain Wooster barked. "So you both saw this car hit your friend and back over him. What else?"

"It was my car," Wayne mumbled.

"What?"

"The car that hit Steve Summers was mine," Wayne said more clearly. "My Jaguar."

"Who'd you give the keys to?" the captain demanded.

"No one."

"Oh, come on!" He banged his fist on the table. "Mary's handbag! You expect me to believe that?"

"Yes, sir," Wayne answered quietly but firmly.

Then, countless variations of this conversation were played out, seemingly as endless as the time I'd taken chasing down the car. I wasn't even being questioned and my head was spinning, not to mention the sudden ache in my legs. I closed my eyes for a moment—the wrong moment.

"Awfully convenient, Ms. Jasper," Captain Wooster's voice broke into my reverie. "You being there while your hubby's car takes this guy out."

"Huh?" I replied reasonably.

The captain thrust his face into mine, sneering. I just hoped he wouldn't hit me with his jaw.

"You wouldn't just be making up this little story, would you?" he asked.

"No, sir," I said firmly, taking my cue from Wayne.

And then countless variations on the captain's *new* theme were carried out. Maybe he hadn't been born with that jaw I thought. Maybe it'd just grown and grown after years of interrogation.

Finally he settled back into his seat and tried another tack.

"Okay, what did you see?"

Wayne and I both said "huh" together, then made the inner cranial turn necessary to follow the captain's new direction.

"The driver was wearing some sort of black cowl," Wayne murmured thoughtfully.

"Yeah," I agreed. "Like a big scarf wrapped around the head."

"A cowl? A scarf?" The captain sneered some more. "Did you see their face?"

"No," Wayne answered. "Whoever it was wore dark glasses, too."

"That's right," I muttered, remembering.

"Man or woman?"

"Couldn't tell," Wayne told him. I just nodded. Even without the scarf and dark glasses, it had all been too fast, a blur.

"Real convenient, sorta like Moses being found in a basket," Captain Wooster put in. I wasn't sure what he meant exactly, but I nodded anyway.

"I chased the car—" I began.

"You what?" he shouted.

"I ran after the Jaguar—"

"On foot?" he demanded incredulously.

"Yeah, and I found it, too." I crossed my arms and sat back in my seat. I couldn't help it.

The captain leaned forward in his chair and asked, "And who was in the car when you found it, Ms. Jasper?"

"Um," I muttered, uncrossing my arms. "No one."

"No one! Noah's tub toys!"

After what seemed like a few hundred other questions, Captain Wooster finally stopped to ask where I'd found the car and sent one of the uniformed officers to call the location into headquarters.

"And have them seal it off!" he hollered. "That car's a murder weapon."

Wayne looked sick, even sicker than he had before. His battered face was white, and his eyes were rolling in their sockets under his low brows.

"Someone else must have seen the . . . incident," I interjected, giving Wayne a chance to take a breath before he keeled over.

The captain snorted. He looked at the two remaining officers. "Anyone come forward with a report yet?" he asked them.

"No, sir," they replied in unison.

"Got any more bright ideas?" the captain asked, and went on before I had a chance to answer.

"Why were you and your friend here, anyway?" he asked Wayne. I snuck a peek. At least Wayne's eyes weren't rolling anymore. His skin tone had ripened to a bilious yellow.

"We were here for the meeting of our Heartlink Men's Group," Wayne informed him.

"You mean there were other people here?" the head of the

Cortadura Police Department demanded. "Ice cream in hell, why didn't you tell me that in the first place?"

I thought Wayne was prudent in not attempting a reply. Anyway, the captain was changing directions again.

"So you and some other guys were at some wuss group?"

I opened my mouth to object to the wording, but Wayne just nodded.

"Were any of them still around when your friend got hit by *your* car?"

"Don't think so," Wayne murmured.

"But each of them knew what time Steve Summers was leaving the group?"

Wayne nodded.

"Hot damn!" the captain bawled. "I want names, addresses, and phone numbers on all of them, you hear me?"

Wayne nodded. He wasn't deaf. Yet.

An officer handed my sweetie some paper.

Wayne began writing, taking out his own notebook from his pocket to work from.

"His wife knew, too," I added helpfully. "I mean, she knew when he was leaving."

"Who's his wife?"

"Laura Summers."

"Damn," Wooster said beneath his breath. "Not the assemblywoman?"

I bobbed my head up and down, glad to hear him whispering for a change. But it didn't last long.

"Quesada!" he yelled at one of his officers. "Get that woman down here, pronto!"

"The assemblywoman, sir?" the officer with the long face asked.

Officer Quesada's clarification was a string of prosaic invective that was apparently reserved for the captain's own staff.

"Here are all the names, addresses, and phone numbers, sir," Wayne declared, handing the captain his list.

"Okay, you, Orr, get all of these clowns down here now, and I mean now!"

Officer Orr didn't ask for clarification. She just got up and grabbed the list. I hoped all she had to do was call these guys, not pick up each one personally.

"And where in purgatory is Marge?" Captain Wooster whined.

"Here, Captain," a good-sized woman with large hands and strong features answered as she came into the room. I could hear the South in those two words. And I smelled something like lilac. It was a nice change from the scent of communal sweat. "Lord, lord," she went on. "You gonna calm down and act like real folks now?"

Amazingly, Wooster did calm down. He filled her in on the situation, at length. "So we got this car. And him." He pointed at Wayne. "And a wife. And a group of 'sensitive' guys who mights have seen it—"

"And their wives, kids, and partners?" I couldn't help adding.

Wooster whirled his head my way.

"Well, it makes sense," I explained. "They probably all knew about the group and when it ended. I did."

So Wayne had to write-out a whole new list of names, though most of the addresses and phone numbers were the same.

"I want them all in here!" the captain bellowed at the last officer standing, the one who'd phoned in about the car.

And he got them. Assemblywoman Laura Summers was first. Officer Quesada led Laura Summers in, announcing that she'd been alone at her house, hers and Steve Summers' house.

I watched Captain Wooster. How would he handle the soon-to-be-grieving widow? Wasn't there supposed to be some gentleness here, some protocol? Wouldn't it be better to give her the news in the privacy of her home? Assemblywoman Laura Summers was a large woman with an all-American face, blue eyes, golden hair, and a pert nose. And a concerned expression that didn't look any more feigned now than it ever did. Laura was always concerned—about the rights of children, the rights of senior citizens, the rights of—

"Tell me what's going on *now*, Captain," she demanded

quietly. Determination was in her eyes, but there was fear there, too. My chest hurt, watching her. Was that my heart?

Captain Wooster asked her to sit, with all the consideration he was probably capable of mustering, which consisted of lowering his voice into normal range and contorting his features into something less angry.

"That won't be necessary, Captain," she replied, her voice slow and serious. Even slower and more serious than usual.

"Would you like to find somewhere more private?" he asked her.

"No," she replied. She glanced at Wayne and me. "These are my friends. Whatever you have to tell me you can tell me here. And now." There was no mistaking the command in her voice. The captain complied.

"Your husband was hit by a car," he told her. "The car then backed up and ran over him. He's dead."

Laura Summers stood like a rock, the only change her skin tone, which seemed to be graying. And her eyes; her eyes sparkled with something. It might have been tears, or anger, or something else entirely.

"Oh, Laura, I'm so sorry—" I began.

The captain's glare cut me off as efficiently as a chain saw.

I suppose it was just as well. I couldn't think of the right words to say, anyway. And I lost sight of Laura's face as Marge got up and put her arms around the new widow. Laura stiffened at her first touch, but then seemed to melt into the support Marge was offering. Big as Laura Summers was, Marge was bigger, at least for the time being.

My own eyes filled then. Poor Laura. Steve was gone. I literally couldn't imagine what she must have been feeling. And she wouldn't be able to grieve privately for long. Her whole life belonged to the public. Damn. It just wasn't fair.

I heard voices from the other room. Garrett's, I thought, and Jerry Urban's. And maybe Van Eisner's.

Did Laura hear them, too?

Suddenly, she pushed her way out of Marge's arms and turned to face Captain Wooster, eyes still glittering.

"Who did it?" she demanded.

"We don't know," the captain replied, and I almost felt sorry for him.

"I will expect you to find out," Laura told him.

"Expect away, then," the captain challenged, whatever gentleness he'd been exercising gone now. "Eve's apples, for all we know it might have been you, Assemblywoman." He made fists with his hands. "It's the wife every other time. If they can't divorce you, they kill you."

Laura Summers seemed to grow taller in front of us.

"I am a member of the California State Assembly," she pronounced.

"Well, I'm a member of the royal donkey society," the captain countered. "I'm trying to be fair here, so don't pull rank on me. I don't care if you're the president. You're a suspect."

Laura didn't even flinch. Maybe this rude treatment was what she needed to keep her sane. "Are you courting a lawsuit?" she asked.

"Nah," the captain answered. "I'm courting an early retirement."

"Ma'am, I'm Sergeant Marge Abbott," Marge intervened. "Ya gotta forgive the captain. His mouth's enough to make ya wanna wear earplugs sometimes, but he's going through a rough time."

And Laura Summers wasn't going through a rough time? Marge must have caught my thought.

"Ma'am," she said, her voice tender now. "You aren't going to get over this easy, I know. And you're angry now. That's good. Real good. But the captain isn't the one to take it out on. We'll find your husband's killer. Make it easy for us."

Laura shrunk back down to normal size.

"Is there someone who can take care of you?" Marge asked.

"I called my personal assistant," Laura mumbled, her head down. "She should be here by now. Our son is away at college."

The captain nodded at Officer Quesada. The officer went

to the other room and brought in a well-dressed young woman with a frightened look on her face.

"Ms. Summers?" she asked.

"Julie, take me home," Laura Summers ordered.

Julie took her arm to lead her out of the room. Laura Summers didn't look like an assemblywoman anymore. She looked like a widow.

"One last thing, Assemblywoman Summers," the captain interjected. "Where have you been for the last hour?"

"Shopping," she mumbled, her voice sounding drugged. "And then I went home to wait for Steve."

Now my chest really hurt. I glared at the captain as Laura's assistant led her from the room.

Wayne stood up then. "May we leave, sir?" he asked.

"Siddown!" the captain thundered. "Women!" he snorted.

Wayne sat back down as Captain Wooster gave his orders. "Bring in the others, one by one, or in couples."

Van Eisner was next. I knew from the potluck gossip that Eisner had a reputation as a lady's man, but it was hard to believe, looking at him. Van was slight, short and balding, with sharp little features that could have been drawn by a cartoonist—sharp, pointy little chin, sharp nose, and nasty little eyes.

"Look," he whined as he was escorted in. "Whatever happened, it wasn't me, okay?"

It was not okay. Van Eisner shifted and turned in his seat as Wooster prodded and probed. The best Eisner had was an alibi of sorts. He had met with a client some time after the group broke up, but he still would have had time to hit Steve with Wayne's car and make it to the appointment.

After even more questions than my mother had asked me about Wayne that morning, Captain Wooster finally got to a good one for Eisner.

"How come you haven't asked what happened?"

Van looked up, his little eyes squinting.

"I don't wanna know," he cried, and that was that. The captain let him go.

Why Captain Wooster kept Wayne and me there was a mystery. Maybe he did it because he realized we really were blameless witnesses? Nah, not likely, I decided. So we were still there as Garrett Peterson and Jerry Urban were led into the room. Garrett was a handsome man with cinnamon-colored skin and a bullet-shaped skull, offset by wide, friendly features and wide-set, gentle eyes. This was in contrast to his lover, Jerry Urban, who was older and molded more along the lines of a benign bear, with a round face, full cheeks, and a constant smile. Well, almost constant. It wasn't on his face now.

"Are you two all right?" Garrett asked Wayne and me as he entered the room. This was typical of Garrett. He was a psychiatrist, after all.

"Never mind about those two," the captain advised, getting right to the point. "Where were you two for the past hour?" Jerry had been at work at his robotic golf caddie start-up company, and Garrett had driven to visit him after the group meeting. But still, the gap in time was not enough for a perfect alibi.

"Is Steve all right?" Garrett asked after his round of interrogation.

"No," the captain answered.

"But—"

"Why did you ask?" the captain prodded, leaning forward.

"I saw Laura Summers on her way out," Garrett answered solemnly.

They were dismissed.

Before the next interrogatees came in, Wayne had a question of his own.

"Sir, when can I have my car back?"

Well, at least that brightened the captain's day. He sat back in his chair and roared with laughter.

"Your car is evidence, now, boy," he finally answered. "Wanna clue? Think Armageddon."

Then Ted Kimmochi and his wife came in. Ted's perfect oval face was blessed with a round nose and expressive eyes under dark brows. Unfortunately, his expression was usually tragic. Today, at least, it was appropriate. Janet McKinnon-Kimmochi looked a lot like Ted, except that she wasn't Asian, and her round nose was scattered with freckles, her oval face topped with red hair. Her expression was not tragic, however—it was irritated.

"We have clients waiting," she announced as she sailed into the room with Ted in tow. "What's this all about?"

"I'll ask the questions," Captain Wooster assured her. And he did, at length. Ted's alibi was driving to the office (and Janet's, being at the office), but still that wasn't a real alibi because he arrived there after Steve Summers had already been hit by Wayne's car.

"This is awful," Ted murmured. "Just awful. Something terrible has happened, hasn't it?"

"Yep," the captain agreed and let them go.

I had a feeling that even Captain Wooster's energy had its limits, and those limits were sorely tried by the arrival of a drunken Isaac Herrick, accompanied by his soon-to-be-ex-wife, Helen. He had visited her after the group, but, of course, not soon enough to let him off the hook for Steve Summers' death.

The captain's interrogation was interrupted by Isaac's jokes, guffaws, and scatological references. Helen might have been mute. But Isaac, even in his drunken state, was worried. I could tell by the unease with which he delivered his jokes, and by the worry in his weathered red face, its redness accented by his white, wavy hair. He took off his black-rimmed glasses and polished them, and I saw even more worry in his bleary eyes, a look that was reflected on Helen's plump, no-nonsense face.

"Bad?" he asked finally.

Helen looked at the captain, her intelligent eyes searching . . . and finding.

But the captain didn't answer. Marge did.

"Bad," she confirmed.

Carl Russo was the last one to be escorted in. His son Mike wasn't with him. If you wanted to go by looks alone, Carl would be your man for murder. He was a broad man with fleshy features and a habitual, guarded look of disinterest. He squirmed through all of the captain's questions. Carl had no particular alibi. He had driven down to the beach to think after the group. He wouldn't say what he was thinking about, but I would have bet it was his absent son, Mike.

After Wooster had finished with Carl, he turned to Wayne and me with one word: "Go!"

We went. As fast as we could stumble out of the room.

None of the group members were left in the main room of the library. I was initially surprised, but then I saw the policeman who had probably chased them away.

On the way home in my Toyota, I prodded Wayne about Laura. Was Captain Wooster right? Was it usually the wife? I thought of her slumped shoulders and graying skin; but still . . .

"Did Steve want a divorce?" I asked Wayne, not really expecting an answer.

"No, he adored her," he told me, his voice gruff with tears.

"This was her day off," I reminded him. I remembered her talking about it at the potluck, how she had to have one day out of the public eye, one day alone with her husband when the legislature wasn't in session. "Wasn't that awfully convenient for her?"

"She took the day off to be with Steve," Wayne murmured. "You know Laura and Steve, they were Frick and Frack. They agreed on politics, on ethics, on everything." His voice faltered.

"All right," I conceded. "Not Laura Summers. But who else would want to kill Steve Summers?"

"Journalist," Wayne muttered.

"He made someone angry with his articles?"

Wayne made a sound that was somewhere between a cry and a whimper.

"We talked about our worst secrets," he whispered.

THREE

✦

"What?" I yelped, my Toyota swerving to the left. I righted it, the hairs raising on my arms, just thinking of the damage a car could do.

"Well . . . it's all confidential—"

"Wayne, there isn't any more confidentiality. Steve is dead. And your worst secrets—"

"You're right," he mumbled.

Whoa. Did he really say that? Did he mean it? If he did, I wasn't going to waste an opportunity to ask questions. We were almost to the highway entrance, and I wanted to know as much as possible before I had to concentrate on helping my car onto the ramp.

"What happened?" I asked softly, adding, "Tell me everything," a little less softly.

Wayne was silent for a moment, and I thought he'd changed his mind already, but then he began to speak. When he did, his words came faster than usual, as if they'd been waiting at the door to tumble out.

"It was Isaac's idea," he explained. "He thought we should all tell our very worst secrets to test the bonds of the group. So he pressured everyone until they did."

"That sounds like Isaac," I muttered, picturing the elder man's drunken smile. "The man always has been an accident looking for a place to happen." I regretted my choice of words the moment they were out, but luckily Wayne didn't seem to notice.

"Exactly. Isaac just wanted to stir the pot. You know how he always watched everyone. Or maybe you didn't," Wayne amended, remembering suddenly that I wasn't a member of the group. He was silent again.

I quickly glanced his way. His eyebrows were at half-mast, covering a good portion of his eyes. Did he already think he'd said too much?

"What were the secrets?" I prodded, keeping my voice calmer than my tingling body felt.

"Kate, I'm not sure I should say," Wayne objected, his face reddening. Was that heat or shame? Or something else entirely? "What if these secrets have nothing to do with the murder? What if the murderer was somebody who had nothing to do with the group?"

"What do you think the chances of that are?" I shot back, as the entrance sign for the highway loomed.

Wayne sighed in answer.

I urged my car onto the highway gently, realizing I had to handle Wayne the same way.

"Did everyone tell their secrets?"

"Yes," Wayne answered, as if enduring Gestapo interrogation.

And then the Toyota was skimming along in the slow lane, just like Wayne. Warm air whooshed in through the half-open windows.

"Van Eisner's secret was about drugs, I'll bet," I hazarded.

I could feel Wayne stiffen in his seat.

"You noticed?" he asked.

"I guessed."

He sighed again. "Well, you were right," he finally admitted. "Van keeps talking about being a sex addict. All those women. But when Isaac asked him his *worst* secret, he said he did cocaine with a lot of those women and then went on a long spiel about how great it was. I think it took him a while to realize that no one else was as entranced as he was. Then he begged us all not to tell."

"Cocaine use is illegal," I murmured over the groan of the Toyota's engine. "Blackmail material."

"I know," was all that Wayne said in reply. He didn't have to say that Steve wasn't the blackmailing type.

Poor Wayne, my Dudley-Do-Right with confidentiality issues. He'd probably been trying to get Eisner into rehab.

"Have you suggested that Van get some help for his drug problem?" I enquired.

"I even got him the names and numbers of clinics, but it's no use," Wayne replied. My suspicions were confirmed.

I may not have understood the other group members, but I understood my sweetie. In fact, I understood him well enough to know that I should change the subject before he imploded from guilt.

"How about Isaac?" I asked.

"His wife wrote parts of his book," Wayne answered, not even bothering to resist anymore, probably because he considered the whole thing Isaac's fault anyway.

"Helen?" I asked stupidly, my brain slack with shock. Isaac's claim to fame was his raft of books about dyslexia and other developmental disabilities.

Wayne nodded. "From what Isaac said, Helen did the bulk of the research and writing of his books—"

"And he took credit?" I demanded, outraged.

"Isaac claims it was a mutual agreement. Claims that men were more likely to be taken seriously than women when he first began writing, that Helen would have lacked credibility on her own."

I could feel Wayne turning to me. I glanced and saw that his eyes were pleading for forgiveness for a man who he didn't even like very much. I gripped the steering wheel tight enough to whiten my knuckles, but I kept my mouth shut about Isaac. If Wayne was in a pleading mood, he just might answer all of my questions.

"What about Ted?" I probed.

Wayne took a deep breath and dived into further betrayal.

"Ted meditates. Feels he's very spiritual. But he admitted that he thinks of food a lot when he meditates."

I chuckled. "Is his mantra 'chocolate'?"

Wayne didn't share my amusement.

"We laughed, too," he announced solemnly. "Until he told us that his *real* worst secret was his affair with some woman he met at Spirit Rock."

"Uh-oh," I said slowly.

I could feel Wayne's nod. "If Janet ever found out, Ted would have to meditate on broken bones," he predicted.

I thought about Ted's wife, Janet McKinnon-Kimmochi. She was a strong woman, a woman with children (including Ted, I thought sometimes), a woman who ruled the financial advice firm they owned jointly with an iron hand. Nope, I wouldn't want to risk exposure to that iron hand, and I was sure Ted didn't want to, either.

"So what's he gonna do?" I asked.

"He cut off the affair with the woman from Spirit Rock. Told her his spirit guides advised him to."

I bristled, but kept it internal. No wonder Wayne hadn't told me this stuff. Now I wanted to punch out Isaac *and* Ted. I felt the blood run to my face. Spirit guide consultation, the Marin excuse for anything. And who was this poor woman who'd been attracted to the king of self-tragedy, anyway? A needy woman, I answered myself. It was time to move on. We were almost to our exit.

"Russo's worried about his kid, right?" I guessed.

"How'd you know?" Wayne replied.

"My spirit guides told me."

"Kate!"

"I'm sorry," I said and reached over to pat his thigh. "I can just tell, sweetie. Carl Russo's worried sick over Mike. He's always watching him like he'll explode or something. And Mike seems like a perfectly nice kid, for a sixteen-year-old."

"It's sad, Kate," Wayne began slowly. I could tell he was weighing how much he should divulge. And then he just let it spill. "Carl's wife had a big drug and alcohol problem, but Carl left Mike with her anyway when he went to work. One day, when Mike was a toddler, he came home to find that his wife was passed out, and Mike had a big lump on his head. Carl was afraid to take Mike to the doctor, was trying to protect his wife. And then it happened again. Carl finally left her, but not until he was really afraid for Mike. He's sure that Mike's a problem now because of the head injuries and general abuse. Isaac agrees with him."

"But Mike doesn't seem like a problem to me," I protested.

"He's not, really. You've seen the kid. He can be a clown, make people laugh. Still . . ." Wayne paused and took a deep breath. "Mike and his friends stole a car and went joy-riding recently. Luckily, they didn't get caught. And he's vandalized things. Done all the stuff a troubled teenager does. Carl's worried it'll get worse."

I shook my head. What constituted a "normal" teenager? I couldn't help but think that Mike would make it through his teenage years without major mishap, but then I wasn't his parent.

"How about Garrett?" I asked as I aimed the Toyota toward the highway exit. "What could he have possibly done that he thinks was wrong?"

Wayne's voice slowed as the Toyota pulled onto the road that would lead us home.

"You know Garrett, how much he cares for his patients?"

"Yeah."

"There was this kid, six years ago. Garrett was his psychiatrist. The kid told Garrett he was going to commit suicide, but Garrett thought he was bluffing. He wasn't. He killed himself that night."

Damn. Poor Garrett. I was sure the group had assured him that it wasn't his fault. Patient suicide had to be a professional risk for any psychiatrist. But Garrett would feel guilty. He was like Wayne that way.

I didn't have to ask Wayne's secret—I already knew it. He'd failed to protect the man who'd hired him as a bodyguard. Or at least that's the way he perceived his boss's death, a boss who had become his friend. And Wayne had never gotten over that perceived failure.

We were almost home when I realized I hadn't asked what Steve Summers' worst secret was.

"Wayne," I started. "What about—"

"Kate, stop," Wayne ordered.

"Huh?" I spit out, startled. "I thought you were willing to talk to me."

"I am. I meant stop the car," he explained sheepishly. "We have to get groceries."

And then I realized we'd never had lunch. That was why my insides were gurgling and growling for attention. Though neither of us had an appetite, Wayne would see it as his duty to feed me.

By the time I'd stopped the Toyota, we'd already passed the local health food supermarket, so I drove around the block and eased my tired car into a parking space, dropping my keys back into my purse, lost in thought.

Wayne and I shopped mostly in silence. Under his instruction, I stalked the aisles for basil, eggplant, and three kinds of marinated tofu as we each thought about Steve. Steve might have been dead, but the market was alive. A man in a business suit and a ponytail raced his cart past me while a mother cooed to her screaming child, "Serena, please be quiet." Bad choice of a name, I thought and found the jasmine rice. Wayne didn't seem to see or hear anyone. He shopped mechanically, dropping healthy groceries into the basket and occasionally asking me to find something for him.

The woman at the checkout counter wished us a "harmonious day" once she'd been paid. *Too late*, I thought, and we headed back out to the car.

Unlike Wayne's Jaguar, my Toyota hadn't moved without us. That was a relief. But there was another car in the parking lot that I hadn't expected to see: Carl Russo's Lincoln Mercury. I caught a glimpse of Mike Russo's face behind the wheel and then the car was gone, backing up and racing out of the lot like it was on fire.

I turned to Wayne.

"Is Mike old enough to drive?" I asked, trying to figure out the logistics. Had Carl driven home and handed his car off to Mike, or had Mike driven Carl to the library? If he had, he hadn't come in with his father for the police interrogation.

"Apparently, he's old enough," Wayne muttered.

We climbed back in the Toyota, but I didn't start it up right away. I was tired of talking to my windshield. I wanted to see Wayne's face.

"What about Steve?" I began again.

Now that I was seeing Wayne's face, I saw that it didn't look good. Or happy. Sweat was beaded on his pitted forehead, and the lower half of his eyes, visible under his brows, looked bleary. And then there was the color of his skin, a mottled red and white combination that would have looked nice on a rose but was a little scary on a human being.

"Honey, are you all—" I began.

"Steve said he didn't write a story he should have," Wayne gruffly interrupted my attempt at consolation. "Said the story would have helped others."

"That's it?" I objected. "Some worst secret."

"You know Steve," Wayne growled, turning his head away from me. I might as well have been looking at the windshield. "Everything was black and white, right and wrong to him."

"And he always did right," I agreed. "But what was the story?"

Wayne turned back to me, the muscles in his face tightening.

"Steve wouldn't talk about the unwritten story to the whole group. That's what he told me today on the way out of the library—that later he wanted to get together with me, alone, and explain."

My brain began to tingle along with my body. Now I really wanted to know about the story.

"Was it about someone in the group?"

"I don't know." Wayne shook his head. "I hate to think so. But the 'worst secret' discussion seemed to upset him. And he was quiet today, even more than usual."

"It could have been any of them," I said under my breath. But what was there to interest a journalist of Steve Summers' caliber? I'd heard the worst secrets, and none of them was bad enough to write home about. Certainly, none of them was interesting enough for an article.

"Where was everyone?" Wayne asked, interrupting my thoughts.

"Does it matter?" I questioned. "Anyone could have done it and been at work or at home by the time Wooster's people got there."

Wayne's shoulders slumped. This wasn't going to be easy. We sat in silence for a few minutes.

"It could have been any of them," I repeated and retrieved the bunch of keys from my purse.

"Or none of them, Kate," Wayne argued. "It could have been a total stranger. It could have been the checker in the store. It could have been—"

"But why *your* car?" I pushed him. "Was someone mad at *both* of you?"

Wayne didn't answer me. His skin just grew more mottled. It was hot in the car. Maybe we should have just gone home to eat. But somehow, I wasn't ready.

"Or it might have been someone's significant other," I added. "Everyone but you probably went right home and spilled the beans."

"What do you mean by that?"

"Wayne," I explained, keeping an incipient whine out of my voice by pure will. "You're the only one who takes this confidentiality stuff seriously. Don't you think Isaac told Helen, and Garrett told Jerry, and Ted—" I stopped myself. "Well, maybe not Ted."

"Kate," Wayne muttered, so low I could barely make his words out. Was there a sob in his voice? "Steve took confidentiality seriously."

It was a sob. Wayne's face was more mottled than ever. I saw tears running out of his closed eyes.

Of course. How could I have forgotten so soon? Wayne had seen Steve Summers' body up close. And he'd cared for the man.

"Wayne, I . . . I . . ." I turned awkwardly in my seat and wrapped my arms around my husband.

He seemed to sink into me then.

"He was a good man, Kate. He helped me with my writing. He never minded looking at it . . ." Wayne's voice faltered as he began to cry in earnest.

"I'm sure he didn't," I soothed.

"And . . ." He faltered again, then spoke through his tears. "And I failed him."

Of course Wayne thought he failed Steve. Wayne felt guilty over unrest in foreign countries, over the fate of the spotted owl, over poverty, over the spiritual condition of the human race. Steve Summers' death had to be his fault. Just like his boss's had been.

"Wayne, it wasn't your fault," I said quietly.

"But—"

"It wasn't your fault," I said more firmly.

"I should have—"

"No should-haves," I insisted. "All we can do now is move on from here."

Wayne straightened up out of my arms. I got back to business, hoping to distract him, to derail his guilt.

"Do any of these secrets add up to a murder motive for one of the group members?" I stopped and thought back for a moment. "Or," I added, lowering my voice, "for their significant others?"

The derailment plan worked.

"Kate, no. How could they?"

"How about Janet's reaction to Ted's affair?" I put in.

"Janet would have killed Ted, not Steve," Wayne responded.

"All right, all right," I conceded. "But how about Helen?"

"The same thing," he insisted. "Helen should have been angry with Isaac, not Steve. And Jerry cares for Garrett. And Laura cared for Steve. And why would Mike Russo be angry with Steve? And Van has too many girlfriends to count anyone as significant. None of it makes any sense."

I lifted the keys in my hand. And I felt them again. They were too light. They jangled differently.

And suddenly I knew why. My spare key for Wayne's car was gone.

"The potluck," I whispered, remembering in that instant when the weight and jangle of my key ring had changed.

Wayne and I looked at each other.

"My key for the Jaguar is gone," I told him.

"But what . . ." He stopped speaking as quickly as he had started, his face settling into plain white now, plain sheet white.

"If the key was taken at the potluck . . ." I began.

₵OUR

"Then someone who was at the potluck killed Steve," Wayne finished for me. "Had to be."

"And whoever it was planned it ahead of time," I added, feeling cold despite the heat inside the car. This was one time I wished I hadn't been right. It would have been a lot better if *Wayne* had been right, and the murderer had been our harmonious grocery checker.

"Kate, are you sure about the time the Jaguar key was taken?" Wayne asked.

I nodded and stuck my Toyota key in the ignition quickly, as if to keep it from disappearing, too. Now it was my turn for a question.

"Wayne, shouldn't we tell the police about the key?"

"Captain Wooster?" he replied incredulously.

"Well, yeah—"

"Don't want to throw suspicion on the group members till we're sure," he stated. And that was that.

We drove the rest of the way home in silence.

As I pulled into the driveway, I realized that Wayne was going to have to do without his Jaguar for the time being. How long could he exist without his car? I turned off the Toyota, feeling protective. I had a feeling it was going to have another driver pretty often now. I just hoped Wayne would be gentle.

If I hadn't been so wrapped up in Wayne, Steve, and the fate of my car, I might have recognized the vintage '57 Chevy parked so obviously across the street. But as it was, we were halfway up the front stairs, a bag of groceries each in our arms, before either of us noticed the car's owner, Felix Byrne, at our door—Felix Byrne, a man who was both my friend Barbara's sweetie and, more importantly, a pit bull of a reporter. Wayne and I halted in the same instant, my muscles cramping, bringing back a kinesthetic memory of my long run after the Jaguar. Felix was a pest, a man who would extract a story with pliers if you didn't stop him. But how had he found out about Steve Summers' death so quickly?

Wayne shot out a palm in Felix's direction, still gripping his bag of groceries with his other hand. "Not now," he growled.

Felix looked at Wayne, his small and slender body vibrating with hurt all the way up to his luxurious mustache, innocence shining in his dark, soulful eyes.

"Come on, Felix, give us a break," I chimed in. I'd seen the innocent act before.

But Felix stood his ground, a momentary look of confusion on his face.

"I've found Brother Ingenio, Kate," he said, and then his dark eyes went out of focus.

"Brother Ingenio?" I repeated, trying to remember if there was a Brother Ingenio involved in the Heartlink Group. Unfortunately, my brain lines were down.

"I think he's my spiritual master," Felix announced, his voice low and resonant.

Spiritual master? I tried to remember if Felix had ever uttered a spiritual word in my presence besides "Jeez Louise" or "Holy Socks." Wayne continued up the stairs. I hastily joined him in his earthly ascent.

"I've been searching for the real whiz-bang all this time, you know," Felix went on. "And I think I've found it. I went to interview this geek for the *Marin Mind*, and I was thinking 'jeez, what a loser,' but then I met him. He's so big it's like he's in a different time zone, man." Felix paused as Wayne and I reached the door.

I looked at my sweetie. Was it safe to let Felix in? Wayne shrugged. It was my call.

"Did you really come to see us about Brother Ingenio?" I asked, wishing I had a truth serum on me.

Felix's soulful eyes narrowed for a moment.

"Why?" he shot back, his voice as suspicious as my own. "Is there another friggin' reason I oughta be here? You find another stiff or something?"

Damn. He really didn't know. Yet.

"All right," I sighed and opened the front door, balancing my bag of food on my hip. "Tell me about your spiritual whiz-bang."

Felix followed us into the house, babbling while Wayne and I dropped off the groceries in the kitchen. He was still at it when he finally sat on the wood-and-denim couch, and Wayne and I plopped into the swinging chair for two that hung from the rafters.

". . . see, this guru guy is the friggin' real thing. He knows all this cool, hot stuff, about finding joy and divine light . . ."

I reached over for Wayne's hand. I couldn't believe this was Felix speaking. I felt like *I* was in a different time zone—maybe the *Twilight Zone*. Wayne's hand brought me back to the present. But it didn't erase Felix. Or shut him up.

". . . and Brother Ingenio channels all these super-cool people from the other side, man—"

"You mean dead people?" I interrupted.

Felix squirmed a little.

"Well, they're dead, but they're super-cool dead people."

I looked over at Wayne quickly. Dead people was not a good topic right now.

"Why are you telling *me*, Felix?" I demanded.

" 'Cause you're a friggin' part of it, Kate," Felix breathed, bending forward, vibrating with excitement now. "See, Brother Ingenio says to trust your dreams, and I dreamt about you. In the dream, you said that life was a great mystery. That you had to ask for the truth. But you didn't say who to ask. You always sleuth the truth, Kate. You know, don't you? You know—"

The phone rang. I thanked the caller internally for interrupting Felix before I disappointed him because I didn't know anything at that moment except how much my legs were hurting and my mind was spinning.

It spun a little more after I picked up the phone. Jade, the head warehousewoman for my gag-gift company, Jest Gifts, was on the phone. And Jade never called with good news. I knew it was her even before I heard her angry voice. Wayne had bought me a new phone for my birthday, a phone that could, among other things, identify the phone number of the caller (Jest Gifts, in this case), block incoming calls from certain numbers (I'd been planning on programming in Felix's number once I figured out how the system worked), and even tell you whether someone else had picked up another extension on the same line (I was sure this feature was for teenage parent-alert).

"You won't believe it," Jade greeted me.

I stiffened. I probably wouldn't believe it. "Tell me," I ordered.

"You know all the terra-cotta planter mugs for the gardeners?"

"The ones that were just shipped," I confirmed as calmly as possible. They were probably just broken, I told myself. I could live with that. I drew in a big breath. "The ones for the national gardening convention this weekend?"

"Yeah, those!" Jade squawked indignantly. "Jean stacked all the boxes on the top shelves—the *top shelves!*"

Then Jade was silent.

Suddenly, I saw it all in my mind: Jean stacking the boxes on the top shelves, then climbing down the ladder, the boxes tumbling down, crushing her on the cold concrete floor.

"Is she still alive?" I whispered.

"Kate?" Jade replied.

"Is she in the hospital?"

"Who?" Jade asked.

"Jean," I answered impatiently. "How badly is she hurt?"

"She isn't hurt at all," Jade told me. "I just wanted you to yell at her for doing something so stupid."

I sat down in the comfy chair at the end of my desk and

began crying. I didn't want to yell at anyone. I was just glad that my two warehousewomen were alive and well. I wished I could have said the same for Steve Summers. As the tears ran from my eyes, I realized that Wayne wasn't the only one in shock about Steve Summers' death. I had simply managed to numb myself with speculation about his murderer.

"Kate?" I heard Wayne's voice from the living room. He sounded worried.

I blew my nose and yelled back, "It's nothing, just some problems at Jest Gifts."

"Kate, what's your problem?" Jade demanded.

"Nothing," I lied again. "Just tell Jean to stack them on the lower shelves. The top shelves are only for soft, light things."

"*I* know that!" Jade shouted.

"Good," I said. "I'll talk to you later, then."

"Wait a sec," Jade stopped me. "I gotta tell you about the acupuncture earrings. They're all bent. They were shipped that way."

"I'll call the manufacturer tomorrow—"

"And the new hollow-tooth computer mouses . . ."

Business reality, no matter how mundane, has a way of bringing you back to, well, business reality. By the time I hung up the phone, my head had stopped spinning.

I was writing myself notes when Wayne's business phone rang. I just hoped that a minor crisis at Wayne's restaurant cum gallery, La Fête à L'oeil, would bring him back to earth, too. A curdled bearnaise sauce, wilted escarole, limp rotini—anything but Steve Summers.

I had actually forgotten Felix until he yelled out from the living room, "Sheesh, Lucy, if no one's gonna friggin' listen to me, I'm outta here."

I kept quiet, but I didn't hear a door slam.

I made my way back into the living room cautiously. Felix was sitting cross-legged on the couch with his eyes closed.

"Felix?" I tried.

"Shush!" he hissed. "Can't you see I'm friggin' meditating?"

I drew myself up to my full height. It wasn't much, but it was all my short, A-line body had to offer.

"Spirit is everywhere, Felix," I pronounced. "Go find it in your own apartment."

He opened one eye.

"Really, Kate?" he asked softly.

"Really," I assured him, belatedly realizing he was actually taking me seriously. I hoped I was telling the truth. He was asking an agnostic, but I didn't have the heart to tell him that.

Finally he left, talking to me, or to himself, or maybe to one of those super-cool dead people from the other side, all the way down the stairs. All I heard that made any sense was "see ya later." I slammed the door behind him and sunk back into the hanging chair.

Wayne came wandering in the minute I heard Felix's car start up. I had a feeling he'd been waiting for that sound. He took his place next to me in the hanging chair.

"Everything all right at La Fête?" I asked.

"Lost a busboy," he murmured. "Kid left without notice. Went back to Canada."

Worse than curdled béarnaise but still no big deal, I decided, and pushed off with my feet, causing our hanging chair to swing gently back and forth. The passing air felt good on my face.

"Felix is in spiritual crisis," I commented after a few silent swings.

"*We're* in real-life crisis," was Wayne's only comment.

"Yeah," I agreed helpfully.

"What happened, Kate?" Wayne asked. I turned to him for clarification of the question, but then I saw his eyes. They were wide open for once, but it looked like someone had turned out the lights behind them.

"Could someone at the group potluck really have killed Steve?" he asked, his voice dazed.

I wanted to tell him no, but I couldn't. So I just put my arm around his shoulders instead.

"Sweetie—" I began.

My cat, C. C., yowled from behind us. It was her opera

yowl, the one she'd been practicing for the occasion.

Wayne and I both jumped and bounced in the chair. It was lucky our combined weight didn't yank the ropes from the rafters. Damn. I jump when yowled at, but Wayne usually doesn't. He must have been well and truly shook up.

"Kate, I can't believe it," he murmured. "But it must be true."

"Sweetie," I began again. "It'll be all right. We'll figure it out—"

The doorbell rang and I was saved an explanation of how Steve Summers' death could ever be "all right."

I approached the door cautiously. What if Felix had found out about Steve Summers and returned? But it wasn't Felix at the door. It was Van Eisner.

"Wayne here?" he inquired, looking over my shoulder. His pointy little features now looked like the cartoonist had drawn them with fear in mind.

I considered lying about Wayne's whereabouts, but Wayne had already extracted himself from the chair and followed me to the door.

"Hey, Van," Wayne greeted his groupmate quietly, shaking his hand.

"Oh God, Wayne," Van replied, his voice shrill. "Did you find out anything from the cops?"

Wayne shook his head.

"Are they looking at drugs?" Van plowed on.

"Why?" Wayne asked, his voice not so quiet now. "Did drugs have anything to do with Steve's murder?"

"How would I know?" Van shrilled. He rubbed his sharp little nose. "It's just, just . . ." He looked my way pointedly.

"You can say anything in front of Kate that you can say in front of me," Wayne assured him.

But Van didn't look reassured. His small eyes widened.

"Hey, I thought you were into this big confidentiality trip. You're the last one I'd think would be shooting off your mouth—"

"Steve was murdered, Van," Wayne reminded him.

"Well, just 'cause I do a little coke occasionally doesn't make me a murderer, for God's sake."

"Are you sure?" Wayne asked.

"Of course I'm sure. You haven't told the police anything about my, you know, personal habits, have you?"

"No," Wayne answered honestly.

"Are you going to tell?"

"Not unless your little habits have to do with the murder," I put in helpfully.

Wayne shot me a glance. I suppose it was a guy kinda discussion or something.

"But I *didn't* have anything to do with Steve's murder," Van insisted. "Why does it have to be someone from the group anyway? It could have been anybody . . ."

Wayne shook his head. Van paled. He didn't even ask what gave Wayne a reason to shake his head.

"Well, it wasn't me, for God's sake," Van said. "I mean, look at Isaac."

"What about Isaac?" Wayne asked.

I stared at Van. This didn't seem to be a conversation that we should be having in the doorway, but I didn't want to invite Van in, either. I could see why Wayne was on his case. If anyone who'd been at the potluck exuded a seeming lack of moral character, it was Van Eisner. Not to mention the smell of bad aftershave and nerves. And he had yet to utter one word of regret over Steve's death.

"Isaac's a drunken old fool," Van finally answered. "And what if it got out that he didn't write his own books?"

"I don't think he'd care," Wayne argued. "He told *us*, didn't he?"

I found myself nodding. It had been Isaac's game to tell secrets, anyway. *He* hadn't been blindsided.

"Okay," Van muttered thoughtfully, scratching the side of his neck. "Well, how about Ted? He's scared to death his wife will find out he's been fooling around."

"Scared enough to kill?" Wayne said.

"How the hell am I supposed to know?" Van yelled. "Man, this has been a bad day all around."

"Especially for Steve," I put in. I couldn't help it.

"Steve! Steve!" Van yelled. "He's dead. How about the rest of us? We should be protecting each other."

"I won't protect a murderer," Wayne warned.

"Well, I'm not a murderer," Van announced, a small but surprising amount of dignity in his voice. "And if you think I am, you're wrong."

"Okay," Wayne told him. "If you're telling the truth, you have nothing to worry about from me."

Van stretched his thin mouth as if to argue some more, but then seemed to rethink his strategy. "Thanks, man," he said instead and slapped Wayne on the shoulder.

Then he turned and left, practically running down the stairs.

I watched him shoot out of our driveway in a bright red Miata before I turned to Wayne.

"What was that all about?" I asked.

"Drugs," Wayne answered, shaking his head. Then he brought his chin back up. "Lunch. We never had lunch," he reminded me.

There is a blessing in Wayne's cooking, and not just because I like to eat. Wayne loses himself in cooking the same way I lose myself designing gag gifts. I could see his color return as he opened a can of lite coconut milk. Even his shoulders began to loosen as he sliced tofu, eggplant, and mushrooms. By the time he was stirring the rice noodles into the boiling water, he looked like a man who was actually present in his body again.

I just sat at the kitchen table and watched him work. And that brought me back into my own body. So did the smells. If I were ever to faint, I think the smell of sauteed onion would bring me back. Add basil, ginger, chilies, and garlic, and I'd be on my feet again for sure.

We were slurping Thai noodles and veggies when Wayne brought up the subject of transportation. Then I really knew he was all right—practicality was triumphing over shock.

"I'll lend you my Toyota when you need it," I offered eagerly.

"Maybe I ought to rent a car," he said, scrunching up his face in thought. "What days—"

The phone rang. I jumped up to get it.

"Ms. Jasper," the voice on the other end of the line greeted me. "This is Laura Summers' personal assistant, Julie."

I peeked back in the kitchen at Wayne and put my hand over the phone. Wayne didn't need to talk to anyone connected with Steve Summers now.

Work, I mouthed his way. Luckily, he wasn't close enough to see the number ID popping up on my new phone. He just nodded and went back to his noodles.

"Assemblywoman Summers wondered if she could drop in on you tomorrow," Julie went on. "She needs to talk about her husband's death."

"Oh, of course," I put in, stricken with guilt. If Wayne was in shock, Laura must be reeling. "How's she doing?" I whispered.

There was a pause. Was Julie trying to decide whether to tell the truth?

"Crying, I think," she whispered back finally. And then more loudly, "And resting. But she'll carry on."

My heart tightened. Laura *had* to carry on. And the media . . .

"Then I'll tell her it's okay?" Julie said.

"Absolutely," I assured her and hung up, willing the tears out of my own eyes.

The phone rang again the moment I put it down. This time it was Jerry Urban, worried about Garrett and, kindly enough, worried about Wayne as well.

Work, I mouthed again at Wayne, and held another whispered conversation.

And finally I was at the table again. I took a bite and savored the perfect combination of spicy flavors.

"Thanks for taking the calls," Wayne growled.

I swallowed too fast, and took a drink of water. Chili interruptus. Of course I hadn't fooled him. I filled him in on the calls, and then we were back to our discussion of cars.

"Can I use the Toyota tomorrow night?" Wayne asked. "I'll probably need to be at the restaurant—"

"Oh Wayne, I forgot," I cut in. In one crisis I'd neglected another. "We have to pick up Aunt Dorothy tomorrow."

"And just who is Aunt Dorothy?" Wayne asked quietly.

FIVE

"Huh?" I replied.

When Wayne uses that special, quiet tone, my brain loses it. I act like someone caught robbing a convenience store in broad daylight. No, worse than that—I act like an environmentalist who's been embezzling ocean water from the whales. Guilty as charged, sir. I'm still not sure why. Maybe that quiet tone resonates with a guilt neuron pathway in my cerebellum. Anyway, I took a deep breath and tried to explain Aunt Dorothy.

"Aunt Dorothy is my father's brother's widow," I said. "She used to be a teacher. And then she was a nurse. Now she does good works—"

"Maybe I should rephrase my question," Wayne interrupted, reaching across the table to hold my hand. Had he noticed I was losing it? "Not 'who is Aunt Dorothy?' but why are we picking her up at the airport?"

I gulped down another "huh?" unpronounced and once again attempted an explanation.

"Oh, it's my mother," I began.

Wayne's eyebrows lowered a little more. He removed his hand. I talked faster.

"My mother sent Aunt Dorothy. See, Aunt Dorothy's big in her church, does all kinds of things—"

"I thought your mother didn't go to church," Wayne put in, confused.

"She doesn't. But see, Aunt Dorothy is a wedding coordinator for *her* church."

Wayne smiled, understanding dawning on his beloved, homely face. Damn, that looked good. Then I realized *why* he was smiling. He still wanted a formal wedding almost as much as my mother did. I had a feeling that my opinion of a formal wedding as an unusual form of torture was not in the majority anymore, if it ever had been.

"So your mother is sending out Aunt Dorothy to plan our 'real' wedding," Wayne guessed. I suppose it was obvious.

I slumped in my chair, only able to nod.

Wayne reached out his hand for mine again.

"Don't worry," he assured me. "No one can *make* you plan your wedding, Kate."

"You don't know Aunt Dorothy," I replied. "But thanks, sweetie." I squeezed his hand back. What a good man.

"Does your Aunt Dorothy carry a whip?" Wayne asked innocently.

"No, no!" I objected, shaking my head back and forth violently. "It's just that she's so, well, nice—"

The phone rang just as sharp claws dug into my shoulder. C. C.!

C. C. had a new game, besides singing opera. She would climb stealthily to a spot above her victim and then swoop down, claws extended. This particular flight path had taken her from the top of the refrigerator to my waiting shoulder. An amazing feat, to be sure, but I definitely preferred the opera trick.

I shot out of my chair, rocket-powered by unbearable tension and slightly more bearable pain. C. C. had disappeared. That was the smart part of her game; I had yet to catch her after one of her stealth attacks.

"Hey, kiddo," my friend Barbara greeted me over the phone. "Don't worry about your aunt. She's a benign force."

Have I mentioned that my friend Barbara is psychic? Her intuitions are amazing . . . except when it comes to murder.

Then her brain "fritzes," as she likes to call it. She is, after all, an electrician as well as a psychic.

"But I really called about Felix," she went on, before I had a chance to demand that she tell me once and for all how she always knows this stuff about me. I hadn't told *anyone* about Aunt Dorothy, aside from Wayne. I certainly hadn't told Felix, Barbara's boyfriend.

"Felix is trying to find his spiritual path," Barbara continued. She didn't need a response from me; she was probably channeling it. "And you know Felix, he's too antsy to take the slow road. He sees me meditating and reading and talking to my guides, and he goes crazy. You know my path is a pretty straightforward one."

I nodded. From Barbara's mind to the astral plane. Who needs an intercessor?

She took my unseen nod as an affirmative and resumed.

"Felix finally realized that my spiritual path makes me happy. Monkey see, monkey do. Only my path isn't his, so he has to find a guru. But he'll find the experience that he needs." She paused and added, "Just like you, Kate."

I opened my mouth to ask what she meant, but I wasn't fast enough.

"I know you feel the power of spiritual presence," she finished up.

I closed my mouth. Had she been peeking into *my* meditation practices, or had she just taken the short route and asked her guides? I was still speculating when she changed the subject.

"Don't get too excited about the murder," she told me.

"How'd you know—" was as far as I got. At least I got in three words.

"I figured it out, kiddo. Your finding the bodies is really a marvelous form of karma—"

"Marvelous?" I broke in. "Marvelous? How'd you like to—"

"See, I finally got it, Kate. You were a resurrectionist in a past life—"

"You mean a body snatcher?" I demanded indignantly.

"No, Kate." Barbara's laughter tinkled across the phone

lines like the sound of shining silver. "I mean someone who resurrected dead people."

Barbara paused, but I had nothing to say in the interval. I was still trying to process her words, and my brain was really tired.

"Isn't that cool, kiddo?" she asked. "You brought people back from the dead."

I was beginning to understand. And the hair on the back of my neck was standing up.

"So, let me get his straight," I began slowly. "I used to bring people back from the dead, so now I'm karmically impaired and get to stumble over dead bodies?"

"Yeah," she agreed enthusiastically.

"And this is marvelous?"

"Yeah!"

"Did one of your spirit guides tell you this?" I asked my friend.

"Nah."

"What, did you just channel it?" I probed.

"Nah."

"Barbara!" I bawled.

"I just thought it sounded neat," she finally admitted.

"You made it up?"

"I thought it would make you feel better," she insisted.

Some psychic. I didn't feel better. I felt totally and absolutely aggravated. But somehow my guilt over Steve Summers' death seemed to be gone—guilt I hadn't even known I was feeling.

"Told ya," Barbara said. "Bye, kiddo."

And then she hung up.

I said goodbye to the dial tone. I was sure Barbara would hear me, anyway. Then I went back to sit with Wayne at the kitchen table.

"Barbara?" he said.

"Are you psychic, too?" I snapped.

"You yelled 'Barbara,' " he explained.

"I'm sorry, sweetie," I whispered. "But Barbara thinks I'm a resurrectionist, and—"

The doorbell rang then. It was probably just as well. Trying to interpret Barbara was a task that made me crazy—almost as crazy as listening to her.

Wayne and I rose together as the bell rang again. We would face whoever was at the door in tandem.

Wayne did the honors, turning the knob and yanking the door back. Then we both stared out onto the deck.

Two pairs of eyes stared back—Sergeant Marge Abbott's and Captain Yale Wooster's.

Sergeant Abbott's eyes were crinkled with good humor. Captain Wooster's were not.

"How are you two doing, then?" Marge greeted us.

I tried to frame a reply, but Captain Wooster was faster with his mouth than I was.

"Typhoid Mary of Murder!" he yapped. His jaw jutted into the entryway.

Whoa. I stepped back from the doorway. The captain wasn't having a good day—not that any of us were. And I certainly hadn't wanted to hear that phrase from a policeman's lips. His mean eyes glinted.

"Now, Captain," Marge admonished. "They can probably hear you all the way back in Cortadura."

"Burning bushes!" the captain erupted. "You could have told us you find bodies as a hobby!"

"My wife does not find bodies as a hobby," Wayne stated, his voice as expressionless as his face. But I could feel the anger vibrating from him.

"Yeah?" Captain Wooster swiveled his jaw in Wayne's direction. "Well, how come every time there's a death in Marin County, she's there?"

"It's not my fault," I threw in, drawing his attention away from Wayne. If the men came to blows, I was pretty sure I knew who would end up in jail—Wayne—and who would end up in a body cast—Captain Wooster. "It's a karmic thing. I was a resurrectionist in a past life."

"You were a body snatcher?" Marge asked, her voice high with amazement.

"No, I raised people from the dead, so now I find them dead." I knew I was babbling, but at least the captain had stopped yelling. Now he was staring at me, his mouth hanging open. Not a pretty sight. "You'll have to ask my friend Barbara for more details," I finished up.

"Hell's bells," the captain finally said. "You going for an insanity plea or what?"

Marge threw her head back and laughed.

The captain turned to her angrily. "I hate Marin, Marge," he whined. "I hate this karmic caboodle, you know I do. I hate all the channeling and crystals and wussy men in their wussy support groups. I hate—"

"Didn't you want to ask Ms. Jasper and Mr. Caruso some questions, sir?" Marge cut him off.

"Right," he answered, straightening his shoulders. He pulled his chin back a notch. "May we come in to talk?"

I looked at Wayne. The Captain had asked permission. I guessed that meant he didn't have the right to just barge in. Was the captain better as a friend than an enemy? Wayne asked with his eyebrows. I gave a tentative nod. Wayne blinked and stepped back from the doorway.

"Come in and have a seat, Captain Wooster and . . ."

I couldn't believe it. I'd forgotten Marge's rank and last name.

"Oh, just call me Marge, honey," she advised, walking past me in a lilac-scented cloud. "Or Sergeant Margel; lots of folks like to call me that."

If the two of them were playing good cop and bad cop, they certainly had their roles straight.

We sat Sergeant Marge and Captain Wooster down on the wood-and-denim couch where Felix had been before. The captain's nostrils flared. Could he smell the absent reporter? Or was he smelling our recent feast? Or Marge's ever-present lilac scent?

"Right," he repeated once he was seated. "Ms. Jasper, how come you were so quick to mention the other group members and—" he paused and rolled his eyes "—and their 'significant others'?"

I glanced at Wayne again. Shouldn't I tell the captain about the key and the potluck? Wayne might as well have had "no" printed on his forehead. I thought maybe I was getting as psychic as Barbara.

"Just logical," I answered, keeping my voice even. Wayne and I both lowered ourselves into the double hanging chair. "They all knew about the group and when it ended."

"Okay, let's go over the timing of these groups," Captain Wooster suggested, sounding almost human for a moment.

Wayne and I nodded like good puppies.

"Okay, Mr. Caruso, you guys had a group meeting today, right?" he asked.

Wayne nodded again.

"When was the previous meeting of your group?"

"Two Wednesdays ago," Wayne answered. His voice was slow and careful. "Heartlink meets every other Wednesday."

The captain bent forward. "What did you talk about at the meeting two Wednesdays ago?"

My body stiffened next to Wayne's—someone from the group had talked to the captain besides us. The way he asked his question made it clear to me that he knew they'd discussed something out of the ordinary two weeks ago. Did he know they'd talked about their worst secrets?

"I can't tell you that," Wayne replied predictably. "Confidentiality."

Wooster turned to me.

"I wasn't there," I stated honestly. I honestly hadn't been there; never mind that Wayne's confidentiality had spread to include me in its confines.

"And Scheherazade told good stories, too!" the captain snapped. He didn't seem human anymore. "You two know plenty—"

"They'll tell us in their own way, sir," Marge interrupted. "Lord, sometimes you're enough to make a gal wanna wear earplugs."

I looked at her gratefully, wanting to tell Marge everything. But maybe that was how it was supposed to work. Marge's crinkly blue eyes were friendly but intent as she searched our faces. I kept quiet.

Finally, the captain began again. "Okay, so your Heartlink group had a meeting today and a meeting two weeks ago. And in between those meetings, the members of the group and their 'significant others' went to a potluck?"

"Potluck was last weekend," Wayne confirmed quickly. He didn't say anything about the missing key.

I wondered once more who'd been talking to the captain. I squirmed in my chair. How much had the captain heard?

"How about you two?" he hissed. "What are your worst secrets?"

My heart rammed itself against my ribs like it was trying to escape. The captain had heard too much, that was for sure. Someone had told him, but who? And what, exactly?

My heart was still ramming like a demented bull when Captain Wooster pointed a knuckled finger at me.

"You hate journalists," he said, accusingly. For a moment, I thought he meant Felix, but then he expanded on the theme. "Heard you karate-kicked one on TV. And Steve Summers was a journalist."

I took a deep breath. "I just used tai chi to get that particular journalist out of my way," I explained. "She assaulted me first."

"Hellfire," the captain muttered, the hint of a smile on his face. "Wish I could do that myself, once in a while."

Marge's laughter made us all one happy family, for about a minute.

"And you," he went on, pointing at Wayne. "You let your boss die when you were supposed to protect him."

The blood pulsing through my veins seemed to pull me up and out of the hanging chair.

"That is not true!" I roared, surprised at my own volume. "Not any more than I could say *you* let Steve Summers die when you were supposed to protect *him*. Wayne did his best—"

"It's okay, Kate," Wayne admonished gently. He reached up and placed his large hand on the small of my back. "It's okay," he repeated.

Only then did I realize how easily I had fallen into the captain's trap.

"Captain Wooster," Wayne said formally. "I often feel that I failed my boss. I feel the weight of it almost every day, but I try to forgive myself. And I've done nothing illegal."

I wanted to clap, to cheer. But I couldn't, so I sat back

down next to Wayne and put my hand on his muscled thigh. My eyes were watering now, with indignation, with pain for Wayne, with love. I blinked and tried to think of anything that would calm me down. I settled on sorbet. I imagined my favorite sorbet, the blueberries melting on my tongue. My eyes dried slowly.

"Captain," Wayne was saying when I tuned in again. "Do you have any ideas you can share with us?"

"No," the captain said. Wooster sorbet, I thought. It wouldn't taste good, but it would sure be fun to make.

"No one saw anything," the captain elaborated. "No one heard anything. Like your wife figured out so logically, it's gotta be one of your little band of fruitcakes—"

"If you're talking about Garrett—" I began, standing again.

"Joseph's garters!" the captain objected. "I can't say one piddly little thing without everyone getting up in arms. No, I didn't mean your 'gay' friend Peterson or his 'gay' friend Urban. I meant all of you, anyone who was in that group or knew when Summers would be leaving."

"Any motives?" Wayne tried again, pulling me back down into the hanging chair by my waistband.

"Why don't you tell me?" the captain suggested. He smiled evilly.

We were mute. How many secrets had the captain heard? And were any of them *the* secret?

"Right," he said. "And then there's the terrorism possibility."

"Terrorism?" I asked, trying to make sense of the word.

"Summers was married to a state assemblywoman."

"So, you think someone who didn't like how their property taxes were being spent retaliated?" I scoffed. "Someone in the group?"

"Not so funny, Ms. Jasper. Do you like the way your taxes are spent? We might be dealing with a lunatic here. Mary's handbag, we probably *are* dealing with a lunatic. And everyone keeps telling me how peachy-keen the Summers' marriage was." The captain leaned forward again. "Though they say that Steve Summers seemed upset lately, maybe at his wife—"

"The Summers were just like anyone else—" Wayne began.

"Some folks have good marriages," Marge put in at the same time. I wondered about Captain Wooster's own marriage, assuming he *was* married. Was his relationship with his wife the reason he was so hostile to Laura Summers?

"So this Summers guy must have known some secret, maybe like Watergate, right?" the captain said, ignoring both of them.

"Watergate on who?" I asked in exasperation. "Not on his wife. And what secret could be bad enough about an educator to lead to murder? Or a shrink, or an accountant, or a computer consultant?"

"A shrink might have plenty under the rug," the captain pointed out.

"Not Garrett," I replied, crossing my arms. "Garrett is a good man."

"And we already know about the accountant's kid," Wooster added. "Trouble brewing there."

"All teenagers have problems," I stated with the assurance of a woman without children.

"And you left out the investment guy," Wooster bulldozed away. "Who knows what he was doing. They screw up, they go to jail these days. And how about his wife? She was in the business, too, right?"

I had a feeling the captain was using the phrase "screw up" in reference to Ted's professional life, not his personal one, but it was funny how close he was getting. Still, at least it seemed that he didn't know everything.

"You're smiling," he accused, pointing his knuckled finger at me again.

"Huh?"

"You were smiling," Marge translated.

"Well, I've stopped. All right?" I said, my voice cranky. Why was I in this conversation, anyway? Wayne was keeping quiet. Why couldn't I follow his example?

"And that Eisner guy looks like a cokehead to me," the captain put in.

I tried to keep my face impassive—no smiles, no frowns, no nothing.

"And just 'cause Herrick is old doesn't mean he has nothing to hide," he ground away. "The longer you live, the more you have to hide. And why's his wife still hanging out with him if she's divorcing him?"

"Why don't you tell me?" I said, taking a phrase from the captain's guidebook.

But Marge didn't laugh at that one. She and the captain were gone less than five minutes of abuse later. With promises.

"You haven't seen the last of me," Captain Wooster informed us at the door. Then he turned to Wayne. "And you can forget your fancy car, *Mister* Caruso."

After we'd closed the door behind them, Wayne murmured, "Well, I guess we're picking up Aunt Dorothy in the Toyota."

I threw my arms around him and hugged him tight. He was warm and solid, and smelled like lunch and Wayne. We had faced the Wooster and survived. How to celebrate? I turned up my face for a kiss.

The phone rang just as our lips touched. This wasn't the kind of electricity I'd hoped for.

Wayne answered it this time, but I could tell who was on the other end just by listening.

"Not to worry, Garrett," he muttered.

Then, ". . . no threat to the group," and ". . . not your fault."

I wondered if psychiatrists were just naturally anxious. Maybe that's what attracted them to the field.

"Don't know any more than you do," Wayne was saying. Then he said "uh-huh," and "uh-huh" again.

I reflected on Jerry's earlier call. He'd been truly worried about Garrett. Well, why not? Garrett couldn't be feeling a lot better than Wayne was. And they were both too caring to successfully navigate the real world and its cruelty sometimes.

"Uh-huh," Wayne said again, then, "Take care," and then he hung up the phone.

"Garrett," he told me.

"Right," I said, imitating Captain Wooster.

Finally, Wayne and I sat back down to our lunch. I don't think either of us wanted to risk the phone call another kiss might generate. There wasn't much left of lunch, but that not much was mostly dessert—coconut milk pudding with strawberry chunks and drizzled carob sauce.

I brought a teaspoon to my lips and licked. It wasn't Wayne, but it was delicious.

"Garrett called Laura," Wayne mumbled through his own mouthful. "Laura told him Steve's death was being treated as a murder. Garrett's calling all the other group members to let them know—"

We might as well have been kissing because the doorbell rang before Wayne could even finish his sentence or I could finish my dessert.

I stomped to the door and flung it open.

A sincere-looking, well-dressed young woman stood in front of me. I'd never seen her before.

"Are you a solicitor?" I demanded.

"No," she said. "Are you Kate Jasper?"

"I . . ." I began.

But then I looked behind her and saw a man with a camera. A truck with a video dish and a TV station emblem on its side pulled into the driveway.

It was worse than a solicitor.

It was the media.

Six

✣

I didn't think to shut the door. Instead, I opened and shut my mouth a few times for exercise as our whole yard sprouted with media beings: animal, vegetable, and mineral. They popped up everywhere. TV vans, cars with press signs on their dashboards, and worse, their occupants, unloading all their instruments for the inquisition: sound and video equipment, cameras, microphones, notepads, and mouths. Especially mouths.

"Ms. Jasper?" the sincere looking, well-dressed young woman in front of me began. Her formal tone told me that *her* station's cameras were rolling, even if some of the other stations' were a little slower. "We're here at your home today to speak to you about witnessing the death of Steve Summers, husband of Marin Assemblywoman Laura Summers. This isn't the first death you've witnessed in Marin County, is it? In fact, some call you The Typhoid—"

"Don't say it," I warned through gritted teeth.

She paused for less than an instant before her mouth opened again. "Steve Summers was the victim this time—a respected journalist, your friend, and, of course, the husband of Assemblywoman Laura Summers."

Then Wayne was behind me, his hand on my shoulder. I didn't have to turn my head to see the gargoyle stare he was aiming at the young woman—I could feel it.

"Is it true that Steve Summers was killed in a botched assassination attempt on Laura Summers?"

"But Laura Summers wasn't killed, *Steve* Summers was," I replied, then gave myself a mental kick for having spoken at all. Still, what was this woman talking about?

"Rumors are that Laura Summers was the intended victim!" a new voice shouted. I saw an older man in a perfect suit behind the young woman. "What did you see—"

"No comment," Wayne broke in.

"Are you Mr. Caruso?" the young woman asked, finding some perverse encouragement from his non-comment.

"Mr. Caruso, isn't it true that you were in some kind of radical political group with Mr. Summers?" another voice shouted. And then everyone was shouting.

"Did Mr. Summers agree with his wife's political stands?"

"Did Steve Summers believe in the violent overthrow of the United States government?"

"Is it true that Steve Summers had a C.I.A. background?"

"Didn't Steve Summers cause a suicide with one of his articles?"

"How did Assemblywoman Summers feel about her husband's political activities?"

"Was the assemblywoman present when her husband was killed?" my original inquisitor demanded, still looking sincere.

"That's it," Wayne announced. "No comment. Goodbye."

He shut the door, but it caught on the foot of the young woman who'd started it all off, leaving at least a six inch gap between us and privacy.

I looked at her blue, high-heeled shoe. Did I dare step on it? Or maybe kick it? I wouldn't want to maim her, at least not terribly. Wayne seemed to be going through the same ethical struggle, unmoving but for his gaze, which was directed down toward the blue shoe.

And then my eye caught a glimpse of something through the gap at the top of the doorway—a flash of fur. Yes! Black and white fur.

C. C. dove and stuck her claws into the young woman's shoulder. The woman screamed, and her foot disappeared from our doorway. I pushed the door shut quickly. C. C. could make her way back in through the cat door. I just hoped none of the reporters were small enough to use it.

Even with the door closed, we could hear the frenzy C. C.'s attack had caused.

"Was that a bobcat?" someone clamored.

"I thought it was a wolf," came another voice.

Our inquisitor was now the inquisitee. Her wounds would heal, I told myself as I heard the flap of the cat door. Our hero had returned.

To reward C. C. or not to reward C. C.? That was the question. What she had done was bad—very bad. But she had certainly picked a good victim.

I stooped down to pet my perfect little cat without even thinking. C. C. had remained to see the audience reaction this time. She knew she was a hero. She purred as I pet her, then slowly blinked her eyes before running off down the hallway to celebrate, her talents recognized at long last.

Once C. C. was gone, I turned to Wayne.

"Why did those guys think—" I began.

He put his finger across his lips. Was it possible that the reporters were still listening? We retreated to the bedroom just in case. Even in there, we sat on the floor and whispered.

"How did Steve Summers' death become Laura Summers' assassination attempt?" I hissed.

"She's more interesting," Wayne hissed back. "Makes a better story."

"If the reporters are on *us* like this, what are they doing to Laura?" I asked a minute later.

Wayne was silent, his brows lowering. "Probably has employees to field reporter questions," he finally answered. "But still . . ."

I reached out and grabbed his hand. How could Laura bear to lose her husband? If he was anything like Wayne . . . I couldn't even complete the thought.

Instead, I bent toward Wayne and pressed my lips against his. Wasn't that where we'd been before? And sure enough, the phone rang.

I took the call on the extension in our bedroom.

"Um, this is Mike Russo, you know?" the voice on the extension informed me.

"Yeah?" I said tentatively.

"Um, my dad is like, really upset," he whispered. "And, um, I wanted you to know that I saw you guys at the store," Mike speeded up. "Dad said I should tell you. I was just shopping. I shop for my dad lots of times when he's busy."

"All right," I assured him, preparing to hang up. But it wasn't that easy.

"And . . . I thought maybe you could cheer my dad up," Mike suggested diffidently. "You know, you or Wayne, maybe?"

I took that to mean that Mike really wanted Wayne to talk to his father. I put my hand over the receiver. "You wanna talk to Carl Russo?" I asked my sweetie.

Wayne sighed but nodded.

"Mike, get your father," I ordered as Wayne reached for the phone.

When Wayne took the phone, I could hear the buzz of Carl Russo's voice on the other end.

"Don't worry," Wayne said when he got a word in ten minutes later. By then he was lying on top of the mattress on the floor that served as our bed, and he was lying backward to accommodate the short phone cord. I lay down beside him.

Another ten minutes later, he said, "Yeah, someone is talking about the group, but—"

"Mike'll be fine," he pressed on after a minute. His interrupt speed was getting better, at least.

Then he said, "uh-huh," a few more times and, "don't worry, he'll be fine," and then he hung up.

Less than a breath later, the doorbell and the phone both rang simultaneously. Wayne and I looked at each other with instant agreement in our eyes. We wouldn't answer either my fancy new phone or the doorbell for the rest of the day. Wayne said he'd leave La Fête à L'Oeil to his manager for the evening; we would work in our home offices.

After a quick hug, Wayne headed back to his little room at the end of the hall, and I heard the clacking of calculator keys. Then I returned to my own office next to the entryway and closed the front curtains. It's lucky no real focus is necessary for paperwork; my brain was throbbing, but my hands shuffled papers, entered numbers in columns, and wrote checks. And all bells rung unanswered.

Wayne and I had a late dinner, followed by an early bedtime. And for once, when our lips touched, no bells rang but the ones in our heads.

When I woke up on Thursday morning, I put out my hand to feel for Wayne, but he wasn't next to me. I rolled off of our mattress bed, put on my robe, and exited the bedroom, looking above me to make sure C. C. wasn't in position to leap on my shoulders. She wasn't. She was behind me, singing opera.

I led the way down the hallway and found Wayne in my office on the phone.

He turned. I didn't think it was to see me in my ratty old robe; C. C.'s opera probably had more to do with it. He smiled, briefly.

Then he put his hand over the telephone receiver.

"They want another group get-together," he whispered.

"All of us?" I whispered back.

"Everyone who was at the potluck."

I nodded, wondering who he was talking to, but he'd turned away again.

"We'll be there," I heard him say into the receiver.

I trundled on into the kitchen to the tones of a feline aria, which stopped abruptly when I opened a can of Fancy Feast.

I was eating oatmeal and blueberries with maple syrup when Wayne joined me at the kitchen table.

"Who was on the phone?" I demanded before his bottom even touched his chair.

"Garrett," he told me brusquely. "He's arranging it. At Ted's house."

"A meeting?"

Wayne nodded.

"When?"

"Today."

We could have been on Dragnet, except for our p.j.s and robes.

"How are you doing, sweetie?" I asked gently, trying to change the tone of the interaction.

"Fine," Wayne muttered, lowering his eyes.

"Right," I said, keeping the sigh out of my voice. Fine, perfectly fine. "Have you eaten?"

"Not hungry."

"Oh, Wayne," I murmured. Then an evil thought gripped me. "I'll make you breakfast," I offered.

Wayne's eyes came back up, and they were panicked. Wayne did not eat my cooking, but he was too polite to ever mention it. He just kept beating me to the culinary punch.

"I, I . . ." he sputtered.

"How about oatmeal?" I suggested.

His face blanched, looking a bit like the oatmeal I'd suggested.

"Okay," he gave in. "Banana pancakes?"

"Yum," I said. Wayne had a dynamite recipe for dairyless banana pancakes. I suspected that carob and a few other spices were involved. But I *knew* that the end result was worth a second breakfast.

So, Wayne got out his mixing bowl and cooked. Minutes later, he ate a big stack of pancakes and I scarfed down a smaller one. And, as usual, cooking did the trick. Wayne was ready for a shower when we finished eating, and he was talking again.

"So Garrett thinks that whoever did it will confess," Wayne told me as he scrubbed my back in the apricot soap-scented steam of the shower.

"Oh, please," I objected. "And this man is a psychiatrist?"

"He thinks loyalty to the group will force a confession."

"So he thinks it was a group member, and not a significant other?" I turned and soaped Wayne's chest.

"Yeah, mmmm," Wayne murmured.

"Why?" I asked.

Wayne stopped mmmming.

"Familiarity breeds contempt, maybe?" he guessed.

"Did you guys feel contempt for Steve Summers?" I asked, not soaping him anymore.

Now Wayne was squirming instead of mmmming.

"Not contempt, never," he muttered.

"But?" I could hear an exception in his voice.

"But, he could be, well . . . a perfectionist sometimes."

"What's wrong with that?"

"Nothing, if you only apply your standards to yourself."

"But Steve applied his standards to everyone, and expected them to measure up?" I tried. But I didn't quite have it.

"No, not really." Wayne struggled in thought, looking like a wet Wookkie in search of the meaning of life. "Steve had his own sense of integrity. He wouldn't allow anyone else to interfere with that integrity."

"And if someone did?"

"Steve wouldn't let it happen."

We rinsed off the apricot soap, each lost in our own thoughts, all sensuality gone.

"It sounds as if Steve Summers could have been ruthless if pushed," I finally concluded as we clamored out of the shower.

"Kate," Wayne said, grasping my arms, "Steve was the victim of this crime, not the perpetrator."

"But *why* was he the victim?" I asked. Wayne dropped my arms.

Neither of us had an answer. Wayne had cared for Steve as we all do for our friends, forgiving them their flaws. But I didn't really know Steve, and what I was hearing now made me feel that I had known him even less well than I had thought. Wayne and I dressed in silence, more quickly than usual, and less playfully. That was actually lucky because the doorbell rang just as I was slipping a vest over my turtleneck.

Wayne and I crept to the living room window like hunted beasts. Should we answer this bell?

But then we saw who was on our doorstep—Laura Summers and one of her assistants—and I remembered that Laura's other assistant, Julie, had asked on the telephone if Laura could visit today.

Wayne and I raced to the door and practically tumbled over each other as we each grabbed for the doorknob. I won. I did the honors: unlocking, turning, and pulling back the door. But Wayne was on hand with the first word.

"Laura—" he began and stepped toward her.

Laura strode in and held Wayne to her. *Poor Laura*, I thought, and then, *this hug is way too long*. Because it was. Laura's grip was a drowning woman's and Wayne was her buoy. I tried to remind myself of Laura's situation. She was grieving. She needed Wayne now. I took a deep breath in, and she was still holding him. I let the breath out and took in another one. Then Laura kissed Wayne, somewhere between the cheek and the mouth, way too close to the mouth.

Wayne was bright red when Laura finally let go of him, and I had a feeling I was, too. Only Laura's complexion had withstood the assault. Her eyes were misty when she turned to me.

She gathered me into her arms for a secondary hug and I forgot my jealousy. This woman had lost her husband. We were lucky she wasn't screaming. Instead, she was finding solace in its most primal form. I could smell the floral fragrance of her soap and deodorant, and I felt the desperate strength of her arms around me. Still, she didn't kiss *me* before she released me from her hug.

"Kate," she said, her voice low and serious, "thank you."

"Um, anything we can do . . ." I began, but stopped myself. I didn't want to offer up Wayne's body through a slip of the tongue. "How are you?" I asked instead. "Has your son come home?"

"Not yet," she answered. "We've talked on the phone. He'll be home as soon as he can. This is a difficult time, but we're taking it day by day." She paused, then said, "We must move forward."

Her all-American face looked haggard, but her hair was still perfectly styled, and she was dressed both for mourning and for political success in a charcoal gray pinstriped suit and low-heeled black pumps.

A petite young woman I'd barely noticed in the hug-fest stepped in behind Laura.

"Ms. Summers' life may be in danger," the woman announced.

My jaw must have dropped. Was this murder really about Laura?

"Now, Tiffany," Laura admonished, and then she introduced the young woman. "This is one of my able assistants."

But Tiffany wasn't finished.

Her gray eyes widened as she spoke. "If only I had been with Ms. Summers that day. But that's her private day."

Laura nodded solemnly.

"Even I need one day a week for privacy. Steve understood. When the Assembly is in session, of course, I have to be there. But when I am at home, Wednesday is my day— our day, mine and Steve's."

My eyes filled with tears. Steve had been killed on her private day. It wasn't fair.

"Laura?" Wayne put in urgently. "*Is* your life in danger?"

Up until now, neither of us had believed such a thing, but suddenly it didn't seem so far-fetched. How many enemies could you make as a state assemblywoman? Could someone have killed Steve to hurt Laura?

"No," Laura said, shaking her head slowly. "I can't believe that Steve's death had anything to do with my role in the Assembly. My people worry, of course. But I think Steve's death had to do with Heartlink."

I shivered. It was one thing for us to talk about a murderer in Heartlink, but it was another to hear Laura state it.

"Please, Wayne, Kate," Laura begged. "Tell me what you know."

I led Laura and Tiffany into the living room, thinking hard and fast. Did we know anything that could lead us to the murderer's identity? Tiffany took out a little notebook and a pen as the two of them sat on the couch. I didn't think we were going to tell her much to put into that little notebook.

"Laura," Wayne asked, once we had plopped down into the hanging chair. "Are you sure there's no link to you?"

Laura shook her head curtly, her blond bob rippling with the effect. Tiffany's gray eyes widened a little further under her own identically styled brown bob.

"No crank notes?" Wayne persisted. "No threats?"

"You don't act as a member of the Assembly without receiving letters, but none of them threatened myself or Steve with any kind of physical violence. Julie reads those letters. She would have told me." She hurried on. "No, it was in Steve's other life, his life as a journalist, his life as a member of Heartlink. I'm sure of it."

This put the ball back in our court. I turned to Wayne. Would he break confidentiality for a grieving widow?

"You know something," Laura stated. I shouldn't have looked at Wayne. This woman could read people, and she had read my look all too well.

"Has Steve been upset over the last couple of weeks?" Wayne asked. I knew he was buying time, deciding where his duty lay—with Steve's confidentiality or with his widow.

Laura shook her head and crinkled her brow. "He was quiet, maybe more quiet than usual. I thought maybe something had happened in the group two weeks ago. But he didn't tell me. Was there something?"

"Nothing that I can equate with murder," Wayne answered. I could tell he'd made up his mind to protect Steve's confidentiality. "Upsetting things were said in that group, but I can't see how any of them could have led to murder."

Laura closed her eyes. "My Steve," she moaned.

I ran over and put my arm around her shoulders. Hugging didn't seem to be one of Tiffany's duties.

"Steve was okay," Wayne assured her. "His death was quick."

"But why?" Laura insisted, clinging to me now. "Why? It must have something to do with the group. It has to."

"You know, the group and everyone from the potluck are meeting today," Wayne sidestepped her question. He paused. "Maybe we'll find out more then."

"You don't know anything that will solve this mystery?" Laura asked again, bending forward, regarding Wayne intently.

No," Wayne said, and I knew he was being honest.

"Do you, Kate?" she asked me.

"Nothing," I said. "I just wish I did. But we'll keep look-ing," I promised.

Laura frowned.

"Thank you," she told us. "Thank you for being dear, dear friends. But please don't put yourself in any danger asking questions. I couldn't bear another death."

And then Laura Summers got up from the couch. Tiffany closed her notebook and followed her to the front door, where Laura hugged us both again. This time she held on to Wayne for a shorter time, but she kissed him again. I can't say exactly where she kissed him because I averted my eyes at the last moment.

Once she was gone, Wayne and I held each other for a long time. I know we were both thinking how awful it would be to lose one another. And there was nothing we could do for Laura—nothing but find Steve's murderer.

We might have held each other for the rest of the day if the doorbell hadn't rung again. But it did.

And, unfortunately, I answered it.

Felix was on my doorstep now, though, not Laura Sum-mers.

"How goes the spiritual—" I began.

But Felix pushed past me, a scowl on his face, anger in his sweat.

"Holy socks!" he began. "You found another stiff, didn't ya? And you didn't tell me nada! Your pal, your compadre. D'ya know what Brother Ingenio would say about that? Huh? Huh?"

SEVEN

"No," I said to Felix, keeping my voice steady. "What *would* Brother Ingenio say about my listening to your spiritual struggle instead of burdening you with the details of a tragic death?"

That stopped him for a second. Exactly one second.

"Some buddy you are, Kate. You, smacking my spiritual beliefs in my friggin' face at a time like this." Felix widened his soulful eyes. "You found another dead body and didn't tell me. All the rest of the media ghouls got it first. Friggin' first, and I'm your friggin' friend. Sheesh, Louise, ya wanna see me out on the street—"

"Is there something you want?" Wayne asked from behind me.

Felix looked up, a forced smile on his face. Wayne had never violently assaulted Felix, an amazing feat of self-restraint, all things considered, but Wayne made Felix nervous, anyway. Maybe Felix had figured out somewhere in his tiny conscience that he deserved a quick karate kick just for all the times he'd made our life miserable.

"Hey, Big Guy," he greeted Wayne. "Just here to get the poop on the Summers' hit, ya know what I mean? Real bummer, and they don't know doodley down at the cop-shop."

"Yes, it *was* a real 'bummer,' " Wayne agreed, his deep

voice vibrating on the word. "Especially for Steve's widow. Have you thought about her at all?"

I knew Wayne was asking Felix about his sensitivity to the widow's grief, but Felix didn't. Sensitivity wasn't big in Felix's repertoire of behavior. Badgering, yes; sensitivity, no.

"Nah, the widow just doesn't play, ya know what I mean?" Felix answered earnestly. "No friggin' motive. But the dudes from your group . . ."

He let his sentence drift off, his eyes taking on an unholy gleam.

"The guys from my group what, Felix?" Wayne demanded.

"Um, they might have friggin' motives. That's all, man. Look, here's this bunch of Mr. Sensitives pouring out their boo-hooey little hearts. And here's this prize-winning, whiz-bang journalist. Whaddaya think's gonna happen? If I'd been in that group, I'd have found a way to make a story out of it."

Oddly enough, he was making some sense. That was kind of scary when I thought about it.

"Felix, what do you know about Steve Summers?" I asked.

"What did the C.I.A. know about Abby Hoffman, man?" Felix answered.

I took that to mean that he knew something. We let Felix in the door and onto the denim couch. Felix was our source of information; we were not his—at least I hoped not.

I plopped down into the hanging chair, but Wayne remained standing, all the better to intimidate Felix. And all the better to be ready to lead the reporter out of the house on a moment's notice.

"Felix, you knew Steve Summers as a writer," I said sweetly. "Tell us about him."

Felix squinted his eyes and crossed his arms, but he talked.

"The man got all the breaks, okay? He wrote for the *New Yorker* and the *Atlantic Monthly*. All that pseudo-intellectual cow patty. He started out like the rest of us, a small-time paper hack, but then he got Big, with a capital 'B.' He even wrote books—one on politics and economics, one about ethical investing. Holy Moly, I can do better than that. Where's the sizzle, man? If it bleeds, it leads; if it thinks, it stinks. And then he gets these friggin' awards—"

"He was a writer of stature," Wayne summed up. "We know that, Felix."

"Maybe he had stature, but just 'cause everyone thought he was a friggin' big deal, just because he was soooo full of himself. Mr. Perfect with a pen."

I resolved to read Steve Summers' work. He must have been good to stir up this much jealousy.

"How about his wife, Laura?" I asked Felix. "Was she cool?"

"Oh, now Laura Summers is the big banana, all right. All her constituents think she walks on water. She votes the right way, she talks the right way, maybe she even thinks the right way. No one but Oz knows, man."

"Any questions of propriety?" I pushed Felix. I already knew about Laura's public persona. I wanted to hear some good gossip.

"Laura Summers?" He laughed. "You gotta be kidding. "We've all been trying to find one stinkin' flaw in that woman for years. Not a friggin' thing. No smoking a little pot, no *leetle* affairs, no nothing. She's bigger than the Pope, man. When she makes a promise, she carries through. And she doesn't need money. Her parents had mucho buckaroos, ya know what I mean? The woman's loaded—what she doesn't give to charity. Mr. and Ms. Perfect, those two."

Felix leaned forward. "So how about your little pals at Heartlink?" he asked Wayne.

Wayne exercised more self-restraint than Felix had. I could see it in the way he held his hands at his sides, sweat darkening the armpits of his blue T-shirt.

"We keep our boo-hooeys to ourselves," Wayne informed Felix.

Felix's face fell.

"Hey, wait a friggin' second," he objected. "I gave you what I know. Now it's payback time."

"If I come up with a murder motive, you'll be the third to know," Wayne promised and moved toward Felix.

Felix jumped off the couch.

"I'll be back," he told us.

"Thanks for the warning," I chirped as he sped out the door and down the front steps. "Have a nice day."

Once we were sure Felix was gone, Wayne and I got ready for the emergency Heartlink group meeting. Wayne made muffins with shredded coconut and chunks of pineapple and banana while I did my part, worrying. Felix had talked sense somewhere in his screed. One of Wayne's buddies was probably a murderer, and we were about to go visit them.

The phone rang just as Wayne tastefully arranged his tropical muffins on a china plate and carefully covered them with a linen napkin.

I don't know why I picked up the receiver. Stimulus-response conditioning is my only excuse. My brother Kevin was on the line when I did.

"Hey, Katie," he greeted me. I almost hung up then. But he was my little brother, so I couldn't hang up, no matter how many times I'd told him not to call me "Katie."

"Xanthe got a flash, and I thought you'd want to hear." I gritted my teeth. Xanthe was Kevin's sweetie, a woman who could curse you one day and hug you the next. "So do you wanna know what she said?"

I kept my sigh internal. "Make it short, Kevin. We're on our way to a meeting."

"Oh, wow, cool!" he replied. Everything was cool to Kevin. Kevin could be enthusiastic about dust settling. "You're targeting your energies, I'll bet. You always do." I smacked the side of my head. Kevin's compliments always short-circuited me. He went on. "You know how Xanthe's in the psychic flow?"

"Right," I agreed, moving things along.

"Well, she was sitting here working on our latest project, solar-powered kelp. It's really cool, Katie—"

"And?"

"Oh, yeah, and she flashed that Mom's planning some kind of sneak attack on you for a formal wedding."

"Thanks, Kevin," I said sincerely. "But I already know. It's Aunt Dorothy."

"Oh, wow, Katie," he whispered sympathetically. You

couldn't grow up in our family and not know Aunt Dorothy. Then his voice came back up to normal volume. "Maybe you need some solar-powered kelp. See, the solar power activates the kelp's healing potential. It's amazing—"

"Thanks, Kevin," I said again, not so sincerely. "And thank Xanthe for me." And then I hung up the phone.

I groaned after I hung up. I was sure I'd hear more about solar kelp soon. And I could almost smell the patchouli oil Kevin and Xanthe habitually wore. I considered figuring out my new phone system and putting Kevin's phone number on permanent block.

And then I remembered what day it was: Thursday. I'd almost forgotten that Aunt Dorothy was coming in today. But it was too late to stop her, anyway. Aunt Dorothy, AKA the wedding warhead, had already been launched.

Wayne and I finally got out the door, muffins and minds intact. Well, at least the muffins were. Wayne scanned our driveway as we left the house. And then he dropped his eyes. Had he forgotten that his Jaguar had been impounded?

"Toyota," he muttered, misery in his voice. He *had* forgotten about the Jaguar.

But my old Toyota ran. In fact, it ran all the way to the Kimmochis' house in the hills of San Ricardo without a hiccup. I guess it had something to prove.

The Kimmochis' two-story hillside house was perfect. At least the living room was. Perfect, that is, if you liked their decorator's use of light and color. Willow green, apricot, and lemon yellow furnishings were softly lit in the living room's perfect balance, as were the quirky but expensive sconces, pendants, and fixtures. Stone lions, candle groupings, faux baroque mirrors, and paintings that might have been quilted with tiny squares in the same colors as the furnishings made the room visually playful—but only visually. Though the Kimmochis had two daughters, Niki and Zora (eight and thirteen, respectively), there were no children's toys in the room, no scrawled pictures beloved only by parents. This was a cerebral room. The only thing out of balance was the buffet table filled with potluck goodies and dishes that was centered in front of the faux fireplace.

"Mo-om, it's Kate and Wayne!" Zora called out as we entered the Kimmochis' perfect kingdom.

Zora was a beautiful young woman, and was just beginning to realize it. She had her father's dark symmetrical eyes and jet black hair, and a scattering of her mother's freckles over her perfect little nose. Niki peeked out from behind Zora, clutching her older sister's blue-jeaned leg. Niki looked like a princess. A heart-shaped face, long dark eyelashes, and a Laura Ashley frock helped the look.

"Mo-om!" Niki imitated her older sister, shattering the princess illusion.

Janet McKinnon-Kimmochi rushed up then, her red hair the only part of her that was mussed. And even that looked professionally mussed. She was wearing a lemon-yellow dress that looked a lot like her youngest daughter's. I guess she didn't get much opportunity to wear ruffles and lace in her role as a financial advisor.

"We don't yell in this house," she instructed her girls loudly.

The girls' eyes widened as they looked at their mother, but they said nothing. I had a feeling that Janet did a lot of yelling in her house. But today, she was a hostess.

"Kate, Wayne," she greeted us, her voice softening. Then she pecked us each on the cheek, smelling of an expensive scent I couldn't identify. "So good to see you."

Somehow the greeting seemed wrong for a group that was minus a murder victim. Still, I smiled and returned a polite hello.

Wayne mumbled something incomprehensible, but probably friendly. Even I couldn't make out his words. All I could tell was that he was uncomfortable. I looked up into his face, searching for an answer, but Ted Kimmochi had made his way through the room to greet us before I had a chance to find it.

"Such a sad day," Ted murmured. At least I could understand Ted. "Such a tragedy. Unbearable."

I nodded. Unlike his wife, Ted recognized the mood of the occasion. Then again, Ted could find a tragedy any time, anywhere, and usually did. Blanche Dubois could have taken lessons from the man.

"Oh, Ted," Janet admonished. "Don't be so negative. Did Ted tell you about the beautification project we've started at the San Ricardo Library?"

I shook my head. Ted rarely spoke of anything but himself.

"Well." Janet took a breath and put her hands on her hips. "That library is a disgrace. Dark and musty. So I offered to help design a new look. Light is the key. When we get the donations, we'll put in skylights. And pick colors. The community is the important thing . . ."

Behind her, Carl's son, Mike, had *his* hands on *his* hips and was bobbing his head in an enthusiastic mime of Janet McKinnon-Kimmochi. I shouldn't have looked because it caused Zora and Niki to look.

"Mo-om, Mike's—" Zora began.

"—being really, really bad," her sister Niki finished for her.

Janet turned around as the girls flew at Mike, pummeling him with tiny but hard fists.

"Ow, ow!" he yelped and leapt over an apricot ottoman to relative safety next to his father.

"Mike, what the hell did you do now?" Carl demanded, wriggling his broad shoulders in his suit.

Mike wriggled his own shoulders and imitated his father's glare. He didn't have his father's fleshy features yet, but he still could have played Carl in the movies—with a little padding.

The girls giggled. Carl didn't.

"Mike—" his father began again.

Garrett Peterson stepped between father and son, a smile on his gentle, wide-featured face.

"Mike's quite a comedian, isn't he?" he asked, his deep voice a soothing vibration.

A smile crept across Carl's face slowly. Mike must have been hard to stay mad at for long.

"But he made fun of Mom," Niki complained.

"Oh, dear," Garrett murmured and squatted down to look into Niki's face. "Is your mom all right?"

"Uh-huh," Niki said, nodding her little head. Then she kissed the tip of Garrett's nose and ran across the room, squealing in delight.

Maybe Garrett could get the murderer to confess after all, I decided. Wayne and I walked all the way into the room. It was then that I noticed the gang was all together—everyone but Steve. Wayne and I had been the last to arrive. Isaac Herrick stood with his soon-to-be-ex-wife, Helen, in the corner. Laura Summers was talking to Jerry Urban. And Van Eisner was filling a glass with wine at the buffet table. Wayne made tracks to get to that table and lay his muffins out just as Garrett stood up and said something I couldn't hear to Carl. Then things got serious.

Garrett extended his arms and brought them together again, clasping his hands in front of his chest. He looked ecclesiastical in his white dress shirt and chinos. Each of us moved to the center of the Kimmochis' living room as if Garrett's arms had pulled us there. We were all standing, even the children, congealed into one small group by Garrett's motion.

Garrett's large eyes narrowed.

"We have gathered together today for a reason," he began.

I wriggled my own shoulders now, squirming in place.

"We're here to find Steve Summers' killer," he went on. He looked at each of us adults in turn. "Some of you may have wondered if the murderer might be in this room, since all of us knew when the group was breaking up, and all of us knew approximately when Steve would walk out onto the street—"

"Garrett," Laura cut in softly. "You don't have to—"

"It's all right, Laura," he told her. "I *do* have to do this. For you. And for Steve."

Could he, though? Our group was certainly mesmerized. Mike Russo's eyes were so round they looked like they'd fall from his head like loose marbles. And I was having trouble controlling the urge to mention the key that was taken from me at the potluck. Something about Garrett's presence made me want to confess. Was the murderer also controlling the urge to confess?

"We must consider the possibility that the murder has to do with us, with the Heartlink group. If one of you did it, you must come forward now. I can tell you that you won't be able to live with yourself afterward unless you do."

And then someone *did* step forward: Jerry Urban, Garrett's lover. There was no smile on his round, genial face. For a moment I thought he had stepped forward to say he was the murderer; Garrett's words had been that powerful. But then I realized that Jerry was just moving closer to Garrett in order to protect him, physically and emotionally.

"Well?" Garrett finished, eyeing us each in turn.

"Hey!" yapped Van Eisner. "Are you accusing one of us? What is with you? I don't get it. We're a support group. We don't accuse each other. We don't spread each other's secrets." He advanced on Garrett, his fist raised. As he passed me, I could smell the wine seeping from his pores. "For God's sake, what is your problem?"

Van's fist was at least a yard from Garrett's actual body, but that was too close for Jerry Urban.

Jerry stepped between the two men.

"Stop that!" Jerry ordered. I had never heard such seriousness in his tone before. "You have no right to speak to Garrett that way."

Van dropped his fist. "Listen," he tried. "This is all screwed up. We're supposed to help each other—"

Jerry went on as if Van hadn't spoken.

"And don't you ever threaten Garrett again. I would protect Garrett with my life. You want to fight? Your fight is with me."

A silence followed Jerry's words.

I knew that Jerry was speaking with absolute sincerity—I felt the same about Wayne as he did about Garrett. And then the hair on my arms stood up. Could there have been a reason to kill Steve Summers that had to do with protecting Garrett? One that Garrett wasn't even aware of? One that Jerry had acted upon?

I had to break the silence before I jumped out of my skin and into the faux fireplace.

"Has anyone here talked to the police about the content of the group meetings?" I asked.

"Oh, you mean 'our worst secrets'?" Isaac responded with a smirk on his elderly, alcohol-weathered face.

I wasn't sure whether everyone in the room knew what he was talking about, but I did, and I wasn't letting his crack go by.

"What did you say to them?" I demanded.

Isaac laughed, baring discolored teeth, but he answered willingly enough.

"I just played a little with Captain Wooster," he told us. "What a horse's ass that man is. I told the captain he ought to ask everyone their worst secrets."

"Did you tell him the secrets yourself?" I prodded.

"Just a few harmless ones," he answered. "Hey, what the hell?"

Van Eisner paled, and Ted Kimmochi closed his eyes. Was he praying? Or meditating?

"What?" Janet McKinnon-Kimmochi demanded impatiently. "What are you talking about?"

Isaac didn't answer her. He just went on, "I told about Wayne's feeling guilty when his boss died. No crime in that. It's a matter of public record." I wanted to reach out and squeeze Isaac's stringy neck, but I didn't. "I told about Ted's . . . meditations." Isaac winked at Ted. Ted looked behind himself, as if for escape. "Thinking about chocolate, ha, ha. And I told him about Van's amazing success with women—"

"Anything else about me?" Van whispered.

Isaac shook his head. "You know me, Mr. Sensitivity." He laughed. "I wouldn't say anything that would really get someone in trouble." He eyed Carl Russo now. Carl's fleshy features reddened.

"How about claiming authorship of things you don't really write?" Carl put in, obviously angry.

Isaac just laughed again. His laugh had a braying quality that wasn't fun. Or funny.

"That can't be proved in court, unlike some of our secrets," Isaac stated, and there was a warning in his voice.

Carl turned his head away, the muscles in his arms and back bunching up under his coat.

"Enough, Isaac," Helen Herrick snapped. She slapped her husband on his shoulder, and it wasn't a light slap. "You think you're just teasing, but these are people's lives you're playing with. And a man's been killed."

"Okay, my sweet," Isaac answered, apparently unfazed by either his wife's tone or slap. No wonder she was divorcing him. Then he bent over and kissed Helen on her cheek and, amazingly, she smiled back at him. They really loved each other, I realized with a jolt.

"Okay, my sweet," Mike Russo imitated.

Niki and Zora giggled, and I wondered if the children should be in the room at all. This was too heavy. Carl turned on Mike and shook his finger.

"Stop it, Mike," he growled. "Stop it now."

Mike stopped it. And Garrett started up again.

"Listen, we need to talk about these issues seriously," he put in. "Maybe even share our secrets with everyone."

"Like my meditating and thinking about chocolate," Ted jumped in quickly. That was a pretty good preemptive strike from a depressed man, I thought, because no one else jumped in and mentioned his affair.

"What else?" Janet brayed. "What?"

Ted looked at her nervously, but she was obviously addressing the other group members.

Van said he had trouble with women, passing up the opportunity to talk about his drug use. He must have been taking a cue from Ted.

Garrett was telling us about the suicide he didn't prevent when the doorbell rang.

Janet marched to the door impatiently and flung it open. Two young women were standing there, one blond and tall, one short and Hispanic.

"I'm a friend of Van's," the two women said simultaneously. Then they whipped their heads around to stare at each other.

"You invited them both?" Isaac murmured incredulously.

He shook his head, but there was an admiring glint in his eye.

"No," Van whispered. "I just told them where I'd be. Jeez, I never expected—" He stopped. The two women were advancing on him in tandem.

"Listen, Claire, Suzi," he said, a broad smile on his weaselly face. "This is a private meeting. I—"

"Who's she?" the Hispanic woman said, pointing at the blond.

"Who's she?" the blond pointed back.

"Look, we're all friends, okay?" Van tried. It was amazing that he could smile at a time like this, but he did. It must have hurt.

"Has he been dating you?" the blond asked. "Dating" sounded like a euphemism to me, but I kept my mouth shut.

"Yeah," the other woman answered. "Has he been dating you, too?"

"Yeah," the first woman snarled. It was a scary sound.

Both women put their hands on their hips. The doorbell rang again.

"Ted, you get it," Janet ordered.

Ted opened the door and a third woman entered, this one a dark, statuesque beauty. You know how they say some women are beautiful when they're angry? Well, she was.

"Van Eisner," she accused. "I followed you here and then I saw these two." She pointed at the first two women.

"But you weren't supposed to come," Van whispered desperately. He began walking backward and tripped over a low couch. No one came to his aid.

The blond woman asked, "Are you with Van, too?"

"Not anymore," the dark beauty answered. "He's pond scum!"

"An earthworm," the Hispanic woman agreed.

"Dog dirt," the blond put in. "And I say we just leave."

"Yeah!" the other two women answered.

"Wanna go for a drink?" one of them asked the others.

And before Van even had a chance to hide, the three women left together, talking about him. At least it looked like they'd made friends, and Van had lost some of his "women problems."

Mike had a field day then, imitating the women. The Kimmochi girls were doubled over with laughter. Even Isaac put his arm around Mike affectionately.

"Way to go, Van," Isaac congratulated our resident amorist. Then he stopped smiling for a moment. "Hey, are we really going to ferret out who killed Steve?"

"How about divulging *your* secret?" I asked. "That would help clear the air."

Helen Herrick grinned. Whether it was at Isaac or with him was hard to tell. Helen was generally as quiet and polite as Isaac was loud and rude.

"Moi, a secret?" Isaac answered in a falsetto. "Me, an author, the world's expert on dyslexia?"

"This is no joke," Laura Summers reminded us. She was right.

Everyone shut up then, even Mike and the kids in the background. The younger generation were huddled by the window now.

"My husband is dead," Laura reminded us, just in case we didn't feel bad enough. "I want to know everything that was said at that group."

Ted argued for confidentiality. Carl looked worried. Van took a convenient trip to the restroom.

Laura turned to Carl Russo. "Carl, is it your son?" she asked gently and slowly.

Carl nodded reluctantly.

"Carl, you're doing the right thing," she assured him. "Nothing your son has done could have had anything to do with Steve's murder. I'm not even convinced that anyone in this group had anything to do with his death." Her expression was bleak, for all the confidence of her words.

"I'm sorry, Ms. Summers," Mike said and then began nervously juggling some heavy bronze candlesticks he'd picked up from the mantel. I wondered how much the candlesticks cost. Not that they looked breakable.

"Mo-om!" Zora called out, but Janet wasn't even looking at Mike. She was looking at Laura.

"She's right," Isaac assured Carl. "Prig that Steve was, he would never have written about Mike."

"Yeah," Janet put in. "Steve always was a little repressed, huh? I wonder . . ."

Wayne glanced at Laura, whose back was stiffening. Time for a distraction?

"No one should be forced to tell their secrets," Wayne interrupted.

"The real question," I followed up quickly, "is whether there was anything said at the meeting that might have been cause for murder."

There was a long silence after that. How could we know what was important and what wasn't? Finally, Ted broke the silence.

"Let's take that as a no," he suggested. "Let's move on to the potluck."

"Are you forgetting Laura?" Garrett asked and walked over to put his arm around the woman whose husband had been killed.

Laura sank back into the support his arm gave her. Slowly, each of us offered our awkward condolences.

"You ought to read a good novel," Janet told Laura when her turn came. I flinched. Did she have any idea how she sounded? Obviously not. "That'll take you out of your funk. It always works for me."

"I don't have time for fiction," Laura replied, her cheeks reddening.

"Hey," Ted said to Wayne. "You and Kate have solved these things before. Why don't you give it a try?"

A chorus of voices, including Carl's and Helen's and Jerry's, seconded the motion.

"Well," Wayne temporized, his pocked skin pinkening.

"We can only try," I put in.

"Maybe it's not fair to put Kate and Wayne in exclusive danger," Garrett argued. "This should be a group effort."

Everyone squirmed then. From guilt? Or from fear?

"Or perhaps the police would be the best in any case," Laura murmured reasonably.

Garrett opened his mouth to add more, and then the room was immobilized by the sound of shattering glass.

"Mo-om!" Niki squealed.

And then all hell broke loose.

EIGHT

I thought *terrorism* as I heard the shattering glass. Van Eisner didn't think at all, he just dived to the floor. It was a better move than none. And nothing was what I did, galvanized into inaction by the sound. Still, I was in the majority. I watched as everyone but Van froze. And I listened for something more over the sound of my own pulse, but all I heard was a gasp here, a yelp there, and a "huh" across the room. At least at first. Then Janet McKinnon-Kimmochi started screaming.

I turned my head. I saw a broken window. Had someone fired a shot through the window? And then I really listened to Janet.

"You broke my window!" she shouted. My shell-shocked brain tried to make sense of her words. Then she added, "Those are bronze candlesticks, you idiot!" She raised her arm and pointed her finger like a well-aimed gun at Mike Russo.

I followed her finger to the unhappy teenager. He stood, his feet apart, staring down at the parquet floor where one of the bronze candlesticks lay. Finally, I figured it out. The sound that had just scared the sense out of the entire Heart-link group and their significant others was merely a failed juggling attempt on Mike Russo's part. The other bronze candlestick had gone out the window the hard way.

"That's it!" Carl roared at his son. "We're outta here."

"But Dad," Mike objected weakly. "I'm sorry. I was just—"

"No 'just' this time, Mike," Carl snapped.

"Carl," Laura Summers said softly. "The boy was only nervous."

"With my things," Janet put in. "That's real bronze, you know, and—"

"Where are your broom and dustpan?" Wayne asked Janet.

"What?" she replied, whipping her head around to look at Wayne. The expression on her freckled face was not happy. She pressed her lips together tightly.

"Your broom and dustpan," he repeated. "I'll clean up."

"Thanks, Wayne," Carl growled. "Sorry, I shoulda thought of that myself. I'm happy to pay the damages."

Janet mumbled under her breath. Was that a thank-you or a curse? Or was she just figuring up the bill?

And then Ted got in on the act. "I remember when we got those candlesticks," he whispered sadly. "At a crafts fair, wasn't it, Janet?" He shook his head as if his heart was broken. Yup, Ted and Janet were made for each other.

"I'm really, really sorry, you guys," Mike tried. And he looked sorry. Sorry and scared, his eyebrows raised and his lower lip sticking out. "I didn't mean—"

"We'll talk about it later, Mike," Carl interrupted. "Everyone knows you're sorry, but sorry isn't enough."

"Carl—" Garrett began.

But Carl shook his head. "We're going home, folks," he insisted. "Kid's got a little problem. I'll take him off your hands."

Mike bowed his head and headed toward the front door. Carl took up the rear. Janet McKinnon-Kimmochi crossed her arms and glared at them both.

I wanted to plead Mike's case. Real bronze or not, Mike *had* been nervous for good reason. But Mike was Carl's boy, not mine.

"Mo-om—" Zora objected as father and son got to the door.

"Pipe down!" Janet shouted. So much for no yelling in her house.

Once the Russos were gone, Laura Summers left, too, taking her time to say goodbye to everyone left in the room . . . and hugging Wayne for the amount of time it usually takes me to cook lunch. It is true that I'm not much of a cook, but still, Wayne was red and sweating when Laura finally let him go.

After Laura was gone, Ted got Wayne a broom and a dustpan, and Wayne cleaned up what was left of Mike's accident. Then it was lemming time.

Van Eisner was out the door before Wayne even dumped the glass remains into the waste basket. Garrett and Jerry followed soon after. And then Isaac and Helen Herrick departed, after a few unappreciated crockery jokes from Isaac.

Wayne and I were the last to say goodbye to the Kimmochis. Janet had calmed down by then, and she smiled her hostess smile at the door, but Ted was sunk into a broken glass depression with bronze undertones.

"Life is so sad," he murmured in farewell. The loss of minor domestic possessions had never been so tragic.

"Right," I muttered.

Wayne didn't even reply as we headed out to my Toyota. Once we were in the car, however, Wayne spoke.

"Sometimes Ted can be a jerk," he muttered.

I was shocked. Coming from Wayne, this was a harsh condemnation.

"Well," I answered cautiously, pulling out from the sidewalk. "He certainly married the right woman."

It took me a moment to identify the sound of laughter coming from Wayne. It burbled up as if he were choking for a moment and then filled the Toyota. I was glad he was laughing, though I wasn't exactly sure why. Post-candlestick stress syndrome? I kept my mouth shut until we were on the highway.

I'd pulled into the middle lane when I remembered the tropical muffins. They were still sitting on the Kimmochis' buffet table.

I was about to mourn their loss when I realized that I would just sound like Ted.

"Whaddaya say we stop at the library and get Steve Summers' books?" I suggested instead.

"I own them, Kate," Wayne told me, and I shrunk back into my seat. Of course Wayne owned his friend's two books. And now he'd stopped laughing again.

We were silent the rest of the way home.

When I opened our front door, C. C. made a perfect four-paw landing onto the top of my head. It took me a few fraught nanoseconds to realize what had hit me. I stood centered and still, my heart playing a loud background beat to the *whoosh* of adrenaline through my body, and then a tail came down to swipe my face. I was wearing a perfect C. C. hat.

Wayne lifted C. C. off my head, smiling a little. I decided not to kill the cat. It was worth one little cardiac shock and a few dislodged vertebrae in my neck to see Wayne smile. I peered at C. C., trying to see into her mind. Had getting Wayne to smile been her purpose? I knew she loved Wayne. But once Wayne had lowered her to the floor, she just blinked and left the room. Cats don't like to give up their secrets, and she wasn't giving up hers.

Wayne and I both dropped into the hanging chair.

"Kate—" Wayne began as I said, "Wayne—"

"What?" I asked.

"We can't just let Steve's death go by," Wayne replied.

I was glad he'd said it first. Ten-to-one, he would have argued if I had.

"But what can we do?" I asked. When all was said and done, I was better at finding dead bodies than at figuring out how they got that way.

"Investigate," Wayne answered simply.

"But how?" I asked, my voice rising with frustration.

I felt, rather than saw, Wayne slump next to me.

"Don't know," he mumbled.

I told myself not to panic because if Wayne was talking in monosyllables, he was probably panicking enough for both of us.

"All right," I said, keeping my voice calm. "Do we agree that it has to be someone related to Heartlink?"

Now I felt Wayne stiffen.

"Wayne, the key," I reminded him. "Someone took the key at the potluck."

Wayne sighed.

Damn. He was the one who'd mentioned investigating.

"All right," I went on, holding down any whine that wanted to come out and play. "Either it's about the group, or it's not. Who else could have killed Steve Summers? Who else—"

Wayne shook his head so hard the hanging chair twisted on its ro_es.

"You're right, Kate," he whispered finally. "It's the group. Something to do with the group. We have to plan."

"Interview suspects?" I suggested brightly.

"Get information about them from other sources," Wayne added.

"Yeah!" I encouraged him. "There's always my hairdresser." My hairdresser, Carol, knew more about the residents of Marin County than C. C. did about getting into trouble.

"Carol," Wayne said, like a man waking up. "Right."

So Wayne and I got in the Toyota and drove to the Golden Rose, a beauty parlor of the old school. It's pink with gold accents, filled with chattering women, and, most importantly, it's inexpensive. There aren't many like it left in Marin County.

When we entered the pink portals of the Golden Rose, an orchestra of feminine voices surrounded us.

"That Martha Lee, why she thinks she can—"

"Polyester is still the best thing since sliced bread. 'Natural' fibers were put on this earth to make women miserable—"

"No, honey, the right side *is* the same as the left—"

"And he's got a woman on the side all along—"

"But will it make me look younger—"

I couldn't see a receptionist, so I grabbed Wayne's arm

and strode into the bullpen of pink vinyl barber chairs. But Carol wasn't at her station.

I looked around me. I'd never been in the Golden Rose without Carol snipping away at me with her scissors. Each station was mirrored, and I saw Wayne's and my reflections staring back everywhere I looked.

"Hey, Kate," Michelle, Carol's station-mate, greeted me, never stopping her hands as she brushed out silvery curls. "Lookin' for Carol?"

"Uh-huh," I uttered with relief. I'd never noticed how scary the Golden Rose was before, especially the women lined up with their heads under dryers. What would aliens think if they landed here?

"Well, Carol went on vacation, hon," Michelle told me.

"Vacation?" I bleeped. So much for my number one informant.

"Why?" Michelle asked. "Ya find another murder victim?"

All the chattering voices went dead.

"Sorta," I muttered.

"Well, Carol isn't here, but maybe we can help," she offered.

I looked at her hopefully. Was it written in the code of hairdressing that all hairdressers had to know everything about the residents of the counties they worked in?

"So who got killed?" Heather asked from across the way.

"Steve Summers," Wayne put in gruffly.

"Oh, yeah," Joy piped up. "He was some kinda reporter or something, wasn't he?"

"Married to the assemblywoman," Michelle added, showing who knew what. "Laura Summers, right?"

A few gasps erupted.

"The assemblywoman's a widow?" a hushed voice asked.

"Poor thing," someone added.

I nodded and waited for more.

It wasn't long in coming, but the direction could have used some work.

"A real tragedy for the assemblywoman," Margo the manicurist commiserated. "So is this your new husband?"

Wayne turned as pink as the vinyl barber chairs.

"Oh, sorry," I apologized. "This is my husband, Wayne, everyone."

"Hi Wayne!" a chorus of female voices called out. It sounded like a twelve-step meeting for a minute.

Wayne forced a smile and waved.

"He the one you ran off with to City Hall?" Michelle inquired.

I cleared my throat. "He's the one," I confirmed, frantically trying to think of a way to segue back to murder.

"I imagine you must want to know something about the suspects in your murder," Margo guessed.

I turned her way and smiled.

"Name 'em," Michelle ordered.

I looked up at Wayne for permission. But he might have been unconscious, or maybe he was holding his breath. The place *did* smell of hair spray, dyes, conditioners, and nail polish remover, among other things. Or maybe he'd just fainted on his feet from shyness. I turned back to Michelle.

"Laura Summers," I began.

The room wasn't silent anymore. Everyone was talking at once.

"That assemblywoman is a saint—"

"Goes too far on the environment, though—"

"Good on education—"

"Good hairdo—"

"Poor thing, her husband—"

"Heard her speech on prescription price gouging—"

"She wears great suits—"

"Medicare reform is due—"

"But gun control doesn't work—"

"The woman understands Social Security—"

I felt like a sheep dog whose flock was scattering.

"Of course, we don't suspect Laura Summers," I hollered into the cacophony. Was I lying? I wasn't sure. "Do any of you know Janet McKinnon-Kimmochi?" I asked at random.

"Ms. High and Mighty McKinnon, we called her in school," came a voice from one of the barber chairs.

"You went to school with her?" I asked, astounded by my luck.

"You betcha. That girl could drive you crazy, even in the fifth grade. No real harm in her, though. Just not real sensitive."

"She's good with money," another voice came from under one of the dryers. "At least I hope so."

"Never gets her hair done here," Michelle stage-whispered. "We're not snooty enough for her."

And then the room was quiet. Too bad Janet wasn't as well known as Laura Summers.

"Helen Herrick?" I threw out.

"Is Helen involved with this?" a sharp voice demanded.

"Possibly," I answered cautiously. I thought fast. "Maybe as a witness or something."

"Oh, dear. Helen has enough to put up with—"

"Her husband ought to be shot—"

"Always gets the same hairdo. You ask me, it's too severe—"

"Sweet woman—"

"No nonsense—"

"But funny—"

As I listened, I realized that the women in the Golden Rose might not have ruled the world, but they were certainly its intelligence agency. And I recognized the score. Helen Herrick lead in popularity, closely followed by Laura Summers. Janet McKinnon-Kimmochi came in a late third.

But these were women. I didn't think I was going to get as lucky with the male suspects.

The names Garrett Peterson, Jerry Urban, Carl Russo, and Ted Kimmochi didn't raise even a ripple of interest, except for a bit of sympathy for anyone married to Janet McKinnon-Kimmochi. And Isaac Herrick was only vilified for Helen's sake. But the mention of Van Eisner's name seemed to push a button in every second woman's mouth in the place.

The ones who hadn't dated Van had girlfriends who had, or sisters, or daughters. As everyone talked, I thought of Van: slight, short, and balding, with pointy little features. What did he have that other women saw in him? I certainly didn't see it.

"But Van was fun," someone finished up.

Maybe that was it. Maybe Van *was* fun.

When the voices finally wound down, there was only one thing left to do.

"Thank you," I addressed the hairdressers, manicurists, and customers of the Golden Rose sincerely. I gave a little bow. "You are truly amazing women."

"Yes, thank you," Wayne's deep voice rumbled.

Someone tittered, and I led Wayne out of the lioness's den.

He was pale when we got in the car, but alive.

"Kate?" he whispered as I started the Toyota. "You don't talk about me down there, do you?"

I took a deep breath and thought of an appropriate answer. "No more than you talk about me to the other Heartlink members."

Wayne's complexion was pink again. Bingo!

And then, all of a sudden, I wanted to know what he'd said about me to the Heartlink members. But the good angel of all foot-in-mouthers stopped me just in time. If I asked him, he'd ask me, and then . . . No, the results were too horrendous to even consider. And the angel must have been doing double-time because Wayne changed the subject abruptly.

"I think we need to know more about Steve," he said as I backed out of my parking space.

"Should we go back to the Golden Rose?" I asked, stopping the car. We hadn't really pumped the women on the subject of Steve Summers.

"No!" he cried out, gripping my shoulder. Damn. It was good we weren't on the highway. I would have been in the next lane. "Oh, sorry," he said, looking at his hand as if it wasn't his. "Didn't hurt you, did I?"

"It's all right," I told him. "I'm fine." I didn't add that he, Mike Russo, and C. C. were now all contestants in the startling-Kate-out-of-her-wits competition. I reparked the car. There was still plenty of afternoon left. I had a feeling we were going to visit someone, and I wasn't moving the car until I knew where I was going.

"How about Steve's friends?" I asked.

Wayne frowned.

"Steve had friends, didn't he?" I asked.

"Well, there was the group . . ."

"I mean outside of the group," I prodded, none-too-gently.

"Steve didn't make friends easily," Wayne murmured uncomfortably. Then he shrugged. "I can't think of any he talked about. He hardly even talked about his son. I'd forgotten he had one till Laura mentioned him."

"Don't worry," I assured him. "We can ask Laura about Steve's friends."

"Or maybe we'll meet some at Steve's funeral," Wayne added.

I restarted the car. It looked like we weren't going visiting after all. I was backing up again when Wayne spoke.

"I do know one person," he announced.

"One person, what?" I stopped the car, braking hard this time.

"Someone who might have known Steve, at least peripherally," he explained. "A guy I went to law school with—Joe Calderon. He was a legislative assistant for a while. He knows the state assembly. Now he teaches law at Beaumont University. I'll bet we can catch him between classes. He's usually in his office between one and three."

I didn't even ask Wayne how he knew that. I just backed up, shifted gears, and took off for Beaumont University. For a quiet man, Wayne had a lot of friends.

Joe Calderon was a large, honey-colored man with a bushy Castro beard so thick he could have hidden a city underneath it.

"Wayne, my man," he roared when we peeked into his open office door. "How goes it?"

"It goes," Wayne answered, and Joe laughed, causing a small earthquake in his small office.

Then the two men did manly things like hand-shaking and shoulder-slapping for a while. Finally, Wayne turned Joe's attention to me.

"Um, this is my wife, Kate Jasper," he said diffidently.

"Whoa, Wayne," Joe admonished him, shaking a big fin-

ger in his face. "This woman is way too beautiful to be your
wife."

Now it was my turn to blush. Wayne had braved the pink
portals of the Golden Rose, and now I was facing masculine
academia in the flesh.

Joe kissed my hand and then flashed me a dangerously
flirtatious look out of his dark eyes.

"What do you know about Steve Summers?" I asked in
response. All right, I admit it was rude. But hand-kissing just
isn't my thing.

Joe laughed again. The glass in his window vibrated. Then
he asked us to sit down. The wooden chairs were hard, but
Joe was easy. Once Wayne had explained our mission, Joe
leaned back and talked.

"I knew Laura Summers," he told us. "Everyone at the
state assembly did. She's one of those people who actually
remembers your name without having to read it." Joe
laughed again, not quite so loudly this time, and I smiled
with him. Maybe the hand-kissing wasn't so bad. "Summers
has a good record: education, environment, Social Security,
Medicare—"

"You mean *Laura* Summers, don't you?" Wayne interrupted. I had a feeling Wayne knew his friend well. Unin-
terrupted, Joe Calderon could probably talk forever.

"And you want to know about *Steve* Summers." Joe
grinned. "I was getting there. It just takes a while these
days." He reached for a bowl of cellophane-wrapped, sugar-
free candies on his desk and offered them silently in our
direction. When neither of us accepted, he took one himself,
unwrapped it, and stuck it in his mouth. I could smell but-
terscotch drifting my way. Suddenly, my stomach wanted
lunch.

"Now, Steve Summers is a little harder to remember," he
spoke around the candy. "I met him, more than once, but he
never said much. Of course, I've read him. His book about
politics and investing was truly brilliant. But he was a cold
fish, if you wanna know the truth."

He was even colder now, I thought, but said nothing. I
resisted looking Wayne's way. That had to have hurt.

Joe must have noticed because his mouth shifted gears.

"Steve was a great helpmeet, though. He couldn't avoid it. It was beyond his sense of ethics to be anything less. A right-minded man of the first degree. He and Laura were a matched set."

Finally, I looked at Wayne. He was nodding politely, but I could tell he was disappointed. There was nothing new here.

"Could someone have attacked Steve to get at Laura Summers, to influence her voting or something?" I asked, desperate for anything that might help.

Joe sucked his candy meditatively. When he finally spoke, his voice wasn't so jolly anymore.

"I would have said no ten years ago. The stakes just weren't high enough in state congress. But these days?" He shrugged. "Who knows?"

We left after that, eating a late lunch at a student hangout near the campus. We filled up on beans and rice on freshly made tortillas smothered in two kinds of salsa and guacamole. We didn't make small talk, and not just because our mouths were too full. What had we accomplished? Had we learned anything that could answer the question of why do-gooder Steve Summers was killed? I thought about Van Eisner. I thought about the Russos and the Kimmochis. And then I thought about my Aunt Dorothy.

"Oh, my God!" I squawked, looking at my watch. "The plane!"

NINE

What had my mother said, exactly? I searched the files in my brain anxiously until I found the one with the time. Four o'clock. Aunt Dorothy's plane was coming in at the San Francisco airport at four o'clock. I checked my watch. It could have been worse. It looked like we had forty-five minutes to get there—forty-five minutes for a drive that usually took me more than an hour.

I must have said "four o'clock" aloud. Or maybe I screamed it because Wayne grabbed me by the shoulder and announced, "I'll drive. It'll be faster that way. You can meet her in the concourse."

It took me two garbled seconds of objections before I agreed to the plan. Wayne did drive faster than me. And of the two of us, I was the only one who was going to recognize Aunt Dorothy when she came down the long tunnel leading from the plane.

We left uneaten food on our plates and cash on the table, then rushed out the door to the Toyota. Wayne climbed in the driver's side and moved the seat back. I winced. Would my elderly car survive the drive?

In minutes, we were squealing down the highway toward the Golden Gate Bridge. Well, my Toyota and I were squealing. Wayne was just driving—driving a lot faster than I thought the car could go.

By the time we hit the bridge traffic, I was ready to talk about anything that would take my mind off the drive and the minutes ticking away on my watch. But there was only one other thing on my mind.

"What was it about Steve?" I asked as Wayne handed the toll collector the bridge ticket. "There had to be something that he did, or said, or was, that killed him."

Wayne grunted, either at me or at the toll collector, and wove his way through the apres-bridge traffic toward Nineteenth Avenue. I wasn't sure he'd even heard me.

"Maybe it *was* what he said," I went on. "What did he say his worst secret was, again?"

Apparently Wayne had heard me because this time he answered.

"Steve's worst secret was a story he thought he should've written and didn't." Wayne's mouth paused as he stomped the gas and darted in front of a tour bus. "A story that might have helped others, he said."

"Was the story about a Heartlink member?" I prodded.

Wayne grunted again, gaining two car lengths as he did.

"All right, maybe the story wasn't about anyone who had anything to do with Heartlink," I said. "Maybe someone we don't even know found out about his story and—"

"The key, Kate," Wayne reminded me quietly. "Had to be one of us. They got the key at the potluck."

I put my head into my hands. How could I have forgotten? Probably the same way I'd forgotten about Aunt Dorothy. Denial is a powerful and effective strategy.

I dropped my hands from my head as we whizzed onto Nineteenth Avenue.

"So *did* Steve want to write a story about someone at the potluck?" I persisted.

Wayne sighed. "Maybe," he conceded. "Or maybe this has nothing to do with Steve's worst secret, maybe it has to do with someone else's worst secret, maybe a secret we don't even know about."

"But who?" I muttered in frustration.

Wayne just shrugged and ran a yellow light.

I reviewed my list of murder suspects in silence as the

cars blurred around me. And then I thought about Steve again. For all the nice things people had said about him, I'd sensed a nasty undercurrent, too. Isaac had called Steve a prig, and Janet had called him repressed. I'd never felt much of anything personal emanating from Steve Summers myself, except a strong sense of righteousness. Self-righteousness? I knew how annoying that could be. But being annoying was not punishable by death. Or was it?

I played out a dozen scenarios in my head. Self-righteousness could lead a person to tell the police about someone's drug use or someone's son's joy-riding, or to tell another person's wife about an affair. But wouldn't Steve's respect for the rules of group confidentiality have inhibited any of those impulses? Wayne was probably right. If there was a secret involved, it was probably one we didn't know about. And now there was another secret—murder.

The road was opening up, even though my brains were snarled.

We were almost to the airport. In rapid succession, Wayne moved from Highway 280 to 380 to 101, and then we were on our way over the overpass and around to the concourse. We sighted the airline logo and I yelled at Wayne to stop. He pulled into an illegal space a bus had just left.

I jumped out of the car. It was three minutes to four.

"I'll park, and then I'll find you," Wayne yelled out at me. I could barely hear him over the roar of shuttles, busses, and cars, and the honking that had just begun behind us.

I gave him a thumbs-up sign and ran into the terminal. I found Dorothy's flight on the incoming airline monitor. It was on time. I jogged though the maze, stopping only for the metal detector. I bumped a young man as I ran and apologized. He had brown skin and deep, dark eyes that seemed to look back into mine as if . . .

I started jogging again. I was a married woman. I shouldn't have even noticed that man's eyes, much less looked into them. This seemed to be happening way too often lately.

Finally, I was at the gate. It was after four, but the plane had just begun to empty itself of passengers.

I panted, wiped the sweat off my face, and belatedly wondered if I looked like the woman my Aunt Dorothy would have wanted me to grow into.

And then my Aunt Dorothy came waltzing down the ramp, looking no different than she had the last time I'd seen her. A well-preserved sprite, Dorothy Koffenburger was not quite five feet or a hundred pounds. But her lack of earthly substance was made up for by the energy she radiated. The lines in her face all pointed to her smiling, mascared eyes. Her white hair was bound up into two twists that ended in curlicues atop her head. That day, she wore a sensible navy blue pantsuit that matched the two small navy canvas bags she carried. When she saw me, she dropped her bags and stretched out her arms.

"Katie!" she greeted me, in a voice that seemed to shimmer with delight.

I didn't correct her, I just galloped the last few steps to meet her and wrapped her tiny frame in my arms. Aunt Dorothy was irresistible. I hadn't forgotten this important fact, but I'd forgotten how it felt to be under her spell. Aunt Dorothy was the magic fairy godmother everyone wanted, and she was mine.

After a good hug, I grabbed her luggage. It couldn't have weighed more than a few pounds.

"Way to go, Aunt Dorothy," I congratulated her. "You know how to pack light."

"Oh, Katie, you're so sweet, just like always," she told me, reaching out her hand to pat my arm. "Of course, there's a lot more where those came from. I checked most of my luggage."

"Oh," I muttered. I kept my groan internal. Everyone's favorite fairy godmother . . . with baggage.

"This is just wonderful, Katie," she chirped as we took the escalator down to the luggage carousel. "I was so thrilled when your mother called to tell me you'd asked for my advice as a wedding planner."

"Um . . ." I began, but decided that this wasn't the time to tell her that it wasn't my idea.

"My favorite niece. What could be more perfect?" No, definitely not the right time.

"Now, I know you and Wayne have some reservations about a formal wedding," she assured me. My spirits lifted. Maybe she'd incurred psychic powers when her plane had landed in the Bay Area. "But it's only the fear of the unknown."

I nixed the notion of psychic powers. I wasn't afraid of the unknown. I was afraid of the known. I'd been married formally once, and look how that had turned out.

"Actually, Wayne and I are happy as we are," I began, but I didn't know how to finish.

"Of course, you are, my dear," she trilled. "That's what will make the ceremony so special!"

We walked to the luggage carousel on that note, and Aunt Dorothy began to point.

"Oooh, that one's mine!"

I snagged a navy blue suitcase that was heavy enough to have held Jimmy Hoffa's remains.

I had grabbed the third piece of luggage when someone put their hand on my shoulder. I spun around, ready to kick if necessary. But it was only Wayne, sweating. He must have run from the parking lot.

"You found us," I said, stating the obvious.

He looked at the luggage that surrounded me and his eyebrows lowered.

"Aunt Dorothy," I said quickly. "This is my husband, Wayne Caruso."

Aunt Dorothy didn't seem to notice Wayne's lowered eyebrows, or his pitted skin or cauliflower nose, for that matter. She just smiled a smile that lit up her face and then attacked Wayne with a hug.

"Oh, goodness," she murmured when she let him go. "You *are* a big man, aren't you? Katie must be so happy with you."

I wasn't sure if I followed her logic, but I loved her for loving Wayne on sight.

Wayne just blushed and mumbled, but I could tell he was under Aunt Dorothy's spell, too.

Finally, we piled my aunt's luggage in a cart. It looked

like it was enough to last a month. I was beginning to panic when I noticed a tall, broad man with long hands and the most beautiful cheekbones standing near us. Damn. It had happened again! I pulled my eyes away. Was it the institution of marriage that was causing these weird hormonal surges? Or did marriage itself give my eyes the permission to roam? Or was it the threat of a formal marriage that was driving me to—

"So, Wayne," Dorothy interrupted my rampaging thoughts. "Katie's mother tells me you own a restaurant that's also an art gallery. What a happy combination."

I expected Wayne to mumble that the combination hadn't been his idea, but for once he didn't.

"La Fête à L'oeil," he replied with quiet pride. "Food to delight the eye and palate, and art to delight the eye and mind." Yes, Wayne was under my aunt's spell, all right.

"Oh, I can hardly wait to find out more. Who are some of your artists?"

And so it went until we'd rolled into the parking lot and stowed away Aunt Dorothy's luggage.

On the way back to Marin, we talked about Jest Gifts, wedding plans, Wayne's writing, our cat, our house. The only thing we didn't talk about was murder. Once we were back in town, we checked Aunt Dorothy into the local hotel on the corner; I didn't think she'd be comfortable sleeping on a futon in our living room. Dorothy's hotel room was decorated in a combination of pinky-beige and dark green with a flowered bedspread and matching draperies. I helped her with her luggage—on a much nicer cart than the airport had provided—while Wayne signed her in. I had a feeling he was putting her bill on his credit card, too. And then we brought her to our house for one of Wayne's home-cooked dinners.

"And you cook, too," Aunt Dorothy cooed at Wayne as she followed the two of us into our entryway. She looked over the living room: overflowing bookshelves, houseplants, hanging chairs, pinballs, and all.

I held my breath, waiting for her reaction, realizing suddenly how much it mattered to me.

"Oh, my!" she exclaimed. Then she clasped her hands together. "I couldn't have imagined a better place for you to live, Katie. This is really fun."

I let out my breath and hugged my aunt again. Even if she was making it up, my Aunt Dorothy had her *heart* in the right place. If only I could get her *mind* off of weddings.

Aunt Dorothy insisted on following Wayne into the kitchen as he began his dinner preparations. Meanwhile, I checked my answering machine. The light was blinking, and the tape was full.

"How fun to watch a real chef in action," Aunt Dorothy's voice said from the kitchen.

I hit the playback button and listened to tinny messages, Wayne's and Dorothy's voices mingling in the background, deep versus high, rough versus tinkling.

"Oh my, I don't believe I've ever tasted Vietnamese cooking before . . ."

"Fresh herbs are the secret . . ."

"This is Helen Herrick," the first message announced. "I just wanted to say that I'm very sorry for any distress that Isaac may have caused you by telling the police what Wayne said in group." I turned down the sound, realizing that if I could hear Wayne and Aunt Dorothy, they could probably hear my answering machine. "He shouldn't have done such a stupid thing, but common sense isn't his greatest virtue." There was a pause, and then she continued. "You don't have to call back. I just wanted you to know he realizes his error."

"Is that tofu?" I heard from the kitchen.

"Carl Russo here," the next message greeted me. "Yeah, well, I just wanted to say thanks, man. Kid screwed up. He didn't mean to, but whaddaya gonna do, huh? Anyway, thanks for cleaning up. And . . . I'll see ya."

"I marinated it in a mixture of . . ."

"This is Laura Summers," the machine recited. "I had a call from Joe Calderon. He mentioned that you two visited. I just wanted to let you know that I appreciate your concern, and that I'm worried for you. Please don't put yourselves in danger. Captain Wooster may be rude, but I assume he's competent. My love to you both."

"Oh noodles, now *those* I understand," Aunt Dorothy said and laughed.

"Hey Wayne, Van here." The next voice came out of the machine. "These police, d'ya think they can search your house for no reason? I've just been thinking. I mean, are we all suspects? Does that give them the right to come into our houses? I'm trying to think ahead here. You know, personal habits and all—" I hit fast forward. I felt like calling Van back and telling him to flush his stash of drugs down the toilet, but it wasn't my business.

"Goodness, are you sure you don't want any help?" Aunt Dorothy inquired from the kitchen.

"Sit, sit," Wayne replied.

I thought about calling Laura Summers back. I wanted to know about Steve's friends, but I couldn't talk in front of Aunt Dorothy. Maybe I could hide in the bedroom and talk on the extension.

"Oh, this smells lovely. No wonder you own a restaurant," my aunt's words came my way on the herb-scented air.

Aunt Dorothy was right. Wayne's cooking *did* smell lovely. And I knew it would eventually taste lovely, too. I decided Laura Summers could wait and joined my aunt and husband in the kitchen.

Wayne was bent over the stove, stirring some kind of broth with his right hand and checking the lid of another pot with his left. I knew he'd already made salad and dessert ahead of time. It was just as well that I'd left some of my lunch uneaten. I'd need room for dinner.

I sat down at the kitchen table across from Aunt Dorothy. Someone had already set the table for three, and I had a feeling it was the sprite I was looking at. I smiled and leaned back in my chair, feeling relaxed for the first time all day.

"Have you decided on your color scheme yet, dear?" Aunt Dorothy asked.

"For what?" I replied.

She laughed her trademark fairy-godmother laugh.

"Your wedding, dear. Your wedding."

The meal was great: Vegetarian Vietnamese pho (noodles and tofu and seitan and a perfect blend of spices and herbs in broth), yam salad, saffron rice with raisins, and orange cake and carob sorbet for dessert.

Wayne and Aunt Dorothy got along famously as we all ate. They talked easily, even exchanging cooking tips. Of course, they were united by a common goal—a formal wedding.

After I'd eaten my final zipper-busting bite of cake and sorbet, I remembered the mail I'd never picked up.

While Wayne and Dorothy discussed the relative spiciness of Tex-Mex and Vietnamese cooking, I made my way out the door and down the driveway to the mailbox.

I grabbed a stack of bills, ads, and catalogs and began thumbing through them as I walked back up the driveway. Then I came to an envelope without an address on it. I stopped in my tracks and opened it. STOP NOW, it said in huge felt-tip pen letters. Only the words weren't right; The "p" in "stop" was turned backward. I immediately thought of Isaac. Was this some kind of dyslexic joke? It didn't look like a joke. Something about the crude letters made me shiver.

I rushed the rest of the way into the house to show the letter to Wayne, but then I remembered Aunt Dorothy. I put the letter face-down on my desk and helped Wayne with the dinner dishes.

Afterward, we all sat in the living room, Aunt Dorothy enjoying the swinging chair for one while Wayne and I sat in the double chair across from her.

"The first thing you have to do, Katie," she told me, "is make a list."

I didn't have to ask her what she was talking about his time.

"A list," I repeated bleakly.

"There are so many decisions: colors, the members of the bridal party, gown, caterers, flowers—"

The phone rang and I sprang out of the hanging chair I'd shared with Wayne, leaving it haphazardly jerking in place with Wayne at the tiller, calming it. My rescuer was none other than Jade, my warehousewoman from Jest Gifts.

"Kate," she greeted me without preamble. "You shoulda

never hired that guy to do your computer mouses. He's a total flake, almost as bad as the first guy."

"What did he do?" I asked, not even dreading the answer. Jade had saved me from wedding planning; she could complain all she wanted. And she did—about unsatisfactory manufacturing, inadequate delivery, stupid hired help, and the idiocy of the world in general. I heard her out until the doorbell rang. Then I said goodbye and hung up.

Wayne got to the door before I did, but I could see who had come to visit. Garrett Peterson and Jerry Urban were standing in the entryway.

"We have to talk," Garrett declared as he stepped forward. And then he saw Aunt Dorothy.

His dark skin seemed to darken even more, and stretch tighter over his wide cheekbones. Garrett was a handsome man, there was no doubt about it. I swore at myself. Now I was noticing a man from Wayne's group, and a gay one at that.

Garrett exchanged a look with Wayne and one with Jerry Urban. Aunt Dorothy was a civilian.

"We came to express our condolences over the death of a dear friend," Garrett explained.

"Oh, my," Aunt Dorothy murmured. "I'm terribly sorry. Was it a long illness?"

There was another quick exchange of heavy looks, and Garrett opened his mouth to speak again. But before he had a chance, a small, slender figure darted through the still-open door.

"So what's the news on the stiff?" the figure asked.

"Felix," I snapped. "Perhaps another time. We have guests."

"No problemo," he replied. "Maybe between all of us, presto-pronto, we can figure out who committed this friggin' murder."

"A murder?" Dorothy's voice asked, and she didn't sound chirpy anymore.

TEN

"Black," I blurted out. Five sets of eyes stared my way. "Black, that's what I'd like as the color scheme for the wedding."

"Black?" Dorothy questioned, her head tilted so that one silver-white curlicue poked upward. It was working. She'd forgotten the murder for the moment.

"Holy socks, Kate," Felix squawked. "Have you gone friggin' gonzo? Back to the—"

"And the flowers," I put in, speeding up my rap. "Black. I've heard of black pansies. And roses. There must be others . . ."

Garrett was staring at me intently. Was his expression that of a concerned psychiatrist?

"Kate!" Felix caterwauled. "What about the stiff? What about—"

"And a long, black bridal gown," I interrupted him. "And Wayne can wear—"

"Katie, is there something you don't want me to know?" Dorothy asked quietly.

My adrenaline pooled in my stomach. Aunt Dorothy was way too smart to fall for my distractions. Maybe I should have suggested a gray color scheme. Black was a definite tip-off.

"Katie?" Aunt Dorothy asked again.

"A friend of ours was murdered," I finally admitted sullenly.

"And Kate saw the whole friggin' thing," Felix put in helpfully. "Presto-pronto, whiz-bang. Man, how she's always got her feet nailed to a murder scene before it even comes down just blows me away. I mean, here I am, an honest-to-God reporter, stories up the wahzoo, and do I find the stiffs? Nooo—"

"You did once," I reminded him. "Twice."

Felix paled at the memory for a moment; maybe a little more than a moment. Good. But then his mouth began moving again.

"This poor geek who got offed was in Wayne's friggin' men's group—"

"Felix," I broke in. Dorothy didn't need to hear all the gory details. "Why don't you tell my Aunt Dorothy about Barbara? She's great at wedding planning."

"Barbara is great at wedding planning?" Felix asked, his soulful eyes squinting in confusion.

"No, my aunt." I took a deep breath and put on my hostess smile. "Has everyone here met my aunt, Dorothy Koffenburger? This Is Garrett Peterson, Jerry Urban, and . . ."

I was having trouble even saying Felix's name. My throat seemed to have closed up.

"Felix Byrne, glad to meet ya." He saved me the trouble, advancing on Aunt Dorothy, hand extended.

Dorothy shook his hand and nodded at Garrett and Jerry, who were still at the door with Wayne.

"You wouldn't believe the deep doo-doo Kate steps in," Felix continued once the introductions were finished. He seemed to be addressing Aunt Dorothy. I could see Wayne stalking Felix out of the corner of my eye. "Here she is, The Typhoid Mary of—"

"That's enough," Wayne broke in.

Felix jumped in place. I was glad to see it. I just wished he'd hop out of our house and down the stairway.

"Whoa, Big Guy," Felix squeaked, taking a couple of steps backward. "I just wanted to tell Kate's aunt here how cool she is, ya know? I mean, how many females find the dead guy at a *men's* group? That takes some chutzpah, and Kate's got it—"

"What do you want here, Felix?" Wayne asked, his voice a quiet growl.

"Hey, we gotta toss this thing around, man," Felix answered. "The local gestapo is definitely not logged on in Cortadura. Dimes to doughnuts, Kate's gonna figure out the poop on the perp, if you know what I mean. And I just want to help."

"Actually . . ." Garrett took a moment to clear his throat, looked at Wayne meaningfully, and then went on. "Jerry and I came to see you on a similar mission. We thought if we talked out what we knew about Steve's murder, we might find something communally that we'd missed individually."

"Yeah, man," Felix agreed enthusiastically. "Brother Ingenio says there are no accidents. We're all here for the same friggin' reason—"

"Felix, my aunt—" I began.

"Yeah, Aunt Dorothy," Felix said, turning his eyes on my aunt. "Whaddaya think of groupthink?"

"Well, I think it might be very interesting," Aunt Dorothy piped up. "The more perceptions on a problem, the less problematic it may seem." She paused to look demurely at her navy blue lap for a moment. "And perhaps I can help."

What a concept. Were fairy godmothers good for more than wedding planning? Yes! Dorothy was a wise woman with more than eighty years of experience with people. If anyone's perceptions would be useful, hers were the ones I'd bet on.

But I wasn't so sure about the rest of our think tank. Garrett and Jerry were suspects. And Felix was . . . well, Felix. Still, a persistent alternative strategy was shuffling up to the front of my mind. We *did* have a variety of viewpoints represented: Felix was a know-it-all, Garrett a psychiatrist, Jerry an engineer, Dorothy a wise woman, Wayne a quiet thinker, and I—

Felix plopped himself down on the couch before I could finish my thought, which was probably good because my major qualification for the group mind experiment was my ability to step in doo-doo, as Felix had so inelegantly put it.

"Why don't we all sit down?" Wayne invited, only a hint of exasperation flavoring his gruff voice. Still, I knew that invitation had to have been hard for him.

Garrett and Jerry took the hanging chair for two. Aunt Dorothy kept her seat in the hanging chair for one. Wayne and I looked at each other. If two pairs of eyes could sigh, ours did. Then we sat on either side of Felix, where he'd staked his spot in the center of the denim couch.

"If you'd be so kind as to tell me about the man who was murdered and the people you suspect, it might prove a useful place to start," Aunt Dorothy suggested. I was lulled by her voice. She might have been a teacher explaining the assignment for a class, a simple assignment that had the potential to be successfully executed.

"Steve Summers," Felix offered up gleefully. "He was this hot-as-hell journalist. Big time. One of those friggin' I'm-so-ethical types—"

"Aren't journalists supposed to be ethical?" I asked Felix sweetly.

It worked. He blushed.

"Steve was what we might call a perfectionist," Garrett put in.

"He set his standards high for himself *and* for others," Jerry added. "He wasn't exactly a get-down-and-boogie guy."

"I see," Dorothy said, and I had a feeling she did. "Was he married?"

"Sheesh, Lucy, you better believe he was married," Felix answered. "To Laura Summers, hotshot assemblywoman for Marin County. She's so hot, you could fry eggs on her, man."

"She does a very good job representing her constituents," Garrett translated. "Very well-respected."

"Was Steve jealous of his wife?" Aunt Dorothy asked.

I looked up, startled. Had he been? I'd never thought about it.

"No," Garrett answered slowly. "I'd guess that Steve was proud of his wife, actually. Intensely proud."

I let myself relax, glad that Steve had been a hero in that regard. Not very many men can handle the Mister-husband-of role.

"Laura and Steve were in sync," Wayne added.

"I don't want to be indelicate," Aunt Dorothy said. "But how was Steve Summers killed?"

I let Felix fill my aunt in on the gory details, which he did with glee. The rest of us tried not to flinch.

When Felix was finished, Dorothy nodded sagely. "And who do you suspect?" she asked. I guess that wasn't as indelicate as her previous question.

"The members of the group," Wayne mumbled miserably.

"And their significant others," I added. I didn't mention the potluck key. There were suspects present, not to mention Felix. "See, they were the ones who knew when Steve would be leaving that day."

"Who are these people?" Aunt Dorothy asked, leaning forward.

"I'm a member of the Heartlink group," Wayne admitted.

"And I knew when he'd be leaving," I added, not to be outdone. "But we both alibi each other, Wayne's car or not."

"Yeah, right," Felix chimed in. He leaned back and crossed his arms. "Married couples are *such* friggin' reliable alibis. Don't even have to do the payola thing with community property—"

"I'm a group member also, Mrs. Koffenburger," Garrett interrupted Felix.

"And I'm his sigo," Jerry stated defiantly, his eyes mischievous behind his glasses. "His significant other, his life partner."

But my aunt wasn't surprised or troubled by Garrett and Jerry's relationship. She'd probably spotted it the minute they came through the door. In fact, she was probably planning their wedding, too.

"Is there any reason I should suspect any of you four?" she asked.

"I don't think so," Garrett said solemnly, looking up at the ceiling as if it might answer the question more fairly.

"Hey, wait uno momento here," Felix objected, bouncing

on the seat between us. "You think they're going to admit anything?"

"No," my aunt replied stoutly. "So why don't we just move on to the other possibilities?"

Felix glared at her, obviously confused by her logic.

"Four other members of the group," Wayne began. "Ted Kimmochi—"

"Ha!" Felix barked. "Hanky-panky Ted. Wonder what his wife, Janet, would do if she found out about his extracurricular bouncy-bouncy? Huh-huh? That woman's meaner than a camel with a bladder infection, man—"

I whirled my head around to glare at Felix.

"How'd you know about Ted, anyway?" I demanded. "Only the group members—"

"I'll give you a friggin' clue," he told me. "Maybe two clues. A big, square auto who'd like to cut off his ear."

"Van Gogh," Wayne said and sighed. I thought I heard Jerry chuckle. "Van." So much for group confidentiality. First, Isaac Herrick, and now Van Eisner.

"Yep," Felix agreed cheerfully. "The Van man himself. He's almost as busy spilling everyone's—" Felix lowered his voice melodramatically—"*worst secrets* as he is doing recreational chemicals. Guy's looney tunes, if ya ask me."

The room was silent. The phrase *worst secrets* seemed to thrum in the air, chanting in our ears and kicking us in our stomachs. Except for Aunt Dorothy; she just tilted her head, bobbing her white curlicues like a bird. Of course, she didn't know what secrets Van and Felix were talking about.

Garrett cleared his throat.

"Ted has told me that he isn't going to see Belinda anymore," he announced. "And I believe him."

"Belinda is the woman who . . ." I didn't want to finish the sentence in front of my aunt.

"Yes, Belinda was the teacher at the tantra and bondage seminar Ted and Janet attended, but Ted—"

"Bondage seminar?!" I gasped. Then I looked at Wayne. He didn't look back. He'd known about this!

"Ted fell in love with his teacher," Wayne whispered, eyes lowered.

"Teacher?" I repeated. "I thought you said he met her at Spirit Rock."

"He did, and then he and Janet took her class . . ."

"Belinda is a dominatrix," Jerry supplied. There was no question that his eyes were laughing now, even if the rest of him wasn't.

"The one with a whip?" I bleated.

Jerry nodded. "Actually," he stage-whispered, as if someone might be listening at the door, "I don't think they really use whips. Just a lot of fantasy. Whoop it up and then go home with your mate for some, um . . ." He looked at my aunt and his speech faltered.

"Marital experimentation?" she suggested mildly.

"Yes, ma'am," Jerry said, his round face flushing. "Mind if I get a glass of water, Kate?"

I nodded, remembering Jerry's diabetes. Was his thirst due to his illness or to a need to be away from Aunt Dorothy's eyes? I wanted to avoid her eyes, too. My mind boggled at the idea of Ted and Janet experimenting at anything, much less fantasy bondage. For a moment, though I *could* picture Janet with a whip. But tantra was supposed to be spiritual, wasn't it? Tantra and bondage? The two words didn't belong in the same sentence, much less the same seminar. But then, maybe I didn't understand. I wanted to ask for more details. But I forced my mouth closed. This wasn't getting us any closer to finding Steve's murderer.

"So," my aunt's voice cut through my tangled thoughts. "Wayne, Garrett, and Ted are group members. Kate, Jerry, and Janet are significant others?"

I nodded.

"Who else?" she prodded.

"Van Eisner," Felix supplied. "The man is some kinda sleaze-ball, if ya ask me. And is he baked on chemicals or what? No friggin' significant other for him, man. He's not even serially monogamous. And that guy gets more humma-humma than—" Suddenly Felix stopped and turned to Dorothy as if he'd forgotten her, closed his mouth temporarily, then turned back to Wayne and started over. "Just a warning, man: Van's a druggie. He'd turn in your whole group for mass execution in exchange for a free stash license."

Wayne wriggled his shoulders. The truth can make your muscles tight instead of setting you free.

"And Isaac Herrick and Carl Russo are group members." Garrett finished the list.

"Isaac Herrick?" Dorothy said, her eyes widening in her wrinkled face.

"Nasty old geek," Felix told her glumly. "Wouldn't tell me a friggin' thing."

An image of Isaac Herrick's alcohol-reddened face flashed through my mind, and I smiled. Maybe Isaac truly had been sorry about breaking confidentiality with Captain Wooster. Or maybe he was just tweaking Felix. Either way, I liked him all the better for it.

"Helen Herrick's his wife," Jerry Urban put in, crossing the entryway from the kitchen with a glass of water in his hand.

"His sigo," Aunt Dorothy said, smiling to show she'd learned a new word.

Jerry smiled back.

"Which leaves—" my aunt closed her eyes to remember—"Carl Russo."

"Yeah, Carl Russo," Jerry agreed. Then he shook his head. "I worry about Carl. The guy never has any fun. He's so uptight about that kid of his; that's all he thinks about."

"Carl has a son—Mike," Wayne explained. "Mike's gotten in a little trouble, and Carl's concerned about him."

"Children can be difficult," Aunt Dorothy said, smiling my way.

I felt my cheeks go hot. Even in their advanced forties, some children can be difficult for their poor mothers, was what I heard Dorothy saying. Maybe she knew I didn't agree with my mother about a formal wedding. For an instant, I was sure I was right.

Then I shook my head to clear it. Dorothy's comment might have meant anything. And we were here to solve Steve Summers' murder, not to talk about weddings.

"So who do you think the murderer is?" Dorothy asked.

There was silence all around. Even Felix didn't offer an opinion.

"Well, then," Aunt Dorothy suggested cheerily, "perhaps we should all think on it for a while."

Garrett and Jerry took her words as their cue for an exit. Wayne patted the two men on their respective shoulders as they left. And then we turned to Felix. How rude could we be in front of my aunt?

I was just opening my mouth to test the limits when Felix leaned back and began talking.

"Been reading the Cortadura police reports," he said casually.

I shut my mouth.

"Pretty friggin' interesting reading, ya know what I mean?" he went on.

I nodded. Wayne sighed and sat back down on Felix's other side.

"So, any whiz-bang guesses what they say?" he taunted.

I shook my head.

"You wouldn't wanna pump your compadre for a little info, now would ya?" he continued. "A little scoop for friendship's sake?"

"No need to pump," Wayne growled. His voice was deep enough to raise the hair on the back of *my* neck, and I was on the other side of Felix. "Tell us now."

"Hey, man!" Felix squealed, flattening himself against me to get away from Wayne. "No reason to go ape-bleep about it. I'm gonna tell you."

"That would be nice," Aunt Dorothy chirped.

Felix swallowed and resumed his casual posture. He was so artificially relaxed, I thought he might shatter if someone tapped him. My finger raised to his shoulder to test that theory, but I pulled it back. I *did* want to know what was in the reports, after all.

"Van Eisner has a prior drug possession conviction," Felix muttered sullenly. I guess Wayne had taken the fun out of torturing us. "If he gets popped again, Van the man could do serious time."

"Oh, my," Dorothy commented.

Felix brightened. "Isaac's got a DUI—"

"A DUI?" Dorothy questioned.

"Driving under the influence, man." Felix pantomimed a bleary-eyed Isaac with one hand on the wheel and the other sipping what might have been a martini. It was actually pretty funny . . . but would have been funnier if it hadn't been Felix.

"Then there's the kid, Mike Russo," Felix went on. "Vandalism. Big friggin' deal, huh? Everyone's worried the kid's going to hell in a hand basket, and all he's done is spray-painted a couple of buildings." He shook his head. "Not a biggie, if ya ask me."

I kept my eyes straight ahead. If no one had told Felix about Mike's unreported joy-riding, I didn't want him to hear it from me.

"And, hey," Felix said, looking at Wayne first, and then at me. "You two are gonna love this one. Guess who got caught with sticky fingers twenty years ago?"

"I don't know, Felix." I forced the words out as politely as possible. "Who?"

"Janet McKinnon-Kimmochi, that's who. What a trip! I wonder how her clients would feel about having a friggin' ex-shoplifter for a financial advisor?"

"Janet?" I asked, dumbfounded. Bondage *and* shoplifting? I was getting a little confused about Janet McKinnon-Kimmochi. In fact, I got so lost in the series of images that flashed through my mind that I missed part of what Felix said next.

". . . something about Carl Russo, some kind of record in another state."

"For what?" I asked.

"I don't know yet, okay? Jeez Louise, even *my* sources don't include New Jersey."

"Anything else?" Wayne prodded.

"Yeah-uh," Felix replied, drawing out the word as if to tease us.

"Now!" Wayne ordered from somewhere deep down in his throat.

"Fine, fine. Keep cool, Big Guy," Felix backpedaled. "Okay, the best poop of the evening is . . ."

He waited for prompting, then turned to Wayne, took in his glare, and went on without a drum roll.

"Jerry Urban used to be a race car driver."

"And a car was used as the murder weapon," Aunt Dorothy finished up for him.

"Don't have to be a race car driver to hit and run," Wayne pointed out.

"Yeah, but it couldn't friggin' hurt." Of course, Felix had managed to get the last word on the subject.

"You know, Katie," Aunt Dorothy began. "I'd like to talk to some of these, well, friends of yours. Isaac—"

The phone rang before she could plan her strategy verbally. I wondered if our think tank had unleashed a sleuthing monster in my aunt.

"It's Van," I heard the voice say from the answering machine in my office. "For God's sake, if you're there, pick up—"

I beat Wayne off the couch and to the phone. I didn't want him to deal with the Benedict Arnold of the Heartlink group until Felix was gone from the premises.

"Hi, Van," I answered casually, all too aware that Felix and Aunt Dorothy were within hearing distance. But Dorothy was talking again by the time Van responded.

"Kate, is that you?" he asked. His voice was shrill.

"Yes," I answered, keeping it short.

"Hey, is Wayne around?"

"Busy," I told him.

"Look, I gotta talk to somebody," Van said. I guessed I was going to be that somebody. His words picked up speed. "Do you think the cops know about my . . . um . . ."

"Stash?" I finished for him.

"Yeah, that," Van answered.

"I have no idea," I said honestly. "Why are you so worried?"

"My house, it looks different!" His words were pinging against my eardrums like hail now. I held the receiver away from my head. "Or maybe it doesn't. But I can't remember.

I'm really freaked. What if they're looking for . . ."

"Your drugs?" I tried to help out.

"Don't even say that over the telephone!" he screamed. "They've probably got it bugged. I don't get it. I just want to have a little fun. I don't want to hurt anyone . . ."

I thought of all the information he'd given to Felix.

"Why don't you just flush the you-know-what?" I suggested coolly.

Van hung up the phone. I just hoped he was running to carry out my advice. But I doubted it.

I listened to the dial tone for a moment and then hung up the receiver. The phone rang again immediately.

I picked it up, angry now.

"Listen, Van," I said. "You want help, how about you try giving some—"

"Kate?" a voice said over the phone. It wasn't Van's. It didn't say much for my mental state that I didn't recognize the voice at first.

"Um, hello," I tried.

"Kate," my mother ordered. "Let me talk to your Aunt Dorothy. And right this minute."

ELEVEN

꙼

I had Aunt Dorothy on the phone for my mother in less than a minute. My aunt didn't seem too upset to be torn away from Felix Byrne's company. Or maybe it was the panic on my face that motivated her. Whatever it was, she excused herself gracefully and stood from the hanging chair with a movement that might have been practiced for years. Then she walked to the phone as I thought of a trio of warnings: Don't tell Mom about my suggestion of black as the color scheme for the wedding; don't tell Mom about my friends, especially Felix; and please, oh please, don't tell Mom about the murder. But Aunt Dorothy had spoken into the receiver before I could give voice to even one of my warnings.

So I stood across the hall from my aunt and stared, hoping she would see the plea in my eyes to withhold information from my mother. If nothing else, though, I was positioned well for eavesdropping.

"Now, Grace," I heard Aunt Dorothy protest.

My shoulders tightened.

"Everything is just fine," my aunt said. My shoulders loosened a thread.

"Van?" she trilled. I opened my eyes wider. I hoped I looked like a cocker spaniel, but I probably looked more like some species of fish. "Oh, dear me, I don't think I actually *know* anyone named Van, dear."

Cool, I saluted my aunt internally. And she was even telling the truth. She didn't actually know Van Eisner.

"Oh, just fine," she said in answer to some unknown question. "You've got to stop worrying, Grace. Wedding or not, Katie's a good girl, a sensible girl."

I blushed and lowered my eyes.

"He's a very kind and good man," she went on. "Just perfect for Katie."

I turned and saw Wayne blushing now. So, he'd been eavesdropping, too.

"Oh, Katie's chosen her colors," I heard her say, and whipped my head back around. Dorothy grinned at me. "Yes, Grace. You just take care. There is absolutely nothing to worry about."

Finally she said goodbye to my mother.

After Aunt Dorothy placed the telephone receiver back in its cradle, she crossed the hall and winked at me. I took two steps and threw my arms around her, hugging her way too tightly. But I couldn't help the intensity of my embrace. She'd done it! She'd finessed my mother, something I'd never been able to do. She hadn't mentioned murder, and even the wedding plans sounded like they were proceeding normally when she spoke. And, best of all, my aunt thought Wayne was kind and good. I gave her an extra squeeze, and then let her go for fear of crushing her fragile body. I didn't want to send her home with broken ribs.

"You always were my favorite aunt," I admitted impulsively.

Aunt Dorothy laughed, and I heard the sound of chimes.

Then I realized that the doorbell was ringing.

Wayne reached the door before I did and opened it.

Laura Summers crossed the threshold and gave Wayne a hug that made my embrace of Dorothy seem nonchalant. Felix's eyes widened as Laura held on to Wayne like a life raft. I took a deep breath and reminded myself that Laura was a grieving widow.

When she finally let go, she looked into Wayne's eyes and murmured, "Is there anything new?" Hers was a husky murmur, not a pathetic one like some people's. Like mine.

I looked away, and my eyes caught Felix's. His eyebrows were raised, and he was actually licking his lips. Of course! He probably hadn't been able to interview Laura Summers yet. Damn.

"Laura," I intervened just as Wayne said, "Don't think so."

Laura turned to me, her eyes focusing with apparent difficulty.

"This is my aunt, Dorothy Koffenburger," I said with a nod at my aunt, who was no longer smiling. "And this is Felix Byrne, a reporter from the *Marin Mind*."

Laura's eyes focused and then narrowed in Felix's direction.

"Good to meet you," Laura said brusquely. And then she stepped forward to take Dorothy's hand in hers. "And it's so good to meet Kate's aunt," she added with more enthusiasm. "I'm Laura Summers."

Dorothy shook Laura's hand, a sympathetic half-smile on her face.

Felix jumped up from the couch.

"Hey, man, this is great!" he told Laura. "You are one whiz-bang assemblywoman! Been talking to my amigos, Kate and Wayne, about your tragedy. You got my friggin' sympathy, man. You ever need to talk—"

"Quite," Laura responded, cutting him off. She turned to me and gave me a short hug, apparently all hugged out after Wayne. "Kate, Wayne, I wanted to let you know that Steve's funeral will be on Saturday . . ." Her voice faltered. She pulled out a hankie and held it to her face.

I turned away, embarrassed to be a witness to her grief. Felix stared at her like a deer spotting an uneaten rosebud.

"I'm so sorry for your loss," Dorothy said, her voice low and respectful. Laura looked up as if really noticing Dorothy for the first time. "I lost my husband not too long ago. I know there's no way to compare experiences, no way to say the right words. But if you need anything at all, please ask."

I sighed. How come I hadn't been able to say those words so simply and eloquently?

"Thank you," Laura replied formally. "I have my assistants to help me with the logistics, but your sympathy is

much appreciated. There *is* no way to explain my feelings."
She paused, then went on. "Wayne, I'd ask you to speak at
the funeral, but I know how you feel about the confidentiality
of the group. Steve would have felt the same."

Wayne looked stricken, his eyes suddenly wide under his
uplifted eyebrows.

"I . . . I . . . it's just . . ." he tried.

"Thanks, Laura," I finished for him.

Standing up in front of a large group to express intimate
feelings had to be Wayne's idea of hell. He'd have probably
gone mute.

"Did your husband have other special friends who might
be able to help you?" Aunt Dorothy asked.

Laura shrugged. "His friends will be at the funeral, of
course," she answered, or didn't answer. She straightened her
shoulders. "Steve wasn't a very outgoing man, socially. His
writing was his life. It was more important than anything
else."

"Not more important than you, I'm sure," Dorothy said
softly.

Laura's perfect skin reddened under her make-up.

"Of course not," she murmured. "Of course not."

"So, Assemblywoman Summers, what can you tell me
about your husband's death?" Felix put in gently—for him.
"Was it an attempt that was directed at you, or do you
think—"

"I've prepared an official statement for the press," Laura
cut him off. "You can get a copy from my assistant."

"But what do *you* think?" Felix bulldozed on. "You must
have your own suspicion of who the perp was—"

"Out!" Wayne ordered. His voice wasn't that loud, but its
intention was. Maybe he felt he couldn't speak at Steve's
funeral, but this task he was up to.

"Hey, wait a friggin' minute," Felix objected. Fear of
Wayne or not, Felix had his political prey in sight and wasn't
about to be distracted.

Wayne strode toward the reporter.

"Listen, Big Guy," Felix whispered loud enough for the
whole room to hear. "This is my chance to scoop it, man—"

Wayne took hold of Felix's arm and steered him toward the door. Felix looked lopsided—the side that Wayne was holding was higher than the other one.

I listened as Felix begged all the way down the stairs. But it didn't do him any good; he wasn't getting a shot at Laura Summers in our house.

"Oh, dear," Aunt Dorothy exclaimed when we heard Felix's car leave, and Wayne came back inside.

"Thank you, Wayne," Laura whispered.

Wayne was the color of his own beet pâté.

"And thank you, Kate and Dorothy," Laura went on. "It's good to have friends at a time like this."

"We'll be here, dear," Aunt Dorothy replied.

There didn't seem to be anything left to say. Laura left without ever having taken a seat, with a quick embrace and an air kiss for each of us.

As I heard Laura's slow, dignified footsteps going down the stairs, I realized that Steve wasn't the only one without a social life. Laura Summers didn't seem to have any close friends, either. Assistants, yes; friends, no. She and Steve must have been there for each other, and now . . .

"Poor woman," Aunt Dorothy sighed.

That said it all. I nodded along with Wayne.

"Let's all sit back down and plan our next steps," Dorothy suggested.

Somehow, I knew I shouldn't let my octogenarian aunt in on a murder investigation. But when she said sit, we sat, back in the hanging chairs.

"We need more information," Dorothy stated. "About Steve and about the group members and their sigos."

Wayne and I nodded, mesmerized. Then we realized that she expected some kind of response.

"My ex-husband, Craig, might know more about Van Eisner," I thought out loud. "They're both in computer consulting. He might even know Jerry Urban. He knows a lot of people in start-up businesses."

My aunt nodded sagely, wisely forgoing any comment or question concerning my ex-husband's reason for being my ex-husband.

"Steve's friends," Wayne muttered. "Gotta find Steve's friends. They might know what he was up to."

"The funeral," I reminded him.

"I want to meet everyone," Aunt Dorothy announced. And I didn't object. What could I say? This woman had finessed my mother, so I was no match for her.

We talked a while longer, and then my aunt brought up her hand to cover a ladylike yawn. Whoa. Jet lag. I hadn't even thought about it.

Wayne and I drove Aunt Dorothy back to the hotel on the corner. She left us in the lobby, insisting that she could tuck herself in.

At the elevator, she turned and waved.

"Nightie-night, lovies!" she chirped, and then she stepped into the waiting maw of the elevator.

"Like your aunt," Wayne commented after we got back in the Toyota.

"She thinks you're good and kind," I shot back, starting up the engine.

Wayne snorted, clearly embarrassed.

I put my arm around his shoulder before pulling out of my parking place. "I think you're good and kind, too," I whispered.

Now he was really embarrassed. But he was smiling. He smiled all the way home.

I opened the front door and let out a blissful sigh of relief. Wayne and I were finally alone.

"Let's turn off the house," he suggested.

"Except for me," I purred back. "You can't turn me off."

But my hormones vaporized when we got to my office and I saw the letter face-down on my desk. I'd forgotten all about the letter.

"Wayne?" I said tentatively.

"What?" he growled back affectionately.

"Um, I got a weird letter in the mail."

"What weird letter?" Wayne asked, his voice all business now.

I showed it to him. It hadn't changed any. It still read, STOP NOW, in outsized felt-tip pen letters. Its words were still twisted, the "p" backwards, and a possible "e" on the end of now. And it still raised the hair on the back of my neck.

"Dyslexic?" Wayne hazarded.

"That's what I thought," I told him, excited now. "But we don't know anyone dyslexic."

"Maybe the handwriting is disguised this way."

"Isaac would know how to write a fake dyslexic letter," I told him.

"And Helen," he reminded me.

"But if Isaac or Helen wrote it, wouldn't it just point suspicion their way?"

"Yeah." Wayne held the letter in his hands and scanned its two misshapen words as if he could discern something from their form.

"Wayne, have you seen the handwriting of everyone in the group?" I asked. "I mean, what if this is the best someone could write?"

Wayne's eyebrows dropped over his eyes. "Haven't really seen much in writing from the group, except from Steve. But Kate, everyone in the group, and all the people who were at the potluck, for that matter, have jobs. They must be able to write."

I mulled this over for a while.

"How about Mike Russo?" I came up with finally. "He doesn't have a job."

"His school would have to notice if he was dyslexic," Wayne argued. "And Carl would have talked to the group about it."

"Okay, how about Ted and Janet Kimmochi?" I tried. "One could be dyslexic, and the other one could be covering."

Wayne shook his head. "They took tests to become certified financial advisors—written tests."

I ran the possible suspects through my head. Van Eisner? A dyslexic couldn't write computer code, could he? Garrett Peterson? How many tests had he taken to become an M.D. and a psychiatrist? And Laura Summers? She'd taken the state bar exam. Good luck to her if she was dyslexic. Carl Russo was an accountant, Jerry Urban an engineer—

"Kate, you do realize, whatever its form, that this is a threat?" Wayne cut into my analysis.

"What?" I said.

"This note is a threat to us, or to one of us."

"There wasn't any address on the envelope," I put in helpfully.

"So what are we being threatened about?" Wayne asked.

"Investigating?" I answered in a very small voice.

"Kate, I'd like to take care of this mess myself," Wayne said carefully. "Maybe you and your aunt could go on a little vacation while I—"

"Don't even suggest it, Mr. John Wayne," I snarled. "Would you go on a vacation and leave me to take care of it?"

"But you're . . . you're—"

"Female?"

"No, I was going to say that you're not a member of the Heartlink group."

Sure that's what he was going to say. That's why it took him three tries to come up with it.

"So, big whoop," I said aloud. "I'm with you, got it?"

After a minute of silence, Wayne said, "Got it," and put his arms around me. I nuzzled his herbed chest, redolent of cooking. He kissed the top of my head. I tilted my head back, and he kissed my lips. It was an equal-opportunity kiss, though. I returned it, with interest.

It wasn't until the next morning, Friday, in the middle of our shower, that we talked about taking the letter to the police. My skin tightened, just imagining Captain Wooster's reaction. Would he even believe we hadn't written it ourselves? And even if the sender *had* been dyslexic, I would bet that person was smart enough not to leave fingerprints. So what would be the use?

"Let's wait a little while," I told Wayne.

He grunted in agreement. His grunt sounded as relieved as I felt.

"The only thing we can do is find out who killed Steve," Wayne added.

I would have had a hard time believing he really meant that if he hadn't taken his slippery-clean body to the phone and called his restaurant to let them know he wouldn't be in that day—on a Friday, no less!

I, too, went to my work desk and said goodbye to my stacks of Jest Gifts paperwork.

"So, what do we do first, Sherlock?" I asked my sweetie.

"First, Van," he announced.

I opened my mouth to ask why Van was first and then closed it again. From the look on Wayne's face, I wouldn't want to be Van.

Van Eisner's office was really more of a large room, located on the second floor over a sushi bar in San Ricardo. I'd been there before. I knew he did most of his real work out of his house. His home office was filled with computers, pieces of computers, manuals, and paper. Finding anything in *that* office was something only Van could do. But this office was different. Neat, with teal furnishings and gray carpet against pearl-white walls, it spoke of money. It said, "Buy my services as a computer consultant."

But today, it was saying something else.

"You slimeball!" a voice shrieked through its closed door. "My girlfriend warned me about guys like you. What if I tell my brother about us, huh? He'll kill you!"

Wayne closed his eyes for a moment, then opened them again and knocked on the door of Van's office.

The shrieking stopped, which was a relief. Even the sushi downstairs was probably cringing.

"Come in?" came Van's nasal voice. The uncertainty in his voice made me wonder how much more trouble he was expecting.

Wayne reached out toward the doorknob, but suddenly the door flew open as if by magic and a buxom, well-cared-for woman in a business suit ran past us and down the stairs.

"Client," Van assured us through the open door, the tremor

in his voice ruining his attempt at nonchalance. "Come on in, you guys."

I took a look at this man. What was it about him that attracted these women in the first place? His slight build? His balding head? His pointy features? All I could see was what drove them away. I moved my eyes away from Van and scanned his office.

It was as neat and polished as ever. The only thing that seemed out of place was a mirror lying face-up on his desk next to his computer—a mirror with a hint of white powder and a razor blade and a straw.

Van must have noticed where I was looking.

"Hey, wanna toot?" he asked jovially.

Wayne growled from beside me.

"Just a little joke, heh-heh," Van said, quickly popping the mirror, blade, and straw into one of his drawers.

"Van, are you crazy?" I asked. "What if it had been Captain Wooster who'd visited you this morning?"

Van's pointy face paled.

"Is he really coming here?" he asked, cleaning off the surface of his desk with a tissue like a mad housewife. He should have wiped his nose, but I didn't tell him that.

"No, Van," Wayne answered for me. "The captain isn't on his way as far as I know, but he could be. Why are you risking everything?"

"For God's sake, it's no big deal," Van insisted, his nasal voice high now with indignation.

"Never mind," Wayne said. "Pretend I never asked."

Van put his head in his hands for a minute, then looked back up, a little color returning to his face.

"You've been divulging group secrets." Wayne cut to the chase.

Van squirmed in his chair.

"Why?" Wayne asked.

"They've got me by the short and curlies, that's why," he whined. "I've . . . I've got a record."

"We know." Wayne told him.

"You know!" Van jumped out of his chair. "See, I'm *not* paranoid." He threw his hands in the air. "Even you know!

It's supposed to be secret. Jeez, they could be here any minute. You've gotta find the killer. I don't want any trouble. I just need to be okay for a while—"

"Van, you need help," Wayne said softly.

Van looked at him, intelligence flashing behind his pinpoint pupils for a moment. Then he shook his head.

"I can't," he whispered. "I just can't."

I was glad when we left. I still didn't see what women saw in Van, but now I felt sorry for him. Even without Steve's death, how much longer could he keep on?

"Did he kill Steve, Kate?" Wayne asked seriously, once we were back in the Toyota and heading home.

"But why?" I answered after a few miles. "Van is messed up, that's obvious. But what motive would he have to kill Steve? Steve wouldn't have broken group confidentiality over Van's drug habit. Van knew that."

"Maybe Van didn't know," Wayne put in. "He said himself that he's paranoid. How much trouble could he be in for a second offense?"

"I read an ad in the paper," I said, suddenly remembering. "For 1-900-DRUGLAW. It's a phone number for an attorney's service. You call these guys, and they answer druglaw questions confidentially. Want me to call and find out just how much trouble Van could really be in?"

"Thanks, Kate," Wayne said and put his warm hand on my thigh. I sighed and the Toyota veered. Wayne removed his hand.

After we got home, I found the ad for 1-900-DRUGLAW in an old paper. I was just dialing the number when I heard a car popping gravel in the driveway through the still-open front door.

A familiar voice chirped in the doorway—my Aunt Dorothy. Once again, I'd completely forgotten about her. I put down the phone and went to greet her.

My fairy god-aunt was not a happy camper.

"You left without me this morning," she accused. She patted her goofy white curlicues, looking forlorn. "I got my own rental car at the hotel. Now, I can investigate with or without you, dear. But of course, I'd rather be part of the team."

"But Aunt Dorothy—" I began

"I know," she told me, her eyes suddenly twinkling behind her mascara. "I'm old. Who better to take risks? You have years ahead of you."

"Don't even say such a thing!" Wayne admonished, stepping up behind me. "We're just trying to figure out—"

"So, I'm with you on this," Dorothy stated.

Wayne and I looked at each other, and then both nodded reluctantly. How were we supposed to stop her?

So, we put my aunt in the back seat of the Toyota and took off to talk to Isaac Herrick.

Isaac lived in a condo in Cortadura. We knocked on the front door and heard grumbling from inside.

"Just a minute! Just a minute!"

Then Isaac was at the door and we were ushered into his living room, a room filled with equal amounts of books and empty whiskey bottles.

He turned to us, his ruddy face bleary for the early visit. He was wearing what looked like pajama bottoms and a ratty flannel robe. His bleary face lit up when he saw Dorothy.

"Whoa!" he said. "My little Dot, still as cute as a button."

"Isaac, you old fraud," Dorothy replied and willingly embraced the fraud in question, ratty robe and all.

TWELVE

Wayne and I must have looked like mismatched twins, staring at Aunt Dorothy and Isaac Herrick with our mouths wide open. How could my sweet aunt be hugging Isaac the Terrible? The smell alone would have put me off. Whatever Isaac had drunk last night was emanating from him quite odoriferously now, not to mention whatever he'd added to the brew this morning. And that ratty robe and those pajama bottoms . . . How much of him was really covered? Would I have to rescue my Aunt Dorothy's virtue?

But Isaac unhanded my aunt before I had to intervene. He even seemed a little embarrassed, straightening his robe and tying the sash tighter.

"How many years has it been, Isaac?" Dorothy said softly.

"Too many," he replied, rubbing the stubble on his face. "Too many."

"How's Helen?" Dorothy asked, her voice a little louder now.

"Helen's great," Isaac told her. "Still as feisty as ever. And as smart. She's divorcing me." He laughed, then returned the question. "How's Claude?"

"Claude passed on," Aunt Dorothy answered. A sad little smile played on her lips. "He would have loved seeing you."

"Oh, I am sorry," Isaac murmured, and I saw the truth of his words on his face—a one-time hint of his humanity.

He gave my aunt a one-armed squeeze. "Damn, they don't make them like Claude anymore," he eulogized.

"Or you," Dorothy pointed out. "I remember you and Claude playing at that old nightclub like it was yesterday."

Isaac Herrick and my Uncle Claude? Playing at a nightclub? My mother hadn't ever told me about this.

"Too bad we had to grow up, huh?" Isaac put in.

"Oh, I'm sure you never did, pumpkin-pie," my aunt chirped and tweaked his cheek. Isaac leaned back and brayed. Yuck. This was as bad as Barbara and Felix. I just hoped my aunt didn't plan on becoming the next Mrs. Herrick after Helen divorced Isaac. If she did, *I* certainly wasn't going to help plan *her* wedding.

Wayne cleared his throat. "Came to ask a few questions about Steve," he told Isaac firmly. Maybe he was as tired of the cooing as I was. "Dorothy is Kate's aunt, by the way."

"Whoa," Isaac said, pulling his eyes away from my aunt to look at me for a moment, and then looking back. "Sorry about the mess. If I'd known you were coming, I'd have called my cleaning lady."

I wasn't sure if he was joking. Maybe he wasn't. He cleared off a couple of straight-backed chairs and a naugahyde sofa before disappearing into the next room with a promise to be back in a "cat's whisker."

My aunt was still chuckling as she lowered herself into one of the straight-backed chairs, delicately pushing an empty bottle aside with her foot.

"Aunt Dorothy . . ." I began and then didn't know how to finish.

"We're very old friends, Katie," she explained. "Helen and Isaac and Claude and I. We had a lot of fun back then. He and your uncle were musicians, did you know that?" Her eyes moistened as I shook my head. "They were beautiful musicians. It was a magic time."

Wayne lowered himself onto the naugahyde sofa.

"But—" I began.

My sweetie tugged at my hand before I said anything stupid.

I sat down next to him.

"Helen and I exchanged cards for years," Dorothy went on. "But then, somehow, we lost the connection. I think they must have moved. It's been so long. I was certainly surprised to hear Isaac's name come up last night."

"And you're as beautiful as ever, Dot," Isaac purred, suddenly back in the living room. He was at least dressed now—in a Hawaiian shirt and khaki pants—though not shaved. And he smelled better. I suspected he had taken a quick sponge-bath.

"Steve," Wayne stated, setting the agenda quickly.

Isaac flopped his long frame onto the remaining chair.

"Steve," Isaac repeated. Then he grinned. "A prig, and hen-pecked to boot," he summarized.

"What do you mean by 'hen-pecked'?" Wayne demanded. I noticed that he didn't challenge Isaac's designation of Steve as a prig.

"He was never in the spotlight around his wife. How could he shine? Hey, I'm a horse's ass, but at least I'm my own horse's ass. Steve was nothing but—"

"A prize-winning journalist," I cut in. I couldn't help it.

"Yeah, I suppose," Isaac admitted. He straightened up in his chair, looking serious for a change. "But that was because Steve knew how to tap the self-righteousness of a self-righteous public. He did a great job at it, but still, where was the man? I never saw him. I saw a shadow."

"So, it must have been his wife's fault?" I pressed.

He bared his teeth at me in a simian smile. "Remind me not to engage in a debate with you, Ms. Jasper. You're too, too right." He bowed my way. "Laura didn't have to hen-peck the man; he was a self-made wimp."

Wayne's face reddened. I reached out and laid my hand gently on his vibrating arm.

"So, I understand you've written extensively about dyslexia," my aunt cut in sweetly—too sweetly. I whipped my head around to look at her. She knew Helen Herrick had helped write those books. I could tell. Had Helen told her in the cards they had exchanged over the years?

And then I wondered if Dorothy knew about our threatening note. But she couldn't have.

Isaac leaned back and chortled. "Ah, yes, dyslexia. My
raison d'être. Why couldn't I have picked the study of wit?
But no, I chose to study the sluggards of language commu-
nication. Ack. But then, it interested Helen." He paused and
smiled wickedly. "And she is, after all, the writer in the family."

"Isaac, can you show me a sample of your writing?" I
asked. I had to know if he'd written our threatening letter.

Isaac's smile faded. "You mean one of my books?" he
responded, confusion in his bleary eyes.

"No, I mean your handwriting," I specified. A weird idea
was going through my head: What if Isaac had chosen to
study dyslexia because he himself was dyslexic? What if Helen had covered for him all these years? It was possible.

Isaac stood and picked up a lined notepad and pen from
a littered coffee table. In elegant cursive, he wrote, ISAAC
HERRICK IS A JERK, then handed the note to me.

All right, he wasn't dyslexic. But he still could have faked
that letter.

"Why?" he asked when I looked back up.

I blushed.

"I . . . I . . ."

"Kate does as she pleases," Wayne growled.

It was a good save. Isaac wasn't going to press me, al-
though both he and my aunt were staring at me with the
curiosity of cats locked out of the bedroom.

"Got any idea who killed Steve?" Wayne went on.

Isaac sighed. "I have a lot of ideas, but that's all they are—
ideas."

Wayne nodded approvingly. At least Isaac wasn't spread-
ing rumors.

"I've got one idea in particular," Isaac added, his voice
softening, his eyes losing focus. "But I have to check a few
things to see if it pans out."

"If you've really got an idea, you ought to go to the police," Dorothy admonished him. "Don't do anything dangerous."

Isaac leaned back and roared with laughter.

"Since when were *you* ever careful, Dot?" he asked finally.

Aunt Dorothy laughed with him. "Since I got old," she told him.

"It never happened," Isaac insisted gallantly.

Dorothy put her hand over her face. "Oh, Isaac," she cooed.

Yuck. Were we going there again?

Apparently, we weren't. Wayne stood up, and I followed his example. Aunt Dorothy didn't balk. She got up and gave Isaac a farewell hug. And then we were out the door of his condo and in the fresh air again. I took a big breath. A little car exhaust scented the sidewalk, but at least the air didn't smell of dust and distillery out here.

"Dot, don't be a stranger!" Isaac yelled from his doorway.

"I won't lose you and Helen again!" she sang back. "You can't keep me away now that I've found you."

I was glad to hear her include Helen. Maybe my aunt *didn't* want to be the next Mrs. Herrick.

Once we were back in the Toyota, Dorothy still insisting on the back seat, we took a moment to plan our next visit.

"I want to talk to Carl Russo—" Wayne began.

"But perhaps Helen Herrick first," Dorothy suggested in such a sweet voice that neither of us even considered arguing. I headed back toward Mill Valley, toward Helen Herrick's house.

"Was Steve really hen-pecked?" Aunt Dorothy asked once we were rolling.

"No couple is perfect," Wayne answered slowly. "But I never heard Steve complain about Laura's public life making him feel small. That wasn't an issue for him. At least, not as far as I could tell."

"And look where Isaac's coming from," I added. "His wife's divorcing him. How do you think he feels about the institution of marriage?"

"Not like you two," Aunt Dorothy answered. "You two do my heart good. Your wedding will be enchanting."

Wayne smiled next to me. I kept my groan internal.

"Your Uncle Claude and I loved each other very much," she went on. "He was playful, but not hurtful. Maybe that's the secret."

I thought about this. Wayne was playful and not hurtful. And Garrett and Jerry seemed to be the same way. But Steve and Laura Summers hadn't been playful, as far as I could tell. Still, I doubted that either would be purposefully hurtful. And Isaac was plenty playful, but he was hurtful as well. And the Kimmochis? I giggled for a moment, trying to decide if bondage was playful or hurtful. It probably depends on the rules.

I was busy imagining scenarios when we arrived at Helen Herrick's. Helen still lived in the house that she and Isaac had shared. Her garden was a well-tended explosion of colors and shapes.

We walked up a pebbled walkway flanked by zinnias, pansies, and towering snapdragons and foxgloves. Heaven. I wondered where the deer were. This time, Aunt Dorothy knocked on the front door.

The door opened slowly. I peeked over Dorothy's shoulder and watched Helen Herrick's expression evolve from a no-solicitors-please scowl to a radiant smile when she recognized my aunt.

"Dot!" she squealed and hugged Dorothy like a long-lost child, which is exactly how Dorothy looked in the larger woman's arms.

"Helen," my aunt whispered from the embrace. "Oh, it's good to see you."

I breathed a sigh of relief as the two women held each other and tossed questions back and forth. Aunt Dorothy's love affair was with both of the Herricks, not just Isaac. Helen's no-nonsense face was more animated than I'd ever seen it before. She rolled her eyes in surprise when she heard that I was Dorothy's niece and shed tears when she heard of Claude's death. And then she laughed at some long story that she and my aunt were simultaneously telling about an evening when the nightclub where their husbands played had been raided.

"Claude was so solemn when he swore you and I were not prostitutes," Aunt Dorothy reminisced.

"Unfortunately, Isaac wasn't so forthcoming," Helen chuckled. "That man can be so bad."

Suspected prostitutes? Did my mother have any idea?

I calmed myself down by thinking of counter-wedding blackmail possibilities and breathing deeply.

"Oh, I haven't even invited you in!" Helen apologized in surprise, some minutes later. For a usually self-contained woman, Helen was acting very silly. But I liked it on her.

She ushered us into her living room, a room with bluish lights, neatly arranged bookshelves, and comfortable corduroy couches. The cinnamon smell of what might have been morning tea lingered in the air.

"Dot," she said, once we were all seated. "How in the world did you ever find me?"

"We're investigating Steve Summers' death," my aunt answered succinctly.

Helen's strong features lost their animation, but her eyebrow still crooked ironically.

"Only you could come to Marin and get mixed up in murder, Dot," she said.

Dorothy laughed. "It's my niece's influence," she defended herself, head tilted to the side, hand over her heart, innocence personified. And then I wondered if anyone had mentioned to my Aunt Dorothy that I was known as the Typhoid Mary of Murder. My brother, Kevin, flashed into my mind. He might have told her if he could have held the thought long enough. Damn.

"Any ideas about Steve's murder?" Wayne inquired.

Helen turned his way unsteadily. I didn't think it was guilt that caused the lack of steadiness. I thought it was my aunt. I was feeling a bit like Jello myself.

"I don't have a clue," Helen said. "But Isaac acts as if he knows something. I've told him to share his idea with the police, or at least with me, but the old goat will not listen."

"He never did, did he?" Dorothy put in.

"No," Helen sighed, then smiled a smile of great sweetness. "I still love him, of course, but living with him is like living with a whirlwind."

My aunt just nodded. History with Isaac notwithstanding, she was still my wise aunt.

"I read the books on dyslexia," Aunt Dorothy said, surprising me. "I recognized your voice."

Helen blushed.

"Not much of a feminist, am I?" she admitted, shaking her head. "I wrote the principle parts of most of the books. But the ideas really were Isaac's. He just lacks the patience to sit down and write. And I cared for the old sot, so I went along with it. I don't think it's much of a secret anymore. Isaac delights in bragging that he persuaded me to do the donkey work."

"And he's cute," Dorothy added mischievously.

Helen laughed.

"Cute, lovable . . . and a drunk," Helen agreed.

Wayne and I were quiet as Helen and my aunt talked. Were we both thinking that Isaac's motive for murdering Steve was not very strong if his non-authorship of his own books was no longer a real secret? Or did Isaac have a worse secret he wasn't sharing? And I wouldn't have put it past him to pretend he knew something about the murderer to remove suspicion from himself. I was so lost in my own thoughts that I almost missed it when Aunt Dorothy said goodbye to Helen Herrick.

Dorothy hugged her and kissed her cheek. Helen's eyes misted—Helen, a woman I'd perceived as being repressed. I realized that I didn't really know Helen. In fact, I wasn't certain I really knew my own aunt anymore. Wayne grabbed my hand, and I was glad to be reminded that there was one person in the room who I knew for sure.

We left Helen Herrick's house and got back on the road to visit Carl Russo's place of business.

"Aunt Dorothy, does my mother know about your past?" I asked, truly curious.

"Yes, dear," my aunt answered. "And I know about hers."

"My mother?" I squealed.

"But you know very well that I keep secrets, dear."

Wayne laughed at my side. I barely noticed; I was too caught up in Aunt Dorothy's words.

"But my mother can't have secrets . . . she—"

"Everyone's mother should have a few secrets," Dorothy

pronounced, and I drove in stunned silence the rest of the way to Walters Ng and Thompson (Tax, Accounting, and Financial Services), Carl Russo's employer.

Carl's accounting firm was housed in a redwood two-story building with heavily carpeted, sound-proofed rooms, expensive furnishings, and quiet calculators.

The receptionist was a young man with an earring in his left ear. He buzzed Carl, who met us in the lobby and then led us back to his office. Even as he walked, Carl's agitation showed in his tense back, which rippled though the expensive suit that didn't seem wide enough in the shoulders for him.

His office contained the same heavy carpet and gray-blue furnishings as the lobby. Only a computer, calculator, and a few papers showed the work he did for Walters Ng and Thompson.

Once the door was closed, Carl leaned forward and asked, "What happened? Is Mike all right?"

"Nothing happened to Mike, Carl," Wayne assured him.

All the energy seemed to drain out of Carl's body. He collapsed into his suit and his fleshy features went blank.

"So what's the deal, then?"

"We just wanted to talk to you about Steve's death," Wayne explained, keeping his voice gentle like you would with a dog whose intentions you weren't sure of. "This is Kate's aunt, Dorothy Koffenburger."

"Oh yeah, glad ta meetcha," he said, reaching out a large hand to grasp Dorothy's smaller one. "Jeez, I'm being stupid. Siddown, you guys."

So we all sat around Carl's desk in office chairs with more controls than my Toyota. I pressed one button and the back of my chair flew back. I was suddenly looking at the ceiling.

"Heh-heh," I heard and realized that Carl was laughing.

It was a good sound, and it broke the ice.

"Listen," Carl told us once I was upright again. "Steve could be a pain in the rear, but he was still a cool guy. He was honest, good-citizen material. I've thought about it, and it just doesn't make sense. Who'd wanna kill the poor guy?"

"Someone with something to lose?" I tried.

"Yeah, but what?" Carl insisted. "Oh, there was that big
deal about our secrets, but nobody would kill over our stupid
secrets. None of them was big enough. And Mike didn't
know anything about the secrets, in case you're interested. I
know the kid looks bad, actin' out all the time, but his counselor says it's just a stage, ya know? So what's left? Van
and his dumb drug habit. Why'd he talk about it if he was
so afraid somebody would tell? And then there's Ted's roll
in the hay . . . Betcha his wife wouldn't care that much; she's
a strange one. There just ain't nuthin' to justify a murder. I
don't get it."

Unfortunately, Carl was talking sense. I didn't get, it either.

"Well, that's it, then," Wayne declared and rose from his
chair gracefully. *He* hadn't played with the buttons on *his*
chair. Nor had my aunt. I got out of *my* chair slowly and
carefully.

Carl said, "Glad ta meetcha," again to my aunt, and we
were out of there.

Ten minutes later, we were parked in the driveway in front
of our house. Dorothy came in with Wayne and me for a
brainstorming session. As we walked through the doorway,
I saw a shadow above us. C. C.

"C. C.—" I began.

"Now, you wouldn't want to jump on any of us, would
you?" my aunt finished for me. C. C. tilted her head, considering my aunt's words. "Of course you wouldn't."

C. C. jumped to the floor like that's all she'd been planning, anyway. Someday soon, I'd have to introduce my aunt
to my psychic friend, Barbara. I'm sure they'd have lots to
talk about.

"Now, don't you two get frustrated," Aunt Dorothy ordered once she was settled into her hanging chair, C. C. in
her lap. "This isn't a dead end." I winced at her wording.
"We still have more suspects to interview. But what we really need are people who knew the suspects, and people who
knew Steve." She cocked her head, waiting for us to come
up with something.

Wayne cleared his throat.

"Well, there's always Ray," he growled.

"Who's Ray?" I prodded.

"The guy who set up the Heartlink group originally. He knew Steve. He knows about groups."

"Very good," my aunt trilled. Wayne smiled at her. I just kept my thoughts to myself. Did we really need a kindergarten teacher running this investigation? My aunt turned my way. I had a feeling it was my turn to recite.

"My friend Ann runs a psychiatric facility," I finally spit out. "She might know Garrett. And she might be able to give us a psychological slant on things."

My aunt nodded. I realized that I longed for a "very good" like the one she'd bestowed on Wayne.

"I know an investment advisor," Wayne jumped back in. "Guy's gotta know the Kimmochis."

My aunt looked at me again. I was desperate.

"I'll call Craig," I told her. "He's a computer consultant, like Van."

"Craig?" she asked, her face crinkled as if she were trying to place the name. Or maybe it was crinkled in distaste.

"Craig, my ex-husband!" I nearly screamed. I'd already told her this.

Craig, the reason I didn't want a formal wedding.

Craig, who answered my phone call on the first ring.

THIRTEEN

✤

"Kate, is that you?"

The longing in Craig's voice stirred up the guilt that I had to quell every time I spoke with him. The way Craig acted, you'd have thought that I was the one who'd left him, instead of the other way around. But it *had* been the other way around, and it had been painful. Then, once he'd decided divorcing me had been a mistake, he'd tried every way known to man—or at least every way known to Craig—to remedy the mistake. But I'd found Wayne by then.

And to think that Craig and I had married formally fourteen years before our divorce. Weddings, ha!

"It's me," I answered, using the light tone I always used with Craig. True, he'd been a philanderer and had divorced me, but he wasn't malicious, just insensitive. I thought of Isaac for a moment. Then I went on. "Wayne and I are looking into a death—" I began.

"The Men's Group Massacre?" Craig asked, excitement overtaking the longing in his voice.

"Where'd you hear that?" I demanded.

"I read it in the *Marin Mind*," he told me.

I clenched my jaw. Felix. It had to be his article.

"Yeah, that one," I conceded. "We wondered if you might know Van Eisner—"

"Van the Man? You bet I know him," Craig assured me.

"Want some help, like the sailor said to the pickle—"

"Just what you know about Van," I cut him off. Craig's jokes should have clued me in to the probably inevitable end of our relationship the first time I heard one. But I'd thought they were funny at the time.

"I know a lot about him, Kate," he told me. "Maybe I should come over."

I ignored the shimmy in my stomach and plunged ahead.

"You wouldn't happen to know Jerry Urban, too, would you?" I asked.

"Oh, yeah, Jerry's a really cool guy. He's gay, you know. Did you hear the one about the gay guy who went to the dentist—"

"Heard it," I lied quickly. I was reliving my ex-husband's insensitivity as we spoke. But still, he *did* know both suspects.

"Oh," Craig said, obviously disappointed at the jokus interruptus. "Jerry's a real smart guy. His robotic golf caddie is going places. You sure you don't want me to come over? I'm on top of my workload. And it's time for lunch, anyway."

I held my hand over the receiver and looked across the entryway at Wayne. "Craig knows Van and Jerry," I shouted at him as softly as a person can shout. "Can he come over?"

"Okay, I'll make lunch," Wayne said in the tone of voice he'd use to say, "Gee, I'd love a flu shot."

"All right, Craig," I relayed. "You can come over—"

"I'll be there before you can even blink," he told me.

I blinked and said, "Don't hurry on my account." But Craig didn't answer. He'd already hung up.

Wayne shambled into the kitchen like a zombie, muttering to himself. He put a pot of water on the stove for rice.

Dorothy and I followed him as he began rinsing and chopping. The twin fragrances of ginger and fresh basil floated our way.

"Craig was your previous husband?" Aunt Dorothy asked me softly.

I nodded.

"Do you keep in contact?" she plowed on.

"Um, yeah," I answered, keeping my voice as low as hers. "We're friends, I guess you'd say."

"Craig's still in love with Kate!" Wayne burst out. I took a deep breath.

"Oh, my," Dorothy commiserated.

"Not that I blame him," Wayne added with a sigh. "Poor guy." I let my breath out. Good and kind. That was Wayne. That *wasn't* Craig.

A half hour later, the rice was done, and vegetables, herbs, spices, and marinated tofu were simmering in a combination of soy sauce, sherry, maple syrup, and hot mustard when Craig arrived. I didn't tell Craig how many times I'd blinked since I'd hung up the phone; I didn't get a chance.

Craig barrelled through the doorway like a friendly rottweiler—a lean, handsome, well-dressed, and friendly rottweiler—thrusting a bouquet of roses and daisies my way.

"Hey, Kate," he greeted me. "Any chance of a divorce yet? I've got a great divorce joke. This guy walks into a bar and—"

—And Wayne walked into the entryway, followed by my aunt.

"Hey, Wayne," Craig said, the enthusiasm draining from his voice. Hadn't he heard me say "Wayne" on the phone? His puppy-dog brown eyes saddened. Then he noticed Dorothy.

"Craig, this is my aunt, Dorothy Koffenburger," I introduced. Then I remembered that they'd already met, at our wedding. But I doubted that Craig remembered.

"Wow," Craig murmured. "Now I see where Kate gets her beauty." He didn't remember. But he *did* remember how to treat an unremembered woman on short notice. He switched directions and handed Aunt Dorothy the flowers as if they'd been for her. At least he didn't hand them to Wayne.

"Well, Katie and I don't share the same blood, but I'll accept a little flattery any day," Dorothy said. She didn't say anything about his memory. But despite her kind words, there was a coolness in her sweet voice. "And I'll certainly accept flowers. Though you shouldn't have."

I could almost hear both men's minds agreeing—Craig shouldn't have.

Aunt Dorothy put the flowers in a jar in the middle of our kitchen table, and the four of us sat down to Wayne's lunch. It was wasted on Craig.

"See, there's this old guy at a retirement home," he began through a mouthful of four-star vegetarian food. (And Craig was a vegetarian, so he should have appreciated it.) "He sits down next to this old—"

"Maybe we should talk about Van Eisner," I interrupted quickly, swallowing my own mouthful of unappreciated food. Aunt Dorothy may have been very young at heart, but I still didn't think Craig's joke was going to amuse her. And I was sure it wouldn't amuse me to have Craig tell it in her presence.

"Oh yeah, Van's a genius with computers," he said. At least he wasn't talking through his food anymore. "And he's always got all these women hanging all over him."

"Tell us something we don't know," I tried.

"Well, he does drugs."

"And?" I prompted.

"I don't know!" Craig whined, dropping his fork on the table. "I like Van. Except for the drugs, he's a pretty cool guy. He knows all these computer jokes. You wouldn't believe it."

I would. No wonder I disliked Van—guilt by joke association.

"Do you think Van could murder a man?" Wayne asked, his tone somber.

Craig squirmed in his chair, reminding me of Van himself, minus the drugs. "I just said I liked him," Craig finally answered, defensively. "Do you think I'd like a murderer?"

"I have," I answered him seriously, remembering all too well a murderer I had totally excluded from my suspect list. I shivered.

"Well," Craig admitted, scrunching up his eyes. "Van's good at planning. To be a good programmer, you have to be. And as an entrepreneur, he knows how to strategize. I guess, if Van *wanted* to kill someone, he could figure out how to do it." Craig frowned. "But I still don't think Van would *want* to kill someone in the first place. He plays around and does drugs, but he's not a bad guy."

"How about Jerry Urban?" my aunt asked gently.

Craig looked down at his plate. "I don't know Jerry as well as Van. We met at the Marin Business Exchange. At first, you know, I wasn't that comfortable with him." Craig lifted a limp wrist, and I kept my opinions about males who felt threatened by the mere presence of a gay man internal. "But the guy is funny. Can he mimic people or what? Whoo-boy! And practical jokes! He put Halloween eyeballs in the Jello at our last meeting. And I heard he wired up the speaker's podium to speak back once." Craig leaned over the table and laughed. "I wish I could have been there for that one."

Practical jokes. My stomach felt queasy for a moment. Running over Steve Summers with Wayne's car had the feel of a practical joke—a sick and twisted practical joke.

"Do you think Jerry has the capacity to murder?" my aunt chirped into the silence.

Craig slumped. "I guess I really don't know," he answered honestly. "I don't know what being a murderer feels like. I don't know how to match it to the reality of these guys. I just can't map into their domain. I'm a computer programmer, not a shrink. I'm sorry."

Craig and Dorothy made conversation and dug into their lunches after that. Wayne and I ate silently. And amazingly, Craig offered no more jokes. Maybe the interrogation had sobered him. He finally left the house with a longing glance over his shoulder. He opened his mouth, closed it, and opened it again.

"Bye, Kate," he whispered finally, and ran down the stairs.

He had pushed the guilt button in my heart once more.

"He looks different than I remembered," Dorothy commented at my shoulder.

"It's the suit," I explained briefly. I didn't want to talk about Craig any more.

"And the haircut and shave," my aunt added, then whispered, "You did the right thing, Katie. Wayne is the right man for you."

"And you're the right aunt for me," I whispered back, giving her a quick squeeze and forgiving her for liking Isaac Herrick.

We strolled back into the kitchen and got started on the lunch dishes.

Meanwhile, Wayne was dialing the phone in my office.

"Not about investments," I heard him say, then, "In half an hour?"

Wayne joined us in the kitchen. "Made an appointment with my investment advisor, knows the Kimmochis," Wayne told us. "Should leave soon. I'll dry."

The incomplete sentences were one clue to Wayne's state of mind. His stiff movements were another. Wayne was still upset about Craig.

"You're the man for me," I whispered in his ear. "Aunt Dorothy agrees."

Wayne's eyes widened. He turned to me. "And Craig will be fine," I finished.

He smiled cautiously. "And you think your friend Barbara's the psychic," was all he said, but he was all right again. I could almost see the worry roll away from his shoulders, down his back, and into the ground.

Within ten minutes, the three of us were back in my Toyota on the way to meet Octavia Parker, Wayne's financial advisor.

Octavia was a woman with a straight back, a good-sized body, and sharp eyes. And ethics. So, when Wayne explained what we were doing, her back straightened even further.

"My dear," Dorothy offered mildly. "What you say will go no further than the three of us unless it pertains directly to the murder. And remember, lives may be at stake."

I kept my eyes on Octavia, resisting the urge to elbow my aunt in the ribs. Lives? She made it sound like the *Titanic* was about to go down.

I suddenly realized I could have learned from my aunt because Octavia's tight lips relaxed.

"As long as it goes no further than his room," she began.

"Well, Janet McKinnon-Kimmochi is the brains of that outfit. Ted Kimmochi is too sensitive." Octavia rolled her eyes. "He does pottery, paints, and plays the piano. *And* he does the grunt work for Janet. You know about the trouble they were in a few years back? Well, that was Ted's doing, but Janet bailed her sensitive genius out of the soup."

"Trouble?" Wayne prodded.

"You didn't know?" Octavia demanded. Her face reddened. "I shouldn't have said anything."

Damn. She'd remembered the ethics part again.

"Don't worry, dear," Aunt Dorothy reminded her. "Our lips are sealed outside of this office."

"Still, it's not up to me to say," Octavia insisted.

"Tell us about their personalities, then," my aunt suggested. "Just your opinion. Could either of them kill?"

"Just my opinion," Octavia repeated. The words seemed to satisfy her inner ethics monitor. "Well, Ted probably couldn't organize a murder. Not that he's not smart enough; he's just too self-absorbed. But Janet?" She looked over our heads, nostrils flaring. "Any woman who steals accounts from under my nose—at church, mind you—is capable of anything, in my opinion."

Whoa. I wasn't sure this was exactly an unbiased opinion.

"She took my accountant, too—Carl Russo," Octavia went on. "At least we can share an accountant. If she didn't already have a husband, she'd probably steal mine, too. And another thing . . ."

Now that her output switch had been toggled, there was no stopping Octavia. Janet dyed her hair. Ted was coddled. He could probably find his own way if Janet didn't take care of everything for him. Their kids were spoiled, too. For financial advisors, they spent far too much money and didn't save enough. And on. And on. I was surprised she didn't know about the bondage seminar.

When Octavia's next appointment arrived, I was almost relieved. Almost. We still hadn't found out about the trouble the Kimmochis had been in a few years ago.

"Did you know Carl Russo was the Kimmochis' accountant?" I asked Wayne as soon as we were back on the sidewalk.

"Nope," he growled, opening the back door for Aunt Dorothy. "And he should have told the group. Let's just go ask him about that. I'll drive."

We were lucky my Toyota survived the trip. How Wayne could kick my aged car into warp speed was one of the mysteries of the universe.

The Kimmochis' office was in a converted Victorian in Hutton. The building had been recently painted a pale turquoise, with white and lavender accents. Janet and Ted's office was on the first floor behind a frosted glass door.

Wayne stomped up to the door, raised his hand to knock, and then paused.

I walked up behind him, wondering why he'd paused; then I heard the voices.

"Naughty, so naughty," a voice sang ecstatically.

"Very, very bad?" another voice asked sternly.

"Ooh, yes, soooo bad!"

Was Ted confessing to whatever he'd done wrong in their business?

"Do you need to be spanked?" the stern voice demanded.

"Oh, yes!"

It took me that long to realize what I was hearing.

I heard the rustle of clothing and a giggle. I couldn't tell if the giggle was male or female.

My aunt's eyes were laughing, though her lips were silent. But Wayne wasn't laughing. Wayne was embarrassed. And when Wayne got embarrassed, he got frustrated. And he was *already* frustrated by Ted Kimmochi's lack of forthrightness. Forthrightness was high on Wayne's list of virtues.

Wayne banged his fist on the door so hard I thought the glass would break.

And then we heard more talking.

"No clients, right?"

"I told you we wouldn't be bothered."

"Well, just make them go away!"

"*You* make them go away."

After another short period of rustling, Janet appeared, swinging the door open with force.

"We are not—" she bawled. Then she saw Wayne.

Wayne in his gargoyle mode can be a shock. His scowl encompassed his whole face and body, his brows lowered so that his eyes were invisible. His skin was very, very red. And his body was vibrating with energy—frustrated energy.

"Oh, Wayne," Janet greeted him with a forced smile. She smoothed back her red hair, her freckles dark against her white skin. "What brings you up this way?"

Wayne didn't waste any time. He didn't even introduce my aunt. He looked past Janet at Ted.

"What trouble were you in a few years back?" he demanded. "Trouble that you neglected to share with the group?"

Janet's skin went even whiter.

Ted took his place next to her in the doorway, dishevelled but apparently calm. Maybe all his years of meditation *were* paying off.

"It was very sad, but it's over," he answered quietly, a pretty fast save for a man who was theoretically too sensitive to organize a murder.

I looked around the couple for whips or ropes or something, but saw only a tasteful office with computers, phone banks, and binders.

"Come on, Ted," Wayne pushed. "If you can't be honest with me, who can you be honest with? What else have you been hiding?"

"Wayne, it has nothing to do with Steve Summers' murder, I swear," Ted insisted, not sounding so calm anymore.

"And it wouldn't be any of your business, anyway," Janet added, finally coming back to her senses.

"Is Carl Russo your accountant?" Wayne asked next.

"Yeah, and so what!" Janet answered. She held up a finger and shook it in Wayne's face. "Who elected you detective? Maybe you'd just better go back to your little restaurant business and bug off."

Oddly enough, Wayne seemed to cool down in the face of Janet's angry words. The gargoyle persona was melting before our eyes. *Why*? I wondered. True, Ted had no legal obligation to disclose his troubles or even his relationship with fellow group member Carl Russo. But to hold back that information *was* almost a lie in a group as intimate as Heartlink. And Carl at least had the excuse of client confidentiality for his reticence.

"Sorry," Wayne muttered. "All the lies in the group are getting to me."

"A lack of disclosure is not a lie," Janet proclaimed and slammed the glass door in our faces.

"If Steve's death wasn't enough, the lies, the evasions, will destroy Heartlink," Wayne explained to the closed door. Then he turned from the door and whispered, "I give up."

I led him back outside by the hand.

"Maybe we should have called first," I said as gently as I could once we were inside the Toyota again. Wayne had not insisted on driving.

Dorothy giggled.

It was infectious. When we thought of their sexual antics, all the tensions the Kimmochis had inspired seemed to disappear. I laughed, and even Wayne grinned unexpectedly.

"We should have waited till she tied him up," I added, and Wayne's grin turned into a much-needed belly laugh.

A few miles down the road, Wayne said, "Tell me if I'm ever being a complete jerk again."

"A complete jerk or just a jerk?" I asked innocently. We all laughed. The Three Musketeers were back in form for sleuthing.

"Who was your group facilitator, again?" Dorothy asked Wayne after a few minutes.

"Oh, that's right, Ray," Wayne answered, his face brightening. "We can still talk to Ray. He helped Steve and me start the group. He met all the members. He even facilitated the original group, then turned it over to Steve and me. Let's go see him."

"Call first," Dorothy and I ordered together.

I found a pay phone outside a convenience store, and Wayne made the call. It would have been nice for Wayne to have used his cell phone, but it was locked inside his impounded Jaguar.

Ray was at home. The ramp to his front door should have given me a clue to his condition, but I was surprised that the man who opened the door, dogs barking all around him, was in a wheelchair. I didn't ask why.

"Sit, all of you!" Ray roared, and amazingly, the four black Labrador retrievers sat. Ray rolled forward.

"It's been a while," Wayne said. "Too long."

"Good to see you, too, man," Ray replied. Wayne bent down and gave him a one-shouldered squeeze.

"My wife, Kate, and her aunt Dorothy," Wayne introduced us briefly. "This is Ray, the man I told you about."

Ray smiled, his weathered brown skin wrinkling. He was actually a very attractive man, I realized. And then I stopped myself. I shouldn't be noticing if he was attractive or not. One of the labs whined and wriggled forward, tongue ready to lick. Ray ignored him.

"Glad to meet you all," he pronounced politely. He pulled his wheelchair back, and his dogs moved with him. "Grab your seats."

Wayne, Dorothy, and I all squeezed onto an old plaid couch, the dogs eyeing us as if we were chew toys.

"Damn, I was sorry to hear about Steve Summers. His death is a real tragedy. Hard to believe."

I wondered if Ray was one of the few people to really grasp the fact that Steve had been murdered. And maybe one of the few who really liked him.

"Steve was a good man," Wayne said, and this time he was met with no argument or hesitation.

"Yeah, Steve seemed like an ideal co-facilitator," Ray agreed. "Honest, committed, willing to keep confidences. The whole purpose of these groups is to build community and friendship." Ray shook his head and reached down, burying his hand in the fur of one of the dogs near his wheelchair. "When I heard he'd been killed coming from the group, with your car, no less, I gotta admit I freaked a little."

"That's the problem, Ray," Wayne explained. "We're

pretty sure the murderer is one of the group members or one of the members'—"

"Sigos," my aunt finished for him. She just loved her new word.

"Why?" Ray demanded, leaning forward in his chair.

"Um . . ." I began. Had we told Dorothy this part yet?

"The spare key to my car was lifted from Kate's purse at a potluck," Wayne explained. Obviously, he trusted this man. But of course, Ray wasn't a suspect. "Haven't told anyone else," Wayne added. "Confidential."

"Understood," Ray said, leaning back in his chair.

I turned and glanced at Aunt Dorothy. She was just nodding as if she'd known already.

"Damn," Ray muttered. "I remember all the guys in your group. We tried to screen out anyone who seemed too unstable."

"Ray, give us your feedback," Wayne suggested. "Tell us what you thought of the members."

"At this point, you probably know them better than I do," Ray told him. "But I'll give it a shot. Steve, well, Steve was quiet but observant, a good listener. Though he could have opened up more."

"Did you know Steve outside of the group?" Dorothy asked.

Ray shook his head, and then offered a brief synopsis of each of the other group members. I wondered as he spoke whether I would have done the same synopses myself. According to Ray, Ted needed a chance to turn his attention outward, to make real connections with others. Garrett needed to care more for himself. Van was self-destructive, but needed the support to change. Carl knew how to give support, but needed the approval of others. And then he came to Isaac.

"Isaac has a problem with alcohol. But he's sharp, a lot sharper that he lets on. Isaac notices everyone and everything that's happening. If I were you, I'd talk to Isaac again."

So the three of us all piled into my Toyota once more and headed toward Cortadura.

No one answered when Dorothy knocked on the door of

Isaac's condo, but the door opened an inch or so with every knock. Whether he was inside or out, Isaac hadn't bothered to close his door, much less to lock it.

Aunt Dorothy frowned. "Oh, dear. We should go in and check on Isaac," she said after her final knock. "He might be in some kind of trouble."

Alcohol trouble, I thought, but kept my mouth shut. Then Wayne and I looked at each other. His face had a look I knew well, a look that said "no" as loudly as C. C. could yowl when going to the vet's office.

"We might learn something," I muttered.

"It's still not right," Wayne declared.

"Look, he left the door open—"

"How would you like it if Isaac came into our house if we left the door open?"

"This is different—"

That's when we realized that Dorothy wasn't with us any longer. She was inside Isaac's condo.

And she was screaming.

FOURTEEN

✤

I saw my own expression reflected on Wayne's face: panic. And then we both rushed through Isaac Herrick's open door. We looked around the living room but saw only the same collection of furniture, bottles, books, and miscellany that had been there on our previous visit. I ran a few steps down the hall and entered the first doorway on the right. It was dark in the room, but I could see my Aunt Dorothy there. She'd stopped screaming and was just staring now, staring down, her shoulders rolled forward and her hands clasped in front of her protectively. I followed her eyes and saw a bed— Isaac's bed? It had to be. I looked back up. My mind seemed exquisitely clear as I walked toward Dorothy. I felt as if I could have seen a pin in the dark, as if I could have heard a bird chirping in the next county. But all I was really hearing was the beating of my own heart.

Then, once I was close enough to my aunt, close enough to the bed, I turned my head, and I saw. And what I saw was Isaac Herrick, but it wasn't Isaac Herrick. It was a corpse. Even in the darkened room, I could tell that the purple and blue skin shades didn't belong on a live person; nor did the pale lips and nails. Only the Hawaiian shirt and khaki pants lent a gruesome normalcy to the body. Isaac Herrick was dead. I didn't need to touch him to be sure.

I closed my eyes and felt the room turn over, or maybe it

was my stomach. I couldn't tell anymore. My heart was pounding too loud.

Then I heard a new sound.

"Katie?" someone whimpered. "Katie?"

I forced my eyes open. Aunt Dorothy. She looked at me now, away from the bed and its grizzly contents.

"It'll be okay," someone said.

For a moment, I thought *I'd* said it would be okay, but then I realized that it was Wayne who'd actually mouthed those words from behind me.

I opened my arms, and my aunt's tiny body was pressed against me instantly. I closed my arms around her. I didn't know what to say.

I felt Wayne's warm hands on my shoulders, and strength seemed to pour into me. Isaac was dead, and my elderly aunt was in shock. I had to act.

"Katie, it's Isaac!" Dorothy shouted, pushing out of my arms suddenly. "How can he be dead? He was alive this morning."

"Let me take you out of here," I finally whispered.

"Yes, dear," Dorothy agreed mildly. "Isaac wouldn't want to be seen like this."

Outside, on the sidewalk, the air was bright and incredibly sweet. The noise of traffic, insects, and voices hummed around us. My body ached, inside and out.

Wayne stood in silence with Dorothy and me for a moment, then made a dialing gesture with his hand and reentered Isaac's condo. I guessed that he was going to call the police.

"They'll say it was a heart attack," Dorothy burst out. "Just because Isaac was old. But you know it wasn't a heart attack just as well as I do, Katie."

"Why?" I said. I didn't know what I knew yet.

"Isaac said he had an idea who'd killed Steve Summers, and he was going to check it out, remember?" my aunt said. I had a feeling she wasn't in shock anymore. I wasn't sure if I was.

"So, you think that someone killed him when he tried to check it out?"

"That must be it, dear," Aunt Dorothy proclaimed, straightening her spine. She was almost five feet tall now.

"But who?"

"We'll find out," my aunt assured me. Then the new confidence in her face faded. She looked stricken. "Helen," she whispered.

"Oh, no," I whispered back, closing my eyes. Helen. Not another widow. Divorcing him or not, Helen seemed to have sincerely loved Isaac.

"I know you might not have seen it, Katie, but Isaac was a charming man in his own way. He just mentioned that the emperor had no clothes a few times too many for most. And he drank. He drank even when Claude and I knew him. But he had kindness, and he had a good wit."

I believed her; I'd seen his kindness when she'd told him Uncle Claude had passed way. And yes, he'd had wit.

"I'll find out who killed him," she stated matter-of-factly.

"*We* will," I expanded, putting my arm around her shoulder.

"Thank you, Katie," she chirped.

And then we heard sirens.

Wayne came out of the house to join us.

"The police are on their way," he explained. "Captain Wooster has been notified."

The police car screamed its way to the curb, and then the same two officers who'd arrived after Steve's death jumped out of their marked vehicle. Before they'd even had a chance to speak, the paramedics pulled in behind them. After a few words with Wayne, the paramedics went scrambling into Isaac Herrick's condo, along with the police. Finally, the last car pulled up, unmarked. The back driver's side door opened and Captain Wooster pushed himself out of the seat. Sergeant Marge hopped out of the right side, and we all stared at each other.

Captain Wooster hadn't gotten any better looking since the last time we'd seen him. You could still have hung a hat off of his jutting jaw, his nostrils still looked like he'd smelled something bad, and his eyes hadn't gotten any friendlier. At least Sergeant Marge smiled our way.

"Hell's bells!" Wooster exploded. "You two again? Who'd you run over this time?"

"No one was run over," Wayne said, his voice filled with a deliberate calm that didn't match the tension of his body. "I called in the . . . the death."

"Isaac Herrick was murdered!" my Aunt Dorothy exclaimed.

Captain Wooster's mean eyes narrowed to two thin lines under his eyebrows as he turned toward my aunt.

"Who in all creation are you?" he demanded.

Dorothy narrowed her mascaraed eyes back at him. "My name is Dorothy Koffenburger. I'm Kate Jasper's aunt. And I was Isaac Herrick's friend."

"You're not one of those goofy group people—"

"No, I am not. I am neither a group member nor a sigo. I knew Isaac when I was younger—"

"What century?" Wooster asked, then leaned back his head and neighed through his equine nostrils.

"That's enough, young man," my aunt admonished him. She stepped forward and looked up into his face. "I'm sure you weren't raised to make fun of the elderly. Or to harass innocent citizens."

"But—"

"Answer me," Dorothy ordered. "Do you believe you're behaving in a dignified manner?"

"I'm just doing—"

"Is it doing your job to try to embarrass an old woman and to make fun of a serious situation? Shouldn't you be trying to find out why Isaac Herrick was murdered?"

"Yes, ma'am," Wooster finally conceded, looking at the ground.

I could hear the sound of choked laughter coming my way from Sergeant Marge. I just hoped the captain couldn't hear it.

"If you three will stay here with Sergeant Abbott, I'll just go check the situation in the house," Wooster announced quietly. He turned and strode into the darkness of Isaac's doorway.

"Heh-heh-heh," I heard, and looked up to see Sergeant

Marge Abbott, red-faced, laughing into her hand.

Dorothy looked at her, too, and smiled unexpectedly.

"Petty tyrants are the worst," Aunt Dorothy offered.

"I'd work a week of overtime to have gotten that on tape," Sergeant Marge responded. " 'Yes, ma'am,' " she mimicked in a deep voice. "Har-har-har."

Luckily, she'd stopped laughing by the time Captain Wooster rejoined us on the sidewalk.

"How in purgatory did you know that Herrick was murdered?" he asked my aunt.

"Because he told us he had an idea who the murderer was," she replied calmly. "How do you know?"

"The eyes," he told us. "You can tell by the eyes when someone's been smothered. People think it'll look like a heart attack, but—"

Dorothy blanched at the word "smothered." For all of her guessing, I don't think she'd really known she was right till Captain Wooster said so.

"Ma'am?" the captain said. "You all right, ma'am?"

"I'm fine," she said, adding a wan smile. "And thank you so much for asking."

Our interrogation was polite—or as polite as it could be, as we were standing on a sidewalk buzzing with gawkers and police personnel. But it was long.

The events leading to our discovery of Isaac's body were dealt with exhaustively, and then we discussed our morning conversation with the dead man.

"Did Mr. Herrick give any indication who he suspected?" Captain Wooster asked.

Then he asked the same question at least twenty more times in twenty different ways, with all due courtesy and respect. Dorothy seemed to be faring the best through these questions. I could feel Wayne stiffening into stone beside me, and my own body was dissolving into a state that felt like sandpapered pudding.

Finally, the captain seemed to run out of questions.

"You've been with your niece and her husband since the last time you saw Mr. Herrick alive?" he asked once more.

"I certainly was, Captain," Dorothy answered.

Wooster narrowed his eyes at us and then sighed. "I guess you might as well go," he said.

And we did. Quickly.

"It's lucky Captain Wooster doesn't have the imagination to believe a woman over eighty might conspire in murder," Dorothy commented on the way home in the car.

We all tried to laugh, but we were laughed out. For all that had happened, Isaac Herrick was well and truly dead.

"Will the captain tell Helen?" my aunt asked a few miles later.

Wayne grunted something that sounded like an affirmative.

"Two widows," I muttered. "Is there a pattern here? Is someone killing off the husbands of the Heartlink group?"

Wayne gave me a startled look. "You're my wife," he said slowly.

"Yeah," I answered. I'd already figured that part out. I pulled into our driveway, popping gravel.

We tramped up the stairs, each in our own world of misery. Dorothy was grieving for Isaac. And I would have guessed that Wayne was, too, as well as for this latest blow to the Heartlink group. I felt so sorry for Helen and Laura. And I was frightened: Could someone be planning Wayne's murder right now?

"Hey, guys!" someone yelled, not far from us.

I looked up. Felix Byrne stood at our front door.

"No," I said. It was too soon for him to know about Isaac's death. "How did you find—"

"Kate, ya gotta help me," he interrupted. "Is Brother Ingenio a fraud?"

I blinked.

"Janis said he wasn't a fraud, but, hey, the man's a friggin' wacko—"

"Janis?" I asked.

"Janis Joplin," he answered. "Brother Ingenio channels Janis Joplin and all these other cool rockers."

"Janis Joplin is dead," I reminded him.

"Yeah, but Brother Ingenio can channel her and Jim Morrison and Jimi Hendrix, all of them."

"You mean," I said slowly, working it out as I went along, "that Brother Ingenio's mouth is channeling these dead rockers, and it's his mouth that's telling you he's not a fraud?"

"Yeah. Cool, huh?"

"Cool," I said wearily. I was just glad he didn't know about Isaac.

"But Kate, I still don't understand. See, Brother Ingenio is so far friggin' out, I can't tell if he's really a looney, ya know. But I dreamt about you, Kate. You had the answer."

"What answer?"

Felix blushed.

"The spiritual answer, man. You told me you could sleuth-the-truth in the cosmos, too. You *know*, don't you?"

"Felix," I tried gently. "I meditate, all right? Sometimes I think I feel a faint connection to the higher self, something that makes me imagine there might be a divine spirit, but I don't know anything for sure. I try to trust my body, to trust those feelings. But I don't think I'll ever *know*—really know—in this lifetime, so I live with that faint connection."

"Kate, that was lovely," my aunt said from behind me. Her voice was tired. "Perhaps we could go in now?"

My connection to the earth grew stronger. I reached for my keys and opened the front door. Of course, Felix dived in the entryway before anyone else and was on the couch in a blur of denim and flannel.

Dorothy and Wayne headed for the kitchen.

"Tea," Wayne explained tersely.

I turned to follow them, but Felix lassoed me verbally before I could.

"I had that gonzo dream for a reason, Kate," he insisted. "You know more than you're telling me, just like always. But this woo-woo stuff is important, man."

"Felix, I'm not holding out on you spiritually," I told him, dropping into the hanging chair for two. I didn't mention that I *was* holding out on him about the scoop of the day.

As Felix peered at me with expectant, soulful eyes, I began to wonder if my own individualistic search for spiritual truth was a viable one. Maybe I should be in a group, have someone to follow like Felix did. Felix! I felt like slapping myself.

This had to be a bad dream. I had actually thought of Felix Byrne as a spiritual inspiration.

"Felix, you need to meditate," I said with an authority that was voice deep. If he was meditating, maybe he'd quit staring at me. Maybe he'd even quit talking.

"Wow, Kate," he whispered. "That's the same friggin' thing Brother Ingenio says. Far out."

He brought up his legs and crossed them on top of the couch, then closed his eyes. And he stopped talking.

I leaned back in my own chair, feeling the comfort of its gentle swaying.

The phone rang before I could even sigh.

"Kate, it's Barbara," I heard from the machine.

Felix's eyes popped open.

"Felix, you keep on meditating," the machine went on. "I want to talk to Kate."

Felix closed his eyes again. He'd long ago stopped bothering to ask how his sweetie knew such details.

"Hey, kiddo," Barbara said. "Just a few things. First, don't worry about Felix. It's just one more step in his evolution. Ignore him."

I nodded. That was good advice from someone who ought to know.

"And stop worrying about this Typhoid Mary of Murder stuff—"

"I haven't been worrying—" I began after picking up the receiver. But then I stopped because I had, actually. Discovering two bodies in two days wasn't cool.

"And stop worrying about finding other men attractive. It's natural to look at other men once you're sure of your own relationship." I blushed. I wasn't about to answer her.

"And the fourth thing . . ." Barbara paused. "Oh, now I remember. I know Jerry Urban. I thought you'd want to hear about it."

I wasn't blushing anymore. "You know Jerry?" I demanded eagerly. "Tell me everything."

"Jerry and I worked together on that big community center out in Mariquitas. He is one funny guy, I mean ha-ha funny, a real crack-up. He was the engineer on the project, and I was the electrician."

"What do you remember about him?"

"His practical jokes. He wired doors to talk and walls to say 'ouch' when you hammered them. He knew as much about electricity as I did, maybe more."

"Is killing someone with a car a big practical joke?" I asked Barbara softly.

There was a long silence.

"I don't know, kiddo," she finally replied, seriously. "I can't imagine Jerry ever doing anything really mean-spirited, much less murderous, but—"

"But murder fritzes your circuits," I finished for her. It's nice to beat the local psychic to the punch once in a while.

I tiptoed into the kitchen after Barbara hung up. Dorothy and Wayne were enjoying a peach tea that smelled delicious. Wayne poured me a cup. No one said a word, maybe because a journalist was meditating on our couch. Or maybe just because we were all exhausted. It was nice, though, sitting in the kitchen and watching the dust motes dance.

After I'd finished my tea, I retreated to my lonely desk and worked on some new gags for music teachers and bookstore owners. Work can be therapeutic, especially when you're designing open-book earrings instead of filling out I.R.S. forms. I had actually forgotten all about Isaac, all about Steve, and all about the Heartlink group when the doorbell rang.

The doorbell acted like a Pavlovian shock, bringing everything back in one peal. I rushed to the door. If our visitor had anything to do with the Heartlink group, I didn't want Felix beating me there. But Felix was still on the couch, his eyes closed. Maybe he was asleep.

I opened the door and slipped out onto the deck, hoping to leave Felix out of whatever awaited me.

Laura Summers awaited me. I almost ran into her when I came through the doorway, still looking over my shoulder at Felix.

"Kate," she said and reached out for my hands. "Have you heard anything?"

For a moment, I thought she was talking about Isaac, and then I realized she probably hadn't even heard about Isaac yet. She had to be asking about Steve. My heart clunked.

"No," I told her, and then remembered my manners. "Why don't you come with me into the kitchen? Wayne and my aunt are having tea."

Laura must have seen Felix on the couch, but her all-American features remained neutral as we walked past the living room into the kitchen. As a politician, she'd probably ignored stranger foibles than meditating friends. Or maybe he wasn't a meditating friend; I thought I heard a faint snore behind us as we crossed the threshold of the kitchen.

"Wayne!" Laura cried when she saw my husband.

He got up from the kitchen table and readied himself for the inevitable hug. And he received it, the full-force Flying Walenda of embraces.

"Oh, Wayne," Laura murmured. I took a big breath and reminded myself, again, of Laura's circumstances. Still, she could have hugged me first.

I looked at Dorothy. She smiled back at me, shrugging a shoulder. It was a message, but I wasn't sure what. Men are men? Women are women? You worry too much?

When Laura finally disengaged, she looked up at Wayne's pink face. "Wayne, I've been racking my brain. Why Steve? Did he say anything to you, *anything* that might make some sense of his murder?"

Wayne just shook his head. "Sorry," he muttered.

Laura slumped in her tasteful black suit, now looking more like a widow than a politician.

I wanted to offer her some tea, but that seemed like a paltry diversion when she was asking who killed her husband.

"Laura," I began. "It's early yet. I'm sure the police—"

And then I heard a screech from the living room.

My first thought was that someone had hurt my cat, C. C. I sprinted into the living room just in time to see Felix rise from the couch as if by teleportation, with C. C.'s claws still stuck in his flannel-covered shoulder.

₣IFTEEN

❧

₣elix landed back on the couch with a *thud*. C. C. looked up at me as I came to a skidding stop in the living room, then she casually hopped off of Felix's shoulder. But Felix continued to scream. By this time, Dorothy, Wayne, and Laura had caught up with me and were all watching him scream, too.

Finally, the screaming stopped.

Felix looked at each of us in turn, his rounded eyes scanning for something. Auras? Witches' brooms? Only Barbara might know what he was seeing, and she wasn't here.

"You're all friggin' gonzo," he concluded. He leapt off the couch and ran out the door and down the stairs before I had time to refute or confirm his accusation.

"What happened to that poor man?" Laura Summers asked once I'd started breathing again.

C. C. sauntered up to us as Laura waited for an answer. I thought I heard a rumble outside. Was that Felix's car?

"Isn't he a reporter?" Laura tried again. "He looks familiar. Wasn't he here before?"

"The *Marin Mind*," I answered briefly, listening. Yes, I definitely heard a rumble, and voices, maybe footsteps.

"The what?" Laura asked, bringing my mind back into the room.

"He's a reporter for the *Marin Mind*—you know, the newspaper."

"Oh," she murmured. "Now I remember. I don't read it often. Papers are such a bother."

By now, C. C. had reached us and was stretching her front paws out in front of my Aunt Dorothy. Dorothy squatted down until she was almost eye level with C. C. I expected a reprimand—C. C. had been a very bad cat. But my aunt laughed instead.

"What a wonderful cat you have, Katie! A watch cat."

She scratched behind C. C.'s ear. C. C. purred. Feline and human had an instant rapport. I wondered if C. C. would make a good bridesmaid.

"C. C.—" I began.

A knock on the door interrupted my planned lecture.

I opened the door without really considering who might be on the other side, then wondered how many lifetimes it would take to teach me to think before acting. The front yard was ringed with people, not to mention cars, trucks, cameras, microphones, and notebooks. Felix stood at the front of the crowd, looking slightly bewildered. If it hadn't been for the look on his face, I would have suspected *him* of calling the media to bedevil us. But he hadn't had enough time to call in the troops, anyway. And he'd left Laura Summers alone when he could have harassed her privately. *Laura*, I thought, my pulse jumping in recognition of the probable cause for all the attention. And then the questions began.

"Is Laura Summers here?" a muscular young man with a microphone demanded.

"I . . ." I began, and then I shut my mouth and imagined a clothespin holding my lips together.

"Laura Summers was seen coming to your house. Is she inside now?" a woman in a suit and silk shirt asked.

"We want to talk to Laura!" another voice yelled. And then it sounded like the zoo, all random shouts, squeaks, and rumbles.

I slammed the door and locked it.

"I might as well go out and face them," Laura offered mildly. "They'll just wait for me, anyway." She sighed. "I took Tiffany's car to throw them off the scent. It's around the block. I thought I wouldn't be recognized."

"Would you like to avoid them, dear?" Aunt Dorothy asked her.

"Yes," Laura said slowly. "But I don't think I can."

"Don't worry," my aunt responded cheerfully. "This just calls for a disguise and a little diversionary action."

"But—" I began.

"Wayne, may we borrow some of your things?" Dorothy asked.

Wayne nodded, and Dorothy led Laura back to our bedroom. When my aunt reappeared, she was standing next to what looked like a man in sweat pants, a sweatshirt, and a watch cap. Laura Summers had disappeared.

"Do you have a back door?" Dorothy asked next.

Wayne and I nodded our heads in unison, our mouths open.

"Wayne, I'll go out front, and you take Laura out the back," Aunt Dorothy commanded.

"Right," Wayne replied. He didn't salute, but it was implied. "The Donovan's fence. They won't mind."

The Donovans, who lived behind us, wouldn't mind because they were out of town.

Wayne and Laura went to the back door and Dorothy opened the front door.

"Well, hello!" she greeted the press. She threw her arms open theatrically as if to embrace them. "I don't know how you tracked me down, but I would be *glad* to give an interview. Anything for my loyal fans."

The muscular young man at the door squinted at her. He wasn't the only one. All around the yard, people were staring at my aunt, trying to figure out who she was. The only one missing was Felix; maybe he'd gone home to meditate.

"Now, which one of my films did you want to ask about?" Dorothy trilled.

"Ma'am, who are you?" someone asked from the back.

Dorothy's face fell dramatically. She raised her hand to her heart. "You mean you don't remember me after sixty-odd films and countless TV appearances?" she asked, her voice trembling. She pulled a handkerchief from somewhere and covered her face for a moment.

"Uh, sure we do," a young woman assured her.

"Who the hell is she?" a whisper drifted our way.

"I'll give you a clue," Dorothy purred, shedding her handkerchief. "*Funny Face*."

"Audrey Hepburn?" someone shouted.

"No, she's dead," someone else informed the shouter.

"Well, she sure ain't Barbra Streisand!"

As people shouted out guesses, my aunt simpered, threw kisses, and cooed.

"Lillian Gish?"

"Shirley Temple?"

"Meryl Streep?"

Meryl Streep? Yikes. They were getting desperate. And suddenly the cosmetically enhanced reporters were crowding up the stairs, shoving each other to get a better look at my aunt. But no one shoved Dorothy. A few cameras angled for better shots, but Dorothy's petite frame was invisible behind the crowd.

"Another movie?" someone demanded.

"*Little Abner*," she replied without hesitation.

Where was she getting these titles?

Then she raised her arms and recited. "Blow, blow, thou winter wind. Thou are not so unkind as man's ingratitude—"

"I got it, she worked with Ingmar Bergman. What's her name?"

"I thought that was Shakespeare—"

"Nah, Bergman. If only I could remember . . ."

Then my Aunt Dorothy sang a little Cole Porter. Apparently, my Uncle Claude hadn't been the only musical one in the family.

But I could see she was getting tired. Her frail body was beginning to sway, and not just from the rhythm of the music.

When Wayne put his hand on my shoulder, I felt the burden of acute tension leave my body, only to be replaced by anxiety. I swiveled my head and cracked my neck for good measure. If Wayne was back, Laura was probably gone.

"The coast clear?" I hissed.

"Completely," he assured me.

Now it was my turn on the deck. I strode out, put my arm around my aunt, and declared, "This has been really wonderful, but Miss Murphy needs her rest now. She has a busy day ahead of her tomorrow."

"Miss Murphy?!" a roar went up, as if it were feeding time at the zoo.

My aunt shuffled in the door with me just as people began asking who the hell Miss Murphy was.

"Eddie Murphy?" someone suggested, and I closed the door and locked it again.

"Oh, my, that was fun," Aunt Dorothy murmured once she was safely inside again.

"Oh, Miss Murphy?" I breathed. "May I have your autograph?"

Dorothy giggled, but then her face grew wistful "Isaac would have loved it," she murmured.

"This calls for a special dinner," Wayne announced quickly and marched into the kitchen.

Dorothy and I sat at the table while Wayne cooked and told us about helping Laura Summers over our back fence and around the corner to her car.

"You missed a great show," I told him.

"What did you do?" he asked, turning from the stove. The fragrance of curry and garlic wafted our way.

"*I* didn't do anything," I told him. "My aunt is the actress in the family."

Dorothy giggled again, then said, "Meryl Streep." Her giggles crescendoed into loud guffaws. The ladylike Aunt Dorothy was gone; enter the comedienne.

"Did you ever think of really acting?" I asked her once we were seated and slurping down curried peanut and spinach soup.

"Oh, yes," she said. "Many years ago. I did summer stock for a while, you know."

I shook my head. I certainly hadn't known. I would have liked to have known more, but by the time we'd consumed dessert, my aunt was back on the subject of weddings.

She led me into the living room and we took our places on the couch. Wayne stayed behind to do dishes. I envied him.

"Have you considered the size of your wedding party?" Dorothy asked.

"No," I replied, searching my mind for another topic. "So, how's Kevin?" I asked. "Have you seen him lately?"

"Kevin will be happy to attend your wedding, I'm sure," she outbid me. "You need to think of your wedding in terms of scope and theme."

"How about Mom?" I tried.

"Your mother's fine; a little nervous about your wedding, but fine otherwise, Katie. You know this means a lot to her."

I sighed. Did I owe it to my mother to have a formal wedding? Did I owe it to Aunt Dorothy? Did I owe it to Wayne?

"Oh, Katie," Dorothy broke into my thoughts. "Do you mind if we shelve the wedding plans for the moment and talk about Isaac?"

"Oh, that'd be great!" I exclaimed, and then added more sedately, "I know you cared for him."

"Katie, I didn't know this Steve Summers of yours. But I knew Isaac. And I know Helen. We have to do something about this—perhaps hire a private detective."

"Do you really think a private detective would do any good?" I asked. "I mean, we're the ones who know the group members—"

"But a private detective might be able to find out things that you can't. Who knows if any of these people had past connections, perhaps relatives who had dealings with Steve or Isaac? The possibilities are endless."

"How do you think we would find a good—" I began.

The doorbell rang. This time I got up from the couch cautiously, with Aunt Dorothy on my heels, and cracked the door open a few inches. Carl Russo stood on the deck with his son, Mike.

I opened the door wider.

Carl pushed his son through the doorway.

"Tell them you had nothing to do with this," he ordered.

"I had nothing to do with this," Mike complied in a prisoner-of-war voice.

"You mean with Steve Summers or—" I began, but then I stopped. Did they know about Isaac?

"Dad has some goofy idea that I'm, you know, like a prime suspect for murder or something," Mike told us.

"I just don't want you in trouble," Carl said. His broad shoulders seemed to sink in his suit jacket. There was fear beneath the anger in his fleshy face.

"Carl," Wayne greeted his fellow group member. I jumped. He'd entered the room so quickly and quietly, I hadn't heard him.

"Wayne," Carl returned the greeting, then seemed to remember he'd never said hello to anyone else.

"Is there any real cause to think your son might be suspect?" Dorothy asked reasonably once all the hellos were finished.

"The cops called," Carl answered. "Wanted to know where we were today. I was at work, except for lunch, but Mike—" He turned and glared at his son.

Mike tried an ingratiating grin, then finished his father's sentence.

"—Mike was cutting school," the boy said, pointing at himself. "No big deal. No federal crime."

"Except that the police wanna know where he was," Carl put in.

"I was out with my friends, dude," Mike offered.

" 'Out with my friends, dude' " his father parroted. "Great! The cops wanna know where the kid is, and all he'll say is 'out with my friends!' "

"Listen, Dad," Mike whined. "I don't wanna get anybody in trouble. We were cool. We just felt like fooling around, you know."

"So did the police say why they were interested in your whereabouts today?" I asked nonchalantly.

"No!" Carl hollered. "Those toads wouldn't tell me nuthin'. Just all these questions about me and the kid. I told them he was in school. Damn it! What if they find out he wasn't?"

"Maybe you ought to tell them yourself," I suggested. "Tell them where Mike was and who he was with—"

"But that's exactly what he won't do. The kid won't even tell *me* who he was with or what they were doing."

Mike's cheeks were getting very red, though whether with embarrassment or anger, I couldn't tell.

"Mike," my aunt said gently. "Someone else was killed today. Telling the truth is more important than not getting your friends in trouble."

Mike's face went from red to white. Carl's eyes widened.

"Damn it, who?" Carl whispered urgently.

"Isaac Herrick," my aunt answered without a pause.

Captain Wooster was going to put us in jail for sure. If he hadn't told anyone else that Isaac was dead, he probably didn't want us telling them. Curried peanuts and spinach whirled in my stomach.

"You see, Mike, this is important," Aunt Dorothy persisted. "Who were you with today?"

"Jason and Tommy and me all went down to the mall," he gave in. "No big deal. We were just fooling around."

"That's fine," she assured the boy. "But now you need to call the police and tell them what you've told me. And perhaps you should call your two friends as well. Let your friends know that the police might be asking them questions. You all *must* tell the truth. This situation is far too serious to play around with."

"Yes, ma'am," Mike said.

I could hardly believe my ears. Mike was not a boy to "yes, ma'am" his elders. But then again, my aunt had pulled a confession out of him as easily as pulling candy out of a bowl.

"Hey, thanks," Carl said to Dorothy, his voice betraying the same surprise I'd felt at Mike's capitulation. "Ma'am," he added.

"Perhaps a trip to the police station is in order?" Dorothy suggested cheerily.

Carl looked at Mike. The boy nodded.

The phone rang.

"Listen, man," the answering machine said a moment later. "It's Van here. I'm really freaking."

Wayne's brows dropped. He sighed and walked to the phone.

"Hey, I wanna thank you and your aunt for helping us out," Carl rasped. "We'll go down to the cops and get everything straightened out."

"Uh-huh," I heard Wayne say from behind me. I wondered what Van was saying.

"Any time," Dorothy said to Carl, and she seemed to mean it. She gripped his hand and shook it, then did the same with Mike.

"Thank you for coming," she finished up graciously.

Father and son left as Wayne said, "Uh-huh" again.

I closed the door behind the Russos and leaned against it as if an invading army might burst through at any minute.

"Um, Aunt Dorothy," I began.

"I shouldn't have told them about Isaac," she finished for me.

"Captain Wooster isn't going to like it," I said.

"Mike's going to tell the truth now," she countered. "He had to understand the seriousness of the situation."

"Yeah, there's that," I admitted.

"Calm down," Wayne said.

At first I thought he was talking to me, but he was speaking into the telephone receiver.

Dorothy and I exchanged looks.

"You can stop holding the door in place now, Katie," she told me.

"Oh, right," I said. But I locked the door behind me before I joined her on the couch again.

"Katie, I think that boy was telling the truth, don't you?" Dorothy inquired, her eyes troubled.

"Of course he was telling the truth," I answered, but then I really thought about it. My aunt was faster than me on the uptake.

"If he had any connection with Isaac's death, all he had to do was convince his friends to lie for him," she reminded me. "Friends will do that."

"But, Mike . . ." I faltered.

All I really knew about Mike was that he was a lovable clown and a trial to his father. Could a clown be an actor, too?

"Get some rest, Van," Wayne advised from across the hall, and then slammed the phone down.

"It's okay, Katie," my aunt whispered as Wayne came back to the living room. She squeezed my arm. "I was just thinking out loud. Neither of us can really know what goes on in a teenager's brain."

"Van, again," Wayne announced. He plopped down into the hanging chair.

"What now?" I asked.

"Paranoid," Wayne answered brusquely.

"And?" I prompted.

"Very paranoid."

"Wayne, is Van a good driver?" Dorothy asked.

Wayne did a double take before answering her. This was a question we should have thought about before. Who was a good enough driver to have killed Steve Summers? I thought of Jerry and his race car driving. Then I wondered if it necessarily took any particular skill to hit Steve Summers and kill him.

"Van's good, I suppose," Wayne answered finally. "I know he's fast. Whips around in a red Miata convertible."

"How about the rest of the group?" Dorothy pressed.

"I guess they all drive well," Wayne muttered, looking down as he thought. "Can't remember anything unusual about anyone's driving."

"Except Jerry," I put in.

"Yeah," he agreed dully. "Except Jerry."

He obviously didn't want to think about Jerry Urban as a suspect. I didn't really want to, either. But then again, I didn't want to think about anyone as a murder suspect.

Wayne, Dorothy, and I all sat in silence then. But it wasn't a comfortable silence. Dorothy had to be mourning Isaac, and there were far too many unanswered questions for comfort in any case.

The doorbell was almost a relief when it rang—except that Felix was the one ringing it.

"That cat was a friggin' omen!" he squealed when I opened the door.

I just looked at him, my brain still on murder suspects.

"Sheesh, Lucy, how could I have missed it?" he went on. "Brother Ingenio is a fraud! All that presto-pronto stuff, what a crock! How do I know he's even channeling these guys? All this whiz-bang, and he's not even logged on . . ."

My brain seemed to retreat. Felix ranted, and I watched him, my ears refusing to pick up any more. Then he snapped his fingers in my face. He must have noticed that most of me was elsewhere.

"Two more friggin' things, Kate," he told me. "One: I found out that Carl Russo spent hard time in the joint for stealing a car. He was in college when he did it. Probably majored in shoplifting."

I flinched. Carl? No wonder he was so worried about his kid. But why hadn't he told us?

"And numero two, amigo," Felix hissed, his hands on his hips. "Why didn't you tell me you found another stiff?"

SIXTEEN

✄

"Where'd you get your information about Carl Russo?" Wayne demanded before I even had a chance to defend my nondisclosure of Isaac's death. Wayne's voice was a low and dangerous growl.

"Huh?" Felix said, dropping his hands from his hips and taking a step backward. All ready to rant and interrupted. I almost felt sorry for him.

"Are you sure that Carl went to prison for auto theft?" Wayne pressed, closing the gap between Felix and himself with one stride.

"Sure as the friggin' New Jersey penal system," Felix answered, looking up into Wayne's scowling face with bravado.

Wayne shook his head as if he couldn't believe it. But I believed it. It made sense of Carl's behavior toward his son in a way that little else could.

"Anyway," Felix jumped back in, gearing up for his original rant. "Isaac Herrick—"

"Isaac Herrick was my friend," Aunt Dorothy put in, her voice as soft as a plush bunny. "Katie and Wayne were protecting me."

Felix's mouth hung open. Rantus interruptus was not a pretty sight.

Finally, he said, "Herrick was smothered."

"Smothered," my aunt whispered. She rose from the couch, then flopped back down. Damn, all of a sudden, she looked her age. No one would mistake her for a vivacious movie star now.

"Yeah, well," Felix went on, his voice subdued now; even Felix could sense the shock in Dorothy's posture. "It was supposed to look like some whoop-de-do heart attack, but the cop-docs can tell. They do all this whiz-bang, and then they tell you everything. Isaac Herrick was smothered with a pillow. While he was sleeping, probably." He glanced at my aunt and quickly moved his eyes back to us. "Pretty painless, the cop-docs said."

That was kind, especially for Felix.

"Thank you," Dorothy whispered. "That's good to know."

"Yeah, that's cool," Felix muttered, looking down at his feet, obviously embarrassed by his momentary lapse into humanity.

"Do they know what time he was killed?" Dorothy rallied.

Felix shrugged. "My source didn't get anything but crumbs, man. Just that Herrick's wasn't a natural death, no way, no how. Captain Wooster is spitting ingots, though. He doesn't want any cop-talk getting out."

"Do they have any suspects?" Dorothy pressed on.

"Same old, same old," Felix answered, shrugging again. "Gotta be tied up with the Summers stunt, though. Bunch of looney-tunes playing sensitivity—"

Wayne cleared his throat. It was an impressive sound; a dog across the street barked, as if in response.

Felix stopped and began again.

"So, the potato-brains at the cop shop have got doo-doo, as usual."

"You were good to let us know," Dorothy told Felix. She rose wearily from the couch. "I'll let you alone now."

"Will we see you tomorrow for Steve Summers' funeral?" I asked her quietly. I could see Felix's eyes light up, but I knew he'd never get in. "You can ride in with us," I finished.

"I'll meet you here," she promised, heading toward the door.

I'd almost forgotten her rental car. Now I was worried about her driving. I looked at Wayne.

"Would you like a ride—" he began.

"No. You're very sweet, but the drive will do me good," she assured him.

So we followed her outside to her rental. She rolled down the window after she started the ignition. I could see the moisture in her eyes glimmering in the darkness.

"We'll find out who killed Isaac, Katie," she declared.

"Right," I agreed weakly.

And then she drove off, not wasting any time as she accelerated onto the main road with a mechanical roar. Now, *she* could have been a race driver.

"Your aunt's a pretty cool old broad," Felix offered.

I didn't object to his wording.

"Your aunt wants to solve Isaac's murder," Wayne informed me once we were back inside, with Felix in place on the denim couch.

"Uh, yeah?" I said, not sure where he was going.

"What is it with you Koffenburgers?" he asked. "Do you have an extra gene for sleuthing?"

Felix closed his eyes. Whether he was meditating, sleeping, or eavesdropping, I wasn't sure.

"Wayne, Aunt Dorothy and I aren't related by blood," I told him seriously.

Then I really looked at his homely face. He was attempting a smile. He was joking.

"Oh, Wayne," I whispered and threw my arms around him. "We just have a gene for marrying good men."

"Ack," Felix commented. Then he pretended to stick his finger down his throat.

So I gave Wayne a good, long kiss.

Felix was out the door before we'd even disentangled our lips.

It was time for bed. And bed was just down the hall. We locked lips again.

*   *   *

Saturday morning, I woke up and remembered that it was the day of Steve Summers' funeral. I turned back over and shoved my face into my pillow.

"Kate?" I heard Wayne whisper, and then I remembered that Wayne had lost two members of his support group. I remembered that Steve Summers had been his friend. Wayne was the one who should have been shoving his face into a pillow, not me. He was such a rock that sometimes I forgot that he might be hurting, and hurting a lot. I rolled back over, took a deep breath, and started my day holding Wayne and wishing I could do more.

Aunt Dorothy arrived after I'd gobbled down a late breakfast of Wayne's dairyless pancakes with raspberry conserves. She looked better than she had the night before, her silver-white curlicues of hair bouncing jauntily atop her head. And she was dressed in a well-tailored, charcoal-gray coatdress that looked more appropriate for the day's activity than my one and only black pantsuit.

"May I drive?" she offered.

Wayne and I looked at each other for less than an instant. Was he remembering her speedy exit the night before too?

"I'll be glad to drive," Wayne answered quickly.

So, the three of us piled into my Toyota with Wayne at the wheel and Dorothy insisting on the back seat as usual.

Laura Summers had chosen an outdoor setting for Steve's funeral. An area the size of two football fields, or maybe one UFO landing strip, was conveniently located in front of the cemetery. That space was filled with folding chairs beneath white canopies, to protect the attendees from the July heat. As we tried to find a place to park, we realized why Laura had chosen this venue. The people attending Steve Summers' funeral couldn't have fit into a funeral home or a church. There were just too many of them.

For a short while, I wondered if Steve had really had more friends than we'd thought. But then I recognized who, or what, most of the mourners were: reporters. Even from the car, I recognized the too-loud, questioning voices, and I saw the cameras that security guards were shooing out from under the canopies. I heard the sound of helicopters overhead and looked up through the windshield. Were they filled with reporters, too?

Once we were parked, we tried to find familiar faces in the half-seated crowd. I spotted Helen Herrick, standing at the end of a row of chairs. Dorothy spotted her, too, and the two women ran toward each other to embrace. Helen was here to mourn Isaac as much as Steve, I realized as I saw her red-rimmed eyes. My aunt was probably here for Isaac as well. Who was here for Steve Summers? Wayne, I reminded myself. And, of course, Laura. I thought I could see Laura in the knot of people milling around in front of the chairs near the podium.

Helen and Dorothy took seats at the end of the row. Wayne and I sat behind them. I began to sweat in my black pantsuit.

"Think someone will try to take out Assemblywoman Summers, too?" a voice behind me asked eagerly.

"Nah, not here. Too many people."

I turned and saw two men with notebooks. The reporters were beginning to make me queasy. Throngs of people hadn't stopped other public assassinations; *could* Laura Summers have somehow been the target of Steve Summers' death? But, if so, what about Isaac?

"Kate, Wayne," I heard and saw Garrett Peterson and Jerry Urban. Wayne and I gladly moved down to make room for them. And then Janet and Ted Kimmochi were in front of us, next to Aunt Dorothy and Helen. Carl and Mike Russo sat next to them. Even Van Eisner showed up, with a petite, tanned beauty on his arm. They sat behind us. Somehow I felt comforted. *These* were Steve Summers' friends, his family. They were a dysfunctional family, but a family nonetheless. Then, I thought of Steve and Laura's son and wondered if I'd meet him today.

"Please be seated," a deep musical voice ordered, and the milling multitudes did just that.

Chairs scraped and voices called out, muffling whatever introductory remarks were being made, but eventually even the reporters quieted down.

"We are gathered here today to celebrate Steve Summers' life," the voice went on in the silence. A warm breeze passed through the canopy as if to remind us of life's fleeting nature. "To celebrate, not mourn, the life of a talented man whose creativity and ethics . . ."

As the voice continued, I peered over the heads of the rows and rows of mourners to see the speaker. He was a white-haired man dressed in a perfect suit. I wondered if he was a minister, or a politician, or something else entirely. His voice had a hypnotic quality. I fought against closing my tired eyes as he spoke of Steve's contribution to journalism and life in general. The uncomfortable folding chair helped me in my battle, its metal contours impossibly mismatched to my rounder shape. So I wriggled awake as the speaker's words blended together seamlessly and meaninglessly in my mind.

I'd barely noticed when the first speaker finished, but then Laura Summers took the place he'd vacated at the podium. She looked out at the crowd, no notes in her hands. Murmurs flitted around us like mosquitoes.

"I will speak briefly of my husband, Stephen Summers," she announced, and the murmuring stopped. "I could speak of my husband's good works for hours, even days, but my husband believed in brevity. He also believed above all in the truth, in doing the right thing. And so he lived his life. He was a man of high principle. He always did what he felt was right. May he always be remembered for that."

There was a silence as Laura sat down.

I felt the pressure of tears behind my eyes. What would I say if I had to eulogize Wayne?

A couple of Steve's fellow journalists spoke after Laura, citing his prizes and award-winning articles. But nothing they said could top what Laura had already told us. She was right—Steve's legacy had been one of high principles. Still, I took mental snapshots of the two men as they spoke. These were Steve's elusive other friends, men we could interview. What could they tell us about the real Steve Summers?

Finally, the original speaker returned to the podium and told us that family and friends would be welcome for a short reception at the Summers' residence. It would be a private reception, he warned—no reporters who were not friends of the family would be allowed. As members of the crowd scrambled from their folding chairs, I considered the irony of barring the reporters whose ranks Steve Summers had belonged to from the final recognition of his passing.

Making our way to the Toyota in that swarm of people was a slow, hot, and irritating process. Getting out of the parking lot was worse. Then, finally, we were on our way to the Summers' house, deep in the hills of Hutton.

When we got there, I could see that very few reporters had been discouraged by the speaker's final words. The front door was massed with shouting, shoving members of the press. They weren't getting far, though. Laura Summers stood slightly inside the front door, surrounded by a phalanx of security guards. She nodded, and the guards let some people in. But for her every nod there were at least nine distinct shakes of her head, and nine disgruntled reporters. I was glad I didn't see Felix, though somehow, I guessed he was in the crowd.

And then Aunt Dorothy, Wayne, and I were nodded through the door of the Summers' residence, past the roar of the media.

"Thank you for coming," Laura greeted us as we entered the octagonal living room that had so impressed me the first time we'd been to the Summers'. The ceilings had to be at least fourteen feet high, and each of the eight walls had an inset window draped in velvet and lace and graced by a comfortable tapestried couch. I wondered, not for the first time, how Steve had reconciled this room with his ideals. Or maybe he'd just never noticed the room.

"We're glad to come," Wayne murmured to Laura in the relative silence inside the door.

"Of course," Dorothy said, grasping Laura's hand.

"You made a wonderful speech," I added uncertainly; maybe she didn't want to talk about those final words.

But Laura smiled. "Thank you, Kate," she whispered. "I'm so glad you thought so."

A tall, gawky young man in glasses stood next to her.

"Steve Summers," he introduced himself, reaching out a hand.

For a moment, I was confused. Did this young man think he was Steve Summers?

"Our son," Laura put in helpfully. "Steve Junior."

Aha. The young man wasn't suffering from delusions. He *was* Steve Summers. He just wasn't the Steve Summers I'd known before.

"Oh, right," I tried. "You're in college now—"

"University," he interrupted. "I'm doing my Ph.D. dissertation on invisible disabilities—"

"Steve, can you help Tiffany with the buffet?" Laura interrupted and shook her head three times in rapid succession. Three more reporters were turned away. "Steve is a good boy, but he does tend to talk people's ears off about his dissertation," Laura apologized.

"How is he handling his father's death?" I asked.

Laura sighed. "He *seems* okay, but I worry. He and Steve—"

Laura stopped to nod the Russos in, and I felt a tug on my sleeve—Aunt Dorothy's tug. I understood the meaning immediately: Laura didn't need us clogging up the entrance, with all the nods and shakes she was in charge of.

So, the three of us walked over to the elaborate buffet that had been set up in the center of the room. I saw Janet McKinnon-Kimmochi and Garrett Peterson immediately. They were deep in private conversation. And I could hear them.

"I wish we'd brought Niki and Zora, but Ted didn't think it would be a good idea," Janet was confiding to Garrett over a slice of ham.

Garrett nodded solemnly, his dark face taut with some emotion, maybe unhappiness.

"Steve just loved Niki and Zora," Janet went on. "They spent hours together. He only had the one son. I guess he enjoyed the girls. Anyway . . ." She lowered her voice to a carrying whisper. "Someone that repressed probably related better to children."

"Quiet people are not necessarily repressed," Garrett responded. There was a slight tremor in his gentle tone. I wondered how hard it was to keep his words that mild. "Steve just kept to himself."

Janet's face paled under her freckles. She was not a woman to be disagreed with.

"Hey, Kate," someone said from behind me before I could jump into the fray. I turned and saw Carl in his inevitable badly fitted suit with Mike by his side in a suit just as badly fitted. "Sorry about last night."

"Did you go to the police?" I whispered, hoping my voice wouldn't carry like Janet's.

"Yeah," he answered. "They were pretty cool, for cops. I think they believed the kid. Your aunt is sumthin' else. Gotta thank her."

And then he turned to find Aunt Dorothy.

I turned, too, but by now Aunt Dorothy was across the room with Helen Herrick, Jerry Urban, and Ted Kimmochi.

I looked for Wayne. He stood across the buffet table, by Van Eisner's right side. On Van's left was the tanned woman he'd brought to the funeral.

"I thought you said this was a date," she complained.

"Hold on a minute," Van told the woman, turning back to Wayne. He rolled his shoulders and sniffed. "For God's sake, you gotta help me out here," he began.

Ugh. And I had felt comforted by having these people sitting around me.

I looked around the room and saw a number of unfamiliar faces. Friends of Steve's? Friends of Laura's? Relatives? Aides? And then I saw two faces that I recognized: the two fellow journalists who'd spoken at the funeral. One was tall, with thinning reddish hair; the other was burly, with an abundant head of black curls.

I was in front of them, with my mouth moving, in three paces.

"Hi, I'm Kate Jasper," I told them. "My husband was a member of Steve's support group."

"Oh," the tall one managed.

The burly one just stared.

"My husband and I are looking into Steve's death," I murmured. "We haven't been able to find friends of Steve's to talk to—"

"Makes sense," the staring journalist muttered. I caught a whiff of alcohol on his breath.

"What?" I replied, startled.

"Steve wasn't the friendliest guy in the world," he explained. "But I guess I shouldn't be saying that here."

"No, you shouldn't," his tall friend whispered angrily. "Think how Laura feels. And Steve Junior."

"Laura probably—"

"Not now, Gus," his friend erupted. "I'm sorry . . . Ms. Jasper, did you say?"

I nodded. The man went on.

"I'm Neil, and this is Gus. Did you want something in particular?"

"Well, I was hoping that my husband, Wayne, and I could talk to you," I answered cautiously. "We'd like to understand Steve better." I looked behind me to make sure neither Laura nor her son were in sight. "Steve was murdered, and we thought if we knew more about him as a person, we might understand why."

"You just said a mouthful, lady," Gus replied and laughed.

"What?" I blurted again.

"Of course we'll talk to you," Neil told me. He handed me his card. "Just call. No matter how anyone felt about Steve, his death wasn't right."

Gus reddened upon hearing his friend's words. I had a feeling that for a friend, Gus hadn't particularly liked Steve Summers as much as Neil had. I would have liked to have defended Steve, but, as an informer, Gus would probably be better than Neil. I had a feeling the chip on his shoulder was ready to talk. At length.

"Thank you," I told the pair of men. "I'll be calling. It was good to meet you."

And then I scuttled off to find Aunt Dorothy.

She was still standing with Helen Herrick, but the two women weren't talking. Steve Junior was talking—or maybe lecturing would be a better description.

"See, invisible disabilities are even more difficult to deal with than the visible ones," he was explaining. "Your husband writes so well about dyslexia . . ."

Helen's face paled. But how could this boy know that Isaac was dead?

"I'd love to talk to Professor Herrick someday about the psychological effects of dyslexia. He's been a real inspiration for me—"

"Steve," Laura's voice came from behind us. Her voice wasn't loud, but it was firm.

Steve Junior turned immediately.

"Mom?" he asked.

"Steve, Helen has her own issues to deal with now," Laura said gently and led her son away.

Helen made a little bowing motion in Laura's direction as they crossed the room.

"Did Steve say anything about his father?" I asked once the Summers were both out of earshot.

"Only that his father was interested in the Ph.D. project," Aunt Dorothy replied. She shook her head. "I think the Summers bury their feelings very deeply."

"Well, I don't!" Helen interjected angrily. "I grieve for Laura, but my Isaac . . ." She stopped for a moment to grab for a well-worn tissue and blew her nose before going on. "I know he was a drunk, but his passion, his mind . . ." She buried her face in the disintegrating tissue again.

"Helen, we'll find out who did it," my aunt assured her.

I squirmed in place at hearing my aunt's promise, especially since I was clearly part of the "we" to which she referred.

We didn't stay much longer at the reception. Van had departed, with his unhappy date on his arm, while I'd been talking with Gus and Neil. Garrett and Jerry had said good-bye not long after.

Laura hugged Wayne as we left. Then she gripped my hand and Dorothy's. I just wished that I could find words to comfort her.

"You must be very proud of your son," Dorothy offered.

"Thank you," Laura answered, and then we were on the sidewalk with the media again.

Driving home in the Toyota, Wayne spoke of Steve Summers. Maybe Laura's eulogy had been too short for him.

"Steve *was* a man of principle. He had needs, desires, and beliefs. He wasn't repressed. His passion was the truth."

And then I realized that Wayne must have overheard some of the same criticism I had. And he'd taken it hard. What had happened to speaking well of the dead?

"Kate," he said. "We'll find out who did this."

"Of course," I whispered back, though I wished that people—myself included—would stop promising to find Steve and Isaac's killer or killers. How could we possibly make a promise that we had no control over?

"For Laura, and for Helen," Dorothy chimed in.

I squeezed up against my seat and hoped that we really were The Three Musketeers.

The three of us were already climbing the stairs before we noticed that we had a visitor.

It was Captain Wooster. I stopped thinking about promises and started thinking about jail.

SEVENTEEN

❧

"Well, Mr. Caruso, how do you rate your life span these days?" Captain Wooster began conversationally, a Halloween pumpkin smile carved above his outsized jaw.

Wayne looked up at him woozily.

"What do you mean?" he finally asked, slowly.

Wayne shouldn't have ever asked that question because Captain Wooster had an answer—a long answer.

"Mary's handbag!" Wooster bellowed, his smile gone now. He threw out his arms. "Haven't you noticed that you and Ted Kimmochi are the only two husbands left standing? Hell's bells, these women are killing off their husbands. First Laura Summers, and then Helen Herrick. If they can't divorce you, they kill you. Women hate men, it's as simple as that. Only Peter at the Gate knows what we ever did to deserve it, but they're out for our blood."

"I'm not out for Wayne's blood," I put in cautiously.

He turned my way, his chin in full assault mode.

"Huh! That's what you say now. Holy Christmas, that's what they all say at first. Look at that Helen Herrick; she was already divorcing the poor sucker, but nooo, that wasn't enough, she had to put out his lights for him, too."

"Are you accusing Helen Herrick of murder, Captain Wooster?" Aunt Dorothy demanded, raising herself to nearly five feet in her barely restrained indignation.

The captain pulled his head back. He'd obviously forgotten my aunt in his excitement.

"Not necessarily accusing, ma'am," he floundered. He looked upward for inspiration. "Um, suggesting a theory. Yeah, that's it." He looked back at us and enunciated carefully, "One of the many possibilities we're pursuing, ma'am."

"I have known Helen Herrick for longer than you've been alive, Captain," Dorothy informed Wooster, her voice cold with anger. "And Helen is grieving for a man she loved. Don't you dare bully her."

"We don't bully people at the Cortadura Police Department," he tried, adding "ma'am" once more as an afterthought. "For Joseph's sake, we have to get them sandwiches if they want them. Or 'wraps.' It used to be croissants—"

"Well, I'll save you a wrap," Dorothy told him. "Helen didn't do it."

"But—" the captain started. Then he seemed to deflate. For a moment anyway, his chin went back to where most people's chins are. Then he opened his mouth again.

"Felix Byrne," he hissed.

I flinched.

"You know that little Judas weasel, don't you?" he demanded. "Friends like—"

"Yeah, but we didn't tell him anything," I cut in, guessing what was coming. "He already knew. He told *us* that Isaac was suffocated for sure."

"That little blood sucker!" the captain roared. "I don't know who leaked it, but now the whole world knows how Isaac Herrick died. No chance of surprising the guilty party with withheld information—"

"The *Marin Mind*?" I guessed.

He nodded. "If I get my hands on that boy, I'll—"

"Deny him a wrap?" my aunt suggested.

The captain's complexion turned an unhealthy shade of maroon.

"Was the coroner female?" I asked before he started in on Aunt Dorothy.

"What?" he said. "What kind of question is that?"

"Felix has a way of weaseling information out of female officers that I don't understand," I explained. "Maybe he's more attractive before you get to know him very well."

"Well, if the coroner has been talking out of turn, I'll have her hide," Captain Wooster promised. So, we *were* talking about a female officer here. I just hoped the captain didn't really have the power to make trouble for her. As far as I knew, the coroners worked for the county, not the city. "She should have known better than to talk to a reporter without my okay."

"Did you give her explicit instructions to the contrary, Captain?" my aunt asked sweetly. "I thought these details were routinely given to the press."

"No, I didn't give her explicit instructions," Wooster whined. "Mary, Joseph, and the baby, you'd think I was the only one with any sense."

There was a moment of relative silence as Captain Wooster squinted his eyes. Was he thinking of the good old days of rubber hoses?

"Sir," Wayne tried respectfully. "When will I be able to pick up my car?"

"When the bodies stop piling up," the captain shot back. "If you live long enough to see it, that is."

We were obviously back to the captain's original theory.

Then suddenly Captain Wooster shoved his chin my way. "Do you know something you're not telling me?" he asked.

I shook my head so hard I nearly slipped a disk.

"If you know something, you'd better tell me," he finally threatened. "That goes for all of you. Or I'll assume you dunnit, see?"

"But—"

"No buts," he corrected me. "Anything you know, you tell me *now*."

But jutting chin in my face or not, I didn't know anything. I searched what was left of my mind and couldn't find one important tidbit to pass on. At least, I hoped that nothing I knew was important. Wayne and Aunt Dorothy didn't do any better than I did. Even C. C., who'd wandered out for the show, had nothing to offer.

The captain left, fuming. I hoped it was an act, but I didn't think it was—not any more than my thudding pulse was an act.

After he'd gone, the three of us made it up the stairs, staggered into the house, and threw ourselves into the living room: Dorothy on the denim sofa and Wayne and I in the double hanging chair. C. C. brought up the rear, complaining about something—maybe it was Captain Wooster's demeanor, but it was more likely food deprivation.

"That man should learn to control his temper," Dorothy commented mildly. "He might have a heart attack."

"We won't get that lucky," I replied gloomily.

My aunt laughed. I looked up, surprised by the sound.

"I wonder if he'll ever catch up to your friend Felix?" she asked.

"Now you're really trying to cheer us up," I said, beginning to smile again. "Can you see it—"

But the doorbell cut off my imagined Wooster/Byrne interrogation.

Wayne got up and opened the door. I would have just left it shut.

Jerry Urban came through the doorway. He gave Wayne a brief one-armed hug, his round face smiling. But I could see tension in the hug.

"Hey, Kate. Hey, Dorothy," he greeted us.

Then he just stood for a moment. He crossed his arms briefly, then uncrossed them. He began to whistle. The three of us stared at him. Finally, he broke.

"Okay, I'm here about Garrett," he told us.

As if we couldn't have guessed, I thought. My aunt was more gracious than I was.

"Please sit down, Jerry," she offered, pointing to the hanging chair for one.

Once Jerry was seated, Dorothy started in. Captain Wooster might have been the master of interrogation, but my aunt was the mistress of polite inquiry.

"Is Garrett in some sort of distress?" she asked Jerry ever-so-gently.

"Whoa, have you been mind-reading or what?" he

exclaimed. Then his face grew more serious. "See, Garrett is a great caretaker for everyone but himself. Everyone depends on Garrett, but who does Garrett depend on?"

"You," Dorothy answered him.

"I wish," was all Jerry said, and then I saw the real hurt in his eyes. "Garrett won't lean on me, but then he won't lean on anyone. And when he gets depressed, I . . . I just don't know what to do."

"Is he depressed now?" my aunt continued in therapist mode.

"He's so depressed, I'm worried he'll just go into his shell and never come back out," Jerry replied. "I can't even talk to him. You know I've got this diabetes thing going on. I don't even dare tell him when I'm afraid. He'll just try to take on all my fear for me. He's like that, always taking on everyone else's stuff, never dealing with his own."

"And then there're the murders," Wayne put in.

Jerry sighed, long and deep. Finally, he nodded.

"And then there are the murders. I was hoping you guys would have this all wrapped up. Not that there's any reason you should; it's just that I'm desperate. It was bad enough when that kid committed suicide." He shook his head. "And that thing with his sister." Jerry sighed again.

"His sister?" I prompted, propelled by a tiny squirt of adrenaline. Did his sister have something to do with all of this?

"Oh, you didn't know about that?" he asked. Then he answered his own question. "No, I guess you wouldn't. Garrett never talks about his *own* problems . . . His sister was killed by a hit-and-run driver when he was a kid. He never got over it. And this thing with Steve is bringing up all the bad memories. It was a big newspaper thing when Garrett's sister was killed. She was just seventeen, and she was pregnant. None of the family had known about the pregnancy. It wasn't like her. She got good grades, wanted to be a nurse, all of that stuff. And then, bam! It was all over. And to top it all off, reporters hounded Garrett's mother while she was still grieving. It was a really bad scene."

It sounded like a bad scene. And then I wondered, could

Steve Summers have been one of those reporters on that bad scene? Garrett was a good fifteen years younger than Steve. It was possible.

"How old was Garrett when this all happened?" I asked.

"Thirteen years old. He calls it his unlucky year."

Yep, it was possible.

"Did Garrett ever say anything to you about Steve Summers?" I asked.

"Just general stuff. He liked him. Thought he was ethical."

My mouth wanted to ask if Garrett had recognized Steve Summers as one of the reporters that had made his mother's life miserable, or if Garrett had even stalked Steve Summers (all the way to Heartlink?), or—the biggie—had Garrett killed Steve for the pain he'd caused. But my brain told me that you don't ask someone's lover those questions.

"Did they ever find the hit-and-run driver?" I asked instead.

Jerry shook his head. "White man, black neighborhood. That's what all the newspaper fuss was about. But no one ever got any further than that on figuring out who the driver was."

"Did Garrett ever try to find out?" my aunt asked.

"Yeah, he asked around. But no one really saw anything but a big, expensive car."

"Speaking of cars," I began slowly. "I heard you used to drive race cars."

Jerry smiled, and the smile looked genuine. "Whoa, those were the days," he said. "Racing was my life—well, besides sex, drugs, and rock 'n' roll, that is. It was the late Sixties. You know, they say that if you can remember the Sixties, you probably weren't there." Then he guffawed, and I felt like I was seeing the real Jerry Urban again.

"Sometimes, I think it's just because Garrett is so young that he's so damn earnest," he added. "He didn't have fun during the Sixties like the rest of us."

"Hey," I plunged in again, trying to stop my mind from doing a roll call of all the people who *didn't* have fun in the Sixties, most of them in Vietnam. "We have a friend in common, Barbara Chu. She says you're a real practical joker."

"You know Barbara?" he asked, his voice squeaking. He slapped his knee. "That woman's a hoot! Helped me wire up the talking drinking fountain. You shoulda seen the people spit out the water in their mouths. Now, *she* knows how to have fun."

I nodded. I should have known that Barbara would have helped with Jerry's jokes.

"Jerry?" Aunt Dorothy asked quietly. "Do you think that Garrett's depression might have something to do with these murders? Perhaps he might have some idea of the murderer's identity."

My heart seemed to stop. Was that it? Had my aunt stumbled on the reason for Garrett's mood change?

Jerry's good-natured face wrinkled in concentration as he stared at the floor.

"He hasn't said anything like that," he muttered, as if to himself. "He would have told me . . . I think."

"Are you really sure?" Dorothy persisted.

Jerry looked up again and met her eyes.

"No, I'm not," he declared, standing abruptly. "But I'm gonna find out, right now."

And then he strode back to the front door.

"Let us know!" my aunt called after him as he took the stairs.

"You'll be the first!" he promised. And then he walked down the driveway, climbed into his BMW, and disappeared in a low hum of precision engineering. I thought of Wayne's Jaguar and sighed.

"We all need to cheer up," Aunt Dorothy announced.

"It would be nice to know who the murderer was," I put in hopefully. For all I knew, she had it figured out already.

"You really think Garrett might know?" Wayne added, his face as hopeful as mine.

But Dorothy just shook her head.

"Garrett would be upset if he suspected the murderer's identity, but that's no proof that he does," she reminded us.

"Oh," I said. Then I remembered Garrett's sister. "What if Steve was one of the reporters who covered the hit-and-run?" I asked. "Would that be enough motive?"

"What if Steve drove the hit-and-run car?" my aunt countered.

My mouth dropped open. I hadn't even thought of *that* possibility.

Wayne shook his head hard.

"Garrett just isn't a murderer," he proclaimed.

"Then who is?" I fired back.

Wayne looked stung. Sometimes I wished he had thicker skin. Sometimes I wished I could sew my mouth shut.

"Listen," Aunt Dorothy chirped. "I'll bet we can all use a change of pace. Let's all go do something fun—"

"That sounds—" I began.

"—like look at wedding books," she finished up.

"Wedding books!" I objected. "But Aunt Dorothy, we have a murder to solve."

"I am quite capable of multi-tasking, Katie," she told me. She didn't shake her finger my way, but she might as well have.

I turned to Wayne. He turned his grinning face away. Well, at least she'd made someone happy.

I wondered if she would believe there were no bookstores in Marin.

"Kate, how about that little store in Horquillo?" Wayne suggested helpfully. "They have a big section on wedding planning."

My mouth dropped open again. If I kept this up, I'd have more than one reason to sew it shut. But I just couldn't believe that Wayne had noticed they had a section on wedding planning. I certainly hadn't. And worse yet, I realized it was possible that he had actually browsed there.

"Oh, that sounds perfect," Dorothy declared, standing.

"Aunt Dorothy," I began.

"What, dear?" she asked.

"Um, this wedding stuff, I just don't know whether I'm really up for—"

"That's exactly why you need to research," my aunt assured me with a big smile. "It must seem overwhelming, but any task can be broken down to its component parts. And some of these books can be very helpful."

Wayne was standing now, too. What was I supposed to do? Faint? Demand to go to the hospital? Claim aliens had arrived to abduct me? It was no use.

"I'll drive," I muttered glumly.

Wayne obviously didn't hear me. When we got out to the driveway, he was in the driver's seat as fast as Felix Byrne pouncing on a good story. Maybe he was afraid I would hijack the car. In fact, that was a good idea. Too bad I wasn't faster than he was.

Once we were rolling, I worked on the multi-tasking.

"So, Aunt Dorothy, who's your best bet for murderer so far?" I asked.

"Well, I can think of a motive for everyone in the Heartlink group, and for their sigos," she began.

"You can?" I exclaimed. She was a lot farther along than I was. "Like what?"

"Well, Van Eisner is obviously paranoid about his drug problem," she pointed out. I nodded. That was a no-brainer. "Carl Russo would do anything to protect his son. And his son is none too stable, judging from appearances. Ted Kimmochi has secrets he doesn't want his wife to know. Is she, perhaps, the money as well as the brains in their little partnership? Even Helen—"

"Look at that," Wayne interrupted, pointing. We were passing a boy on a bicycle with a cell phone pressed to his ear.

Dorothy laughed.

"Only in California," Wayne told her.

They were bonding. Ack.

"And Helen?" I prompted.

"No more talk about murder," Dorothy ordered. "We're out here to cheer up."

And then she proceeded to talk about wedding books. Funny, I'd never thought of murder as a relatively cheerful subject before now.

"So, I suggest a comprehensive book," she was finishing up when Wayne turned the Toyota into the small, shrubbery-bordered Horquillo shopping center where he'd spotted the wedding books. There were no places directly in front of the

bookstore, so Wayne parked across the lot, in front of the
empty space where a yardage store had once been.

"The book by Murray Lynne is the most comprehensive,
I think," Dorothy continued after the two of us had exited
the car.

She linked her arm in mine, and we began to cross the lot
together while Wayne locked the Toyota. We were almost
to the bookstore when I heard a car gunning its motor. I
turned to look for Wayne. He was in the exact center of the
small lot, in an aisle between two rows of cars, his eyes
lowered thoughtfully as he ambled along.

A black car came barreling down the aisle in his direction.

"Wayne!" I screamed.

He looked up, but he looked at me, not at the car. And he
stopped moving.

I reached him in three leaps, and I shoved him with everything I had. He flew through the air, out of danger from the
car that was almost on us. Then I dropped to the ground and
rolled away from the shrieking engine, smelling exhaust
fumes. As I rolled, I remembered something important: I had
to get the license plate number of that car.

But the car was gone by the time I raised myself to sitting
position again. I could hear the roar of its engine speeding
away, but I couldn't see it over the shrubbery surrounding
the shopping center.

If it hadn't been for the aching of my body, and Wayne
sitting stunned on the ground a few yards away from me, I
would have thought I'd imagined the black car. But I hadn't.

EIGHTEEN

❧

"That vehicle tried to run over Wayne," my Aunt Dorothy announced from somewhere above me. Her voice sounded distant, as if from another planet.

I brought my own body back down to Earth, looked up, and took in the shock on my aunt's elfin face. No, I hadn't imagined the black car.

The last of my adrenaline rush faded away, leaving me weak. I closed my eyes. I was already on the ground. If I fainted—

"But Kate hit me first," Wayne growled. My eyes popped back open. Wayne! He stood up, wincing at me. "Remind me not to ever make you *really* mad." He limped toward me, held out his hand, and then whispered, "Thank you doesn't cover it, Kate. Love you."

"Oh, Wayne," I answered. I couldn't think of anything else to say. I took his hand and let him lift me to a standing position. "Are you really hurt?"

"No, just a little bruised, ego more than body. All that karate training." He shook his head. "Shouldn't have let you throw me. Should have been underneath the wheels of a car. Hate it when I goof up like that."

I giggled, then couldn't believe I had. Wayne had almost been killed, for all I knew. I threw my arms around him and squeezed.

"Ouch," we both said at once, and I let go.

"Oh, no, I didn't look at the license plate!" Dorothy broke in, her voice sounding a little closer now. "Did either of you?"

Wayne and I looked into each others' eyes, and shook our heads.

People were streaming into the parking lot now.

"What happened?" a tall woman in khaki demanded.

"Should we call an ambulance?" a shorter man in a Grateful Dead T-shirt asked.

"Did someone get hurt?" someone I couldn't see threw in.

"It was a car; it almost hit that guy," a red-haired teenager said, pointing Wayne's way.

"On purpose?" asked the woman in khaki.

"Sure looked that way," the guy in the Grateful Dead T-shirt answered.

"Did any of you get a license plate number?" Aunt Dorothy inquired politely.

But these people had more questions than answers. No one remembered the make of the car, just that it had been black. Or maybe dark blue. An American car, kind of big. No one saw the driver, though one woman thought she'd seen dark glasses and maybe a muffler or something. They were actually doing better than I was in the memory department; all I could remember was Wayne's face as he'd looked at me and stood stock still in the path of the speeding car.

"What were you thinking about?" I asked him.

"Thinking about?"

"When the car was coming at you," I explained. "You didn't hear it. You didn't see it."

"Oh." His skin grew pink. "I was thinking that I shouldn't be so judgmental about all the secrets that people have been keeping. Secrets aren't necessarily lies."

I wondered whether Steve Summers would agree, but then people were asking questions again.

"D'ya wanna report this thing?" was the question that came through the loudest.

Did we?

"Perhaps we should call Captain Wooster," Dorothy suggested.

"I'll get my cell phone," Wayne said. That's when I knew he was still shaken. The cell phone was in his Jaguar, not my lowly Toyota.

"Um, Wayne—" I began.

"Right," he muttered. "No cell phone. Home."

So, the three of us said goodbye to the sympathetic crowd that had gathered, got into my Toyota, and went home to call Captain Wooster.

On the way, Wayne, Dorothy, and I all argued over who should call the captain.

"I saw the most," I put in.

"The car was aimed at me," Wayne insisted.

"That young man won't listen to you," my aunt pointed out.

"I heard it first," I tried again.

By the time we got home, we were all tired and cranky. But I was the fastest on my feet into the house, and I was dialing Captain Wooster's number before Aunt Dorothy and Wayne even made it up the stairs. Unfortunately, the captain was in, and my call was put through to his office. I should have listened to my aunt.

First, I told him about going to Horquillo for wedding books. I should have never mentioned the "W" word.

"Weddings! Eve's apples, do you have to marry the poor clod twice before you kill him or what?"

"I don't even want to get married again," I fired back. Then I looked over my shoulder. Dorothy and Wayne were just settling into the living room. I lowered my voice. "But that's not the point. We were in this little shopping center, you know the one that used to have the yardage shop in Horquillo—"

"To get wedding books?"

"I . . . yes. Anyway, I heard this car—"

"Hell's bells, just do up the wedding favors in cyanide and be done with it—"

"So this car came barrelling down on Wayne, but I shoved him out of the way—" I pressed on.

"You're saying this was in Horquillo?" Captain Wooster stopped me, his voice sounding almost happy for a moment.

"Yeah, and then I rolled away—"

"If this was in Horquillo, why are you calling me?" the captain demanded.

I closed my mouth for a minute to digest his words.

"Because this has to be related to Steve Summers' murder—" I finally started up again.

"So *you* say. I say, let the Horquillo Police Department deal with it."

"Are you kidding?" I yelped.

"Listen to me, Ms. Jasper. Noah's giraffes, I've got two murders on my hands, and you call me about a traffic accident in Horquillo? And you ask me if I'm kidding?"

"This wasn't a traffic accident!" I screamed. "Someone tried to kill my husband."

"Were *you* there?" he asked me accusingly.

I took a deep breath. I was seeing pinpoint dots in front of my eyes in colors that would have been more appropriate to the Sixties.

"Captain, I was not driving the car in question," I replied, hoping my voice was calmer than the rest of my body.

"Ha!" he shot back. "Tell that to the guys in Horquillo." And then he hung up.

I walked into the living room. Aunt Dorothy and Wayne were both on the denim couch with expectant faces.

"Captain Wooster feels that the Horquillo Police Department has jurisdiction," I summarized.

Dorothy just nodded. She was not a woman to say, "I told you so." Not out loud, anyway.

"He what?" Wayne asked, squinting his eyes.

"He's nuts!" I moaned.

"Oh, right," he murmured calmly. Maybe he was seeing pinpoints of color, too, but at least Wayne *sounded* calm.

"Sorry," I whispered.

"Oh, now, Katie, don't you be sorry," my aunt told me. "You did your best. And our Captain Wooster *is* missing a few berries from his basket."

Wayne stood up and put his arm around me. "Plus, you

did save my life," he added. "A small thing, maybe, but I appreciate it."

I felt my mouth curve into a smile then. The tension rolled away from my body, leaving me as limp as a Beanie Baby.

"Well, I'll let you two youngsters have some peace," Aunt Dorothy announced. "I'm going back to my hotel for a nice, hot bath."

It wasn't until Aunt Dorothy's car pulled out of the driveway that I began to cry. But once I started, I couldn't seem to stop. And then Wayne was holding me. He might have been crying too, or maybe I just splashed tears on his face. We just held each other, bruises and all. And then we were kissing. And cuddling. And then we were back in bed, where we'd started the day an eternity ago.

Sunday morning, Wayne and I woke up simultaneously, groaning—not from lust, but from sore, aching bodies. It was lucky we'd made love the night before because showing each other our bruises wasn't exactly erotic. But then again, neither of us was afraid anymore.

The phone rang while I was examining a black and blue spot on Wayne's backside. It was the size and shape of Brazil.

"I'll get it," we both said.

Amazingly, Wayne bowed, letting me do the honor. I didn't have time to be suspicious as I threw on a robe and headed to my phone just in time to hear the answering-machine tape end and Garrett Peterson say "hello."

"Garrett," I greeted him, grabbing the receiver.

I wanted to talk to this man. We had something in common—hit-and-run. Did Wayne's close call the night before have anything to do with Garrett's sister's final call years before? Would I have the nerve to ask?

"Kate?" Garrett said, a slight lilt to his deep, slow voice. "It seemed important to call, to take some action."

"Uh-huh," I murmured, feeling very therapeutic.

"I think it's time for another meeting of the group. And not just the members. I . . . well . . ."

"You want all the suspects there," I put in.

There was a brief silence. Garrett *did* realize that all the members and their sigos were suspects, didn't he? Even if he didn't know about the key, he had to realize the implications of the deaths. And then I reminded myself that I really didn't want him to know about the Jaguar key because the only way he could know about it was if he'd stolen it himself. And I truly liked Garrett.

Finally, he replied, his voice barely audible. "Yes, I suppose I mean the suspects."

"Garrett, do you think you know who did it?" I asked.

"No, no," he told me. He sighed much more audibly than he was speaking. "Jerry told me about your aunt's theory. But I have no idea. I just need to talk to everyone. To see them react with my own eyes. If one of us did this thing, I want to know. I need closure."

"So you want the group to meet—"

"See you in a few minutes!" Wayne called out.

I looked up and saw my sweetie at the door, fully dressed. How had he done that so fast?

"Hold on a minute, Garrett," I ordered and put my hand over the receiver.

"Wayne, where—"

"I'll be back in half an hour," Wayne assured me, or tried to assure me.

"But—" I protested.

Wayne was out the door before I could even finish my objection.

"Are you okay, Kate?" Garrett asked me.

His voice invited me to confide in him. No, I wasn't okay. Wayne was going out without me. Was he going to investigate? Why did he run out so fast? But Garrett was the man who took on everyone else's problems. I wasn't going to make him take on mine.

"Fine," I lied, hearing the Toyota start up and leave as I did. "So, when do you want the group to meet?"

"Today?" Garrett suggested. "Maybe I could reach everyone by late afternoon. I know it's short notice, but still, it's Sunday."

Maybe *I'd* be able to reach *Wayne* by then. Damn. Where
had he gone?

"Sounds fine to me," I agreed.

"Is Wayne okay?" Garrett asked softly.

"What do you mean?" I shot back. My skin tightened on
my bruised body. Did Garrett know about last night's car
assault?

"The murders must be affecting him, Kate," he answered
slowly and clearly, as if addressing a mental patient. I knew
the tone; I'd used it myself years ago when I'd worked on a
psych ward. "I know Wayne's a very sensitive man."

"Oh, right," I muttered. "Um, you know Jerry was over
here last night—"

"And told you all about my sister," Garrett finished for
me, his voice speeding up. "I know I should have shared
information about my sister with the group, but it was so
long ago, and the others had more current problems. It didn't
really seem appropriate. Still, I wasn't trying to hide anything."

"Some things just hurt too much to discuss in a group?"
I guessed.

"Yes," he agreed simply.

"It's all right, Garrett," I told him, wondering if it was all
right with Wayne, too.

"Thanks, Kate," he replied. "Wayne's lucky to have you."
And once again, paranoia made me wonder if he was talking
about the car that had aimed for Wayne last night. I rolled
my sore shoulders impatiently, as if I could roll away my
suspicions.

"And Jerry's lucky to have you," I reminded him. "You
know, I'll bet Jerry wouldn't mind if you leaned on him for
support more often." Me, the Dear Abby of the Heartlink
men's group. There was something about Garrett that
brought out the inner meddler in me.

Garrett was silent for a few heartbeats, then he spoke seriously.

"You're right," he conceded. "I've got to start paying better attention to Jerry."

"Well, anyway . . ." I said, suddenly embarrassed by my

meddling. Then we talked about the proposed afternoon get-together. We worked out details, and Garrett promised to call the others, and finally, I hung up the phone.

Wayne hadn't returned by the time I'd finished talking. But then, a half-hour hadn't gone by either.

I went to my desk, still in my robe. Paperwork awaited me. A workaholic tipple would get me through the time left before Wayne returned. Invoices, ledgers, checks . . . The choices were endless.

Within minutes, I was working on invoices, but my mind continued to hum with questions. I hadn't planned to leave Wayne's side until I found out who was driving the black car, until I found out who'd murdered Steve Summers and Isaac Herrick. But Wayne had escaped. And for what? A half-hour wasn't long enough to go into the city to work. It certainly wasn't long enough to investigate. What *was* he doing?

My mind was so loud that I didn't hear the door open at first. But a swishing sound caught my attention—the sound of a lion slithering through tall grass.

I jumped out of my chair and ran toward the entryway.

But the tall grass wasn't grass, it was flowers—a huge bouquet of flowers: gladioli, irises, roses, Shasta daisies, cosmos, and more, swishing toward me. I couldn't even see the lion.

And then the flowers bowed my way.

"To the superiority of fast reflexes over somber thoughts," a deep voice intoned, and then the flowers were standing again.

I opened my mouth to yell at the homely face that peeked over the top of the flowers, but his worried eyes stopped me.

"Damn, you're cute when you're flowers," I drawled in my best Mae West voice.

Wayne smiled shyly, and I remembered again why I loved him.

"Didn't know how else to thank you," he mumbled.

"I thought you did a fine job last night," I reminded him.

He blushed. Too bad I was too bruised to make him *really* blush.

We'd finally found a vase big enough for the flowers when Wayne mentioned Ann Rivera, my friend who worked as a psychiatric hospital administrator.

"She might know Garrett," he reminded me.

"Lunch?" I asked.

"Yeah," he breathed

We were a team again.

I got on the phone and convinced Ann to go to lunch with us. Ordinarily, Ann would have preferred a feast cooked by Wayne's own hands, but Sundays were always busy at the hospital. So, she suggested a trip to Eco-Eats, a vegetarian place near her work. We agreed on a time, and I hung up. Then I remembered Aunt Dorothy, the third member of our team. Wayne promised to call her and shooed me into the shower.

The hot water stung my bruises, but after a while it eased the sore muscles in my neck and back. I leaned into the water and luxuriated, and smiled secretly at the naive sweetness of my husband.

A few hours later, Aunt Dorothy, Ann Rivera, Wayne, and I were seated at a table at Eco-Eats. Our table mats were woven, not paper, and our waitpersons weren't persons at all, but Disneyesque endangered species. We'd been shown in by a sad-looking panther and were being read the specials by a six-foot spotted owl.

". . . avocado-tempeh burgers, six-grain pilaf, and stuffed zucchini with lemon-walnut sauce, and our soups today are mushroom-miso and basil-bean."

Wayne gave a little grunt beside me. Eco-Eats was not his kind of restaurant. Wayne managed to put up with vegetarian food, but only the best vegetarian food.

"I'll give you a little time," the spotted owl said and turned in a flurry of scruffy plumage.

"So, you know Garrett Peterson." My aunt Dorothy returned to the subject at hand once the owl was out of earshot. We'd all taken turns filling Ann in on recent events and suspects while we were still in the car driving to Eco-Eats.

"I certainly do know Garrett," Ann answered. "He's a visiting psychiatrist at our hospital. And let me tell you," she shook a finger here, "Garrett is one of the kindest men I've ever known. You can take him off your suspect list right now."

"You're a loyal friend," my aunt encouraged her.

Ann relaxed into her linen suit, her brown face breaking into a toothy grin.

"Okay, so I'm a little biased," she admitted. "If Isaac wasn't dead, I'd think *he* had a hand in this mischief in some way, though."

"You knew Isaac?" I asked.

"Isaac was a man you couldn't *not* know in the therapeutic community," she told us. "And he was a real joker." Her face turned serious again. "I never really figured him out. He was smarter than he acted, that's for sure."

Aunt Dorothy nodded solemnly.

Ann sat back in her woven hemp seat, her eyes unfocused and thoughtful.

"Did you tell me that the mother of the Kimmochi girls said Steve spent a lot of time with them?"

I nodded.

"Well, if you're looking for motive—"

"Have we made up our minds?" the spotted owl interrupted us.

We all jumped.

Ann and I got the avocado-tempeh burgers. Dorothy decided to try the stuffed zucchini. Wayne played it safe with the miso soup and a vegan chef's salad. We all ordered herbal iced tea, and our owl shuffled away. I wondered how hot it was in that bird suit.

"Have you guys considered sexual molestation?" Ann interrupted my thought.

"Huh?" the three of us replied.

"Steve, the Kimmochi girls," Ann reminded us impatiently.

"But Steve was Mr. Clean," I objected, "ethical at the least—"

"You ever notice how these religious leaders are always the ones fooling around when they shouldn't be?" she shot back. "Child molesters don't wear signs."

"Steve was very quiet," Wayne offered. I didn't know if this was an indictment or a character reference.

We all sat in silence for a while. Steve Summers as child molester. I shook my head, and realized that I was still sore from my dive and roll the night before. Still, I didn't buy it. Steve was too self-righteous to bring himself to do something so despicable. He'd have killed himself first. And then I wondered if he *had* killed himself, had somehow planned his own death. But who'd killed Isaac Herrick? And why?

Our food arrived before anyone voiced any more arguments, pro or con.

The avocado-tempeh burger was stuffed with onions and hot mustard, and it was good, despite Wayne's unspoken disdain. The thought of Steve Summers as a child molester was less appetizing.

We all left Eco-Eats in a more sober mood than that in which we'd entered its ecologically correct doors.

Dorothy and I began to talk once we'd dropped Ann off at the hospital—theories, second theories, conjecture. Could Steve have been a child molester? Wayne cut in authoritatively after a few minutes.

"No," he stated. "It's not possible. Steve Summers couldn't have done it."

Dorothy looked thoughtful, but said nothing. I don't think she believed his absolute no, but she didn't state any further opinion.

"Do you think Isaac's most recent book is in print?" she asked instead.

We both turned to look at her.

"When people write, they leave clues. I wonder if Isaac left any."

So we went to a local bookstore in Mill Valley, far away from Horquillo. The woman behind the counter found the book for us and rang it up.

Then she leaned over the counter and whispered, "You know, his wife really wrote his books."

So much for Isaac's secret.

When we left the store, all three of us turned both ways and scanned the lot before crossing to our car, and we saw a red Miata. It was gone before we could see the driver. Had it been Van Eisner?

And if it had been, was Van stalking us?

None of us had to speak those thoughts aloud.

But, even if it was Van Eisner, would he have used his own car? I remembered the black car from the night before and tensed.

And then someone honked.

NINETEEN

✣

Dorothy, Wayne, and I all jumped in place in perfect synchronization. We could have been the Rockettes.

"Are you guys coming or going?!" a masculine voice bellowed out the window of an SUV. "Jeez, you're standing there like cows!"

In watching the red Miata, we hadn't noticed the other moving vehicle in the lot. Now, it honked again, veered around us, and sped off.

I wanted to run after it like a dog and rip off its bumpers, but I knew I wasn't fast enough.

The three of us walked cautiously across the lot to the Toyota. I took the wheel once we got there—my car needed its true owner's loving touch once in a while.

The engine died the first time I started it up. I swiveled my head around to look at Wayne. It hadn't died on *him*. Could the car really prefer Wayne to its true owner? Could Wayne have alienated my auto's affections? Jealousy isn't a pretty thing, especially when it's over a car. I decided not to challenge Wayne to a duel. Instead, I pumped the Toyota again and turned the key, and we were on the road. Maybe the car had just been sending me a little reminder of how much it had missed me.

"I can't help but think that Van Eisner is the obvious choice for murderer," my Aunt Dorothy began from the back seat of the car once we were scudding along the back roads of Mill Valley.

"But is he together enough to plan a complicated murder?" Wayne asked thoughtfully.

"No," I answered.

"He's certainly paranoid about his drug use," my aunt went on. "Could Steve have threatened him with police exposure if he didn't give up drugs?"

There was a silence in the car. Were both Wayne and I imagining Steve doing just that? It sounded like him, all right.

"Still, whoever planned Steve's murder found another car, disguised themselves, hit quickly, and disappeared," I mused aloud. "Can you imagine Van focusing clearly enough to pull it off?"

"No," Dorothy agreed. "But perhaps he was very lucky. Isaac's murder didn't take a lot of imagination."

"But why would Van kill Isaac?" I asked gently.

"I don't really know," my aunt admitted. "Isaac was an intelligent man; perhaps Isaac figured out it was Van and challenged him with the knowledge."

I just wished Ann was still with us to help with this analysis. Because as much as I would have liked the murderer to be Van, I still just didn't believe it. Van was an insensitive womanizer and a bumbler, not to mention a man with a drug problem, but he didn't strike me as a murderer. Then again, none of the suspects struck me as a murderer. I sighed and guided the Toyota home.

Once we got there and saw who was waiting on our front doorstep, I let out another sigh. Felix was back.

"Howdy-hi!" he greeted us as we trudged our way up the stairs.

Wayne and I mumbled mixed curses.

Only my aunt said, "Hello, Felix."

But it wasn't my aunt that Felix wanted to talk to. It was me. Lucky me. He practically dragged me through the door after I opened it, ranting incoherently.

". . . so whaddaya think, man?" he asked once he was sitting on the denim couch. "Janis and Jimi, man. Gotta be the

Brother. Holy socks, this is the real whazoo, doncha think? I mean, you were there and everything—"

"Slow down, Felix," I told him. I put a restraining hand over his mouth, felt his mustache, and instinctively drew my hand back and wiped it on my Chi-Pants.

"But Kate, it's happening, like the pope and his poodle—"

"The pope and his poodle?" I asked, now hopelessly confused. My brain was swirling in the blender of Felix's words.

"Like Cher and Captain Kirk, man," he expanded.

I didn't want to know. I turned away, but that didn't stop him.

"Listen to me, Kate," he insisted. "You were right— Brother Ingenio is for real."

I turned back to him. "I never said Brother Ingenio was for real," I pronounced very clearly.

"Sheesh, Lucy!" Felix pushed his face into mine. I could smell onions and curry. "You told me he was the Honest Abe incarnation in my dream, Kate."

"In your dream?" I asked, the slightest thread of light dawning. "You mean, you think I'm responsible for what you dream?"

"And Jimi told me, too. Brother Ingenio channelled him, whiz-bang, whoopdee-doo."

"Let me get this straight," I tried. "You believe the words confirming Brother Ingenio's validity as a . . . a what?"

"Like a holy guy, ya know, a visionary, man—"

"All right, so you believe that the brother's for real because he told you with his own mouth—"

"He was only using his mouth to channel Jimi Hendrix, Kate. Jeez Louise, doncha get it?"

"Fine," I said. It was cowardly, but I didn't want to get into a logic-slinging match with Felix. It would just drive me crazy—or crazier—and it wouldn't really be logic, anyway.

"Be that way," Felix sulked. "Ted believes me."

"Ted who?" I asked. I couldn't help it. I searched my mind for dead Teds. "Ted Bundy?"

"Criminy, Kate!" he protested. "Ted Bundy's under the lilies. Ted *Kimmochi*."

It took a second for me to switch gears. I wanted to tell Felix that Jimi Hendrix was as dead as Ted Bundy, but Felix's words led me in another direction completely.

"Have you been bugging the suspects, Felix?" I asked.

Felix raised his eyebrows.

"Of course, I have, Kate. I'm a reporter, remember? I get the poop. No one else has a clue. Betcha you know who did it, though, right?"

His large eyes reflected craftiness as he spoke.

"No, I don't know who did it, Felix. Do you?"

"Nah," he admitted. "My sources are as dry as Martha Stewart's toilet bowl."

"You must know something," I wheedled, wondering if my own eyes looked crafty now, too—and wondering if Martha Stewart really had a waterless toilet bowl.

"Well, he did have these two amigos, ya know—"

"The two reporters at the funeral?"

Felix nodded. "The dude didn't have that many real compadres, Kate," he said. "So tell me about Brother Ingenio—"

"I don't know anything about Brother Ingenio!" I blared.

Felix looked at me with hurt in his soulful eyes.

"Perhaps you'd like to meditate, Felix?" Aunt Dorothy suggested. "The outdoors are especially nice for meditation."

I could have hugged my aunt because now Felix was babbling to *her* as she led him out to sit under our walnut tree. I watched from the window as Dorothy situated him. Felix sat cross-legged under the tree and a stray green walnut fell on his head.

"Nirvana," I muttered.

Wayne snorted next to me.

Then my aunt was back in the living room. She was smiling, but somewhere there was an edge of impatience in her face. It was something about the way her chin was raised. Had she been taking lessons from Captain Wooster?

"Are we doing anything more today?" she asked sweetly. Maybe I'd imagined the impatience.

Then I remembered the group get-together at Garrett's. I glanced at Wayne. He shook his head, ever so slightly. My aunt didn't belong at an extended meeting of the Heartlink group any more than Felix did.

"Not really," I muttered.

Dorothy's eyes hardened. She'd seen the look and the head-shaking.

"All right, there's a group meeting," I confessed, "but, I—"

"I understand completely, Katie," Aunt Dorothy assured me. "The group is for members and sigos only." My muscles loosened. "I won't impose. Anyway, I wanted to go over some wedding ideas this afternoon." My muscles tightened again.

Dorothy gave me a big hug, announced, "You'll call me," and was out the door before I had time to speak.

Wayne and I plopped down together in the hanging chair for two as soon as she was gone.

"Let's try to see Steve's journalist friends after the group meeting," Wayne suggested.

"Good idea," I answered, but I didn't get up. Aunt Dorothy seemed to have taken my energy with her when she left.

"Wayne?" I murmured after a few moments had passed. "What do you think of Felix and Brother Ingenio?"

Wayne grunted.

I turned to him. He was blushing. I had forgotten—Wayne was as embarrassed to speak about spiritual matters as he was to speak about sexual ones. He had no problems experiencing either state, but talking about it was another matter. In all the years we'd been together, we'd had less than a half-dozen conversations about what we felt like when we did our separate meditations.

"Know about contemplation," he muttered finally. "Read a little. Still, can only go with my own feelings. Just don't know . . ." He faltered.

"But Brother Ingenio doesn't ring your chimes," I finished for him. It was too painful to watch him try to explain. "Me, neither," I let him know. "You know how I meditate," I went on softly. "Sometimes, I even feel a certain spiritual presence and a sense of peace, but I don't like to rely on someone

else to interpret that presence. No dead rock stars are talking
to me."

Wayne chuckled.

I pressed up against him.

"Thanks," I said.

"For what?" he asked, his eyebrows lifting.

"For . . ." I paused. I wasn't even sure myself. "For everything," I finished huskily.

And then he blushed again.

"All right, time to call Steve's friends," I declared.

Wayne almost leapt from the hanging chair to do the deed.

I heard the rumble of his voice from across the entryway,
and then he was back.

"We'll see them for an early dinner," he announced. "Time
to go to Garrett's."

I looked down at my watch. It was time. Too bad. I'd
have liked to have sat with Wayne and watched him blush
a little longer.

We passed Felix on the way out. He was still under the
walnut tree. From the tilt of his body, I guessed he was
asleep. Or maybe that's just how he meditated.

Going to Garrett's and Jerry's house in the San Ricardo
hills was usually a pleasure, if only because their home was
so arty. The white living room with its black furnishings and
black-and-white photos could have been clipped from a magazine. But that afternoon, I remembered that this was where
it had all started—this was where someone had stolen
Wayne's Jaguar key from my key chain.

As we walked into their living room, I looked at those
who'd already arrived and wondered if one of them had been
the thief. And the murderer.

The doorbell rang again, and Van Eisner was ushered in.

Van didn't look good. His slight body looked even thinner
than usual, and his sharp features just seemed to accent his
reddened, round eyes. He rubbed his hands together as he
looked around the room.

"Hey, any of you guys tell the cops about my personal
habits?" he demanded.

"You're probably a drug addict, but that doesn't excuse

your behavior," Ted's wife, Janet, jumped in. "Back off."

Van laughed. It wasn't a pleasant laugh; it was way too shrill and way too loud.

"You're protecting your sweet hubby, and he's having an—"

"Janet's right," Jerry interjected, his high voice menacing. He'd entered the room carrying a tray of fresh-baked cookies. A warm, sugary smell floated through the air. But suddenly, Jerry looked scary. "Back off, Van," he repeated Janet's admonition.

"Yeah, back off," Mike Russo parroted from behind Jerry. He stuck out a hand, cocking it like a gun.

Jerry grinned and turned to the boy, and the menacing man I had seen a moment ago was gone. The roly-poly bear was back.

"Make fun of me, will ya? See if *you* get any cookies," Jerry said to Mike.

Mike pretended to re-holster his gun and then grabbed two cookies off the tray.

"You little—" Jerry began affectionately, but Van wasn't finished.

"All you guys think you're so high and mighty," he complained. "Well, I know secrets, too. So just don't be telling mine—"

"Van, no one here wants to tell the police anything but who killed Steve and Isaac," Laura Summers said. Her deep, quiet voice held a certainty that was soothing. "We all understand your wish for privacy and will respect it."

Finally, Van seemed to deflate. He flopped down into a black leather armchair and put his head into his hands, mumbling, "Thank you."

The whole room seemed to expand in relief—almost the whole room.

"So, Ted probably *didn't* call the police," Janet snapped at Van, her hands on her hips. "But I wouldn't blame him if he did. People like you—"

Van was out of his seat in less than a second and headed toward Janet. In that second, Ted stepped in front of his wife.

"I'll kill her!" Van shouted, and I wondered if my Aunt Dorothy was right after all.

"Whoa, Van," Ted said, his arms raised, palms out. "Don't be so harsh. It's okay."

"But Ted, she—"

"I know," Ted commiserated. And I'm sure he *did* know.

Janet peeked out over her husband's shoulder, her face pale beneath her red hair.

"I'm sorry," Van muttered, and then he began to cry.

Ted put a tentative arm around his shoulder. Damn. They really *were* a support group.

"Let's have a time-out," Garrett suggested quietly.

Laura Summers took Janet by the arm and gently led her into the dining room. Garrett, Wayne, and Carl gravitated to the other side of the room to huddle. Jerry and Mike headed back to the kitchen.

I went to the bathroom. I skipped the downstairs one, leaving it open in case someone else needed it. Instead, I went upstairs where I could peek into bedrooms and home offices on the way. Garrett's office looked much like the living room, in miniature. It had the same white walls, black furnishings, and photos. Only he had bookshelves—shelves and shelves of books so weighty, my mouth went dry and my brain went dead just looking at them.

Jerry's office was altogether different. Gadgets, sci-fi and mystery novels, and machine parts were jumbled together in a colorful mess of piles and stacks. Yep, Garrett had decorated the living room, not Jerry. And then I noticed a book on the top of one of Jerry's stacks: *The Deadly Directory*, edited by a woman named Derie, *Kate* Derie. Whoa, that looked serious. I reached for the book—

"Looking for the bathroom?" a voice asked from behind me.

I whirled around, my arms jerking up defensively.

Jerry stood right outside the door. He smiled at me. The smile was pleasant, but still . . .

"Neat room," I croaked. "Cool stuff."

"I think so," he agreed. "Too bad Garrett's taste is more in the line of organization than chaos."

"Heh-heh," I tried.

Now I really *did* have to go to the bathroom. I was just lucky I hadn't already.

Jerry showed me the lavatory, done neatly in mauve and white. I closed the door and sucked in the gasp I hadn't allowed myself earlier. I was shaking. Why did I think I could go sneaking around someone's house without them noticing? I was just glad Jerry hadn't caught me in their bedroom, though I was sorry I hadn't gotten a look at it.

There's nothing like an empty bladder to put things back in perspective. Jerry Urban was a nice man. He hadn't been angry at my presence in his office. I flushed, washed, and marched back downstairs.

". . . today to talk about two murders," Garrett was saying.

I looked around the room. Van was sitting on one side, Janet on the other. Everyone else was scattered. I found Wayne and sat next to him on a black couch, sinking into its leather cushions.

"As a group, we may know who is responsible for these murders," Garrett continued. "But we must all share information. Let me share that my sister was killed in a hit-and-run accident when I was a boy. This has no bearing on the murder, but I feel negligent in having held it back."

"Jeez, I'm sorry, Garrett," Carl Russo put in. "Must have been really bad."

"It was," Garrett admitted, eyes on the ground. "But I mention it only so that we may all open up. If we get to the root of all our secrets, we may get to the root of the murders."

"I did time for car theft," Carl muttered.

"You what?" Janet screeched.

Ted gave her a look. She clamped her lips together. Maybe she didn't want Carl following Van's example, flying across the room at her.

"Long time ago," Carl muttered on. "No big deal. Not related to the murder. But I'm doing like Garrett said, opening up."

"Thanks, Carl," Garrett whispered and looked around at the group.

"Um," Jerry began. "I'm not an actual member of the group, per se, but I guess I ought to tell everyone that I used to be a race car—"

Jerry's confession was drowned out by the peal of the doorbell.

Helen Herrick sailed into the living room. She didn't look much better than Van. Her usually plump face was gaunt and her eyes were swollen.

"Are we talking about the murders?" she asked.

Garrett, Carl, and a few others nodded.

"Well, I just wanted to tell you, if one of you is the killer, I'll never, *never* forgive you," she promised quietly. "Isaac didn't deserve to die." She paused and added, "Nor did Steve."

"Of course—" Laura began.

But Helen put up her hand for silence.

"And I wanted to let the rest of you know that this doesn't affect my affection for you." Tears filled her swollen eyes. I stood up and went to her, holding her as the first tear fell. "I loved Isaac so much," she whispered.

The group talked a little longer while I comforted Helen as best I could in the kitchen. Then Wayne peeked his head in.

"It's time to go, Kate," he said softly.

"But—"

"Helen, should we visit you later this evening?" he asked.

"Please," she murmured.

And we left.

But even at the Toyota, we weren't alone. Mike Russo was waiting for us.

"Is my dad all right?" he asked as we approached the car. He peeked over his shoulder to make sure he wasn't overheard. "Captain Wuss has him all weirded out." I snorted back my laughter. "Captain Wuss," indeed. But Mike went on seriously. "They wouldn't, like, arrest my dad, would they?"

"Did he do anything to be arrested for?" I asked, hoping I already knew the answer.

"No way," Mike assured us.

"Then don't worry," I told him. "Just tell him you love him."

The teenager's face reddened. "I . . . I don't know if—" he began.

"Or something," I added quickly. Maybe when Mike grew up and joined his own men's group he'd be able to tell his father he loved him. I was sure Carl knew, anyway.

When we got home, Felix was gone. That was the good news. The bad news was that my answering machine was blinking.

I hit Play and my Aunt Dorothy's voice spilled out.

"Did the group go nicely?" she asked. "Call me as soon as you can. I think I've come up with the perfect wedding theme."

TWENTY

❧

I thought I heard a muffled chuckle behind me, but Wayne's face showed nothing when I turned around to accuse him. Did he know about this perfect wedding theme? No, I decided, he was probably just laughing at the way all my hair was standing on end.

"Guess we'd better call her," was all he said.

He was right. Aunt Dorothy was not to be left alone for long periods of time with access to wedding books. It was altogether too dangerous.

"We're going out to dinner with Steve's friends from the funeral," I told my aunt once I got her on the phone. "Would you like to come along?" I was ready to do anything to divert her from wedding plans. Though I did have a glimmer of curiosity as to what she thought a perfect wedding theme might be. Murder? Fear? Wedding phobia?

"Oh, my," she breathed. "I'll be right over."

"No," I told her quickly. "We'll pick you up. There's no use wasting two cars." And that way we could drop her right back at her hotel if she digressed into wedding themes. Of course, I didn't say that.

Ten minutes later we drove up to Aunt Dorothy's hotel. Prompt as ever, she was ready for us in the lobby, dressed to interrogate in a forest green business suit and pearls.

"So," I put in quickly once I was safely behind the wheel

of my Toyota with Wayne at my side and Dorothy in the back seat. "We're meeting Steve's friends at this really cool restaurant. It's called Mushrooms because almost everything they serve is made with mushrooms, and—"

"Don't you want to know about the theme, Katie?" my aunt interrupted. I was shocked. Dorothy was usually far too polite to interrupt, but I suppose she knew she wouldn't ever have gotten a word in edgewise if she hadn't. Unfortunately, my shock stopped my mouth long enough for her to insert a whole edge, middle, top, and bottom into the conversation.

"The theme," she announced, "is cats."

"Cats?" Wayne and I both exclaimed at once. So, he hadn't known after all.

"Oh, yes," Dorothy went on, warming to her idea. "I know how you two love your little kitty, C. C., so I thought perhaps you could both dress as cats. Remember how they did in that Broadway musical? And then," she paused breathlessly, "C. C. can be part of the wedding."

I opened my mouth to object. I knew that cat had been plotting something with my aunt! Then I heard a groan escape from Wayne's lips.

"C. C. is such a sweet cat . . ." my aunt went on.

I gripped the steering wheel and whispered into Wayne's ear, "Hardee-har-har." I was tempted to add, "nyah, nyah," but even I have my limits.

Wayne glowered my way. Well, he was the one who'd wanted a formal wedding—let it be cats.

". . . party favors with little cat faces . . ." my aunt persisted.

"And the guests could bring their cats, too," I suggested once Dorothy had burbled to an end, imagining the cat fight that would ensue.

"Oh, dear," she murmured thoughtfully. "Do you suppose they would all get along?"

"Um, almost to Mushrooms," Wayne put in. "The two men we're meeting are Gus Swanson and Neil Lennon." Was *Wayne* diverting the subject from my aunt's wedding plans? "They were journalists who worked with Steve."

"I see," Aunt Dorothy said cheerfully. And I was sure that

she did. Had she been putting us on about the cats?

We hadn't been to Mushrooms in a long time. The windowless cavern of a restaurant was still lit softly, but instead of seashells, there were now small, lit toadstools at each table, along with the lighted aquariums that were scattered around the room. At least whale music still played in the background. And the food smelled wonderful, redolent of garlic, onions, and all the other things that make life worthwhile.

Gus and Neil were barely visible in the murky light, but we finally spotted them at the bar.

"Hey, there," Neil yelled and waved our way, alighting from his bar stool to smile at us. Gus nodded in our direction, then turned back to the bar. The men would have been hard to confuse even if it weren't for Neil's smile and Gus's surly greeting. Neil was tall, with thinning red hair that matched his thin body, and Gus was burly, with thick black waves of hair that somehow matched his personality.

It took a while to get our seats. Even at five o'clock there was a crowd, and Gus wanted to finish his drink. But finally, we were seated at our own table with our own toadstool.

"So, you were friends of Steve's?" my aunt began mildly.

"I wouldn't exactly say 'friends'," Gus muttered.

"Colleagues," Neil tried, blushing.

"You spoke at Steve's funeral," I reminded the men.

"Neil's idea," Gus rumbled. "You know, poor widow, all that cra—junk."

"I take it you didn't particularly like Steve?" I led Gus.

But our waiter arrived before I could lead Gus very far. I was just glad our waiter wasn't dressed as a toadstool—shiny black pants and a white shirt were a nice change from spotted owl feathers.

"Our specials tonight are mushroom crepes, wild rice and mushrooms with fresh herbs and salmon, and vegan mushroom and almond croquets topped with a curried avocado sauce," he recited.

We thanked him. That is, everyone but Gus thanked him. Then we surveyed our regular menus, dipping them into the dim light provided by the toadstool lamp.

"Oh, my," my aunt cooed. "I don't believe I've ever had mushroom manicotti before. It sounds delicious."

"I'll stick with chicken and mushrooms," Gus declared, shutting his menu decisively.

"So," I began again. "You and Steve didn't really get along—"

The sight of our bread arriving at the table knocked the rest of the words out of my mouth. But the bread was worth it: brown and rich, and baked in the shape of fist-sized mushrooms.

I had just taken a bite of the bread when Neil spoke.

"Steve Summers was a really great writer," he offered.

"Just not so great with the old social skills," Gus followed up.

I resisted the urge to ask if he considered himself an expert on social skills.

"Tell us more," my aunt suggested.

"Steve was a quiet man, an observer," Neil complied.

"Had to be quiet with that wife of his dominating his world," Gus explained gracelessly. "He got sucked into her life. His role as a political spouse overtook his job as a writer. Damn shame."

"Did Steve and Laura get along?" I asked.

Neil nodded and opened his mouth, but Gus beat him to the reply.

"Of course they got along," he said. "They were both absolutely sure that they knew what was right for everyone else but themselves."

Gus laughed. Dorothy offered an encouraging smile. I reminded myself that Gus was the best of our two sources. Neil probably wouldn't ever say anything critical of Steve Summers; Gus was more than willing.

Our waiter returned before Gus could say much more, though, and we all ordered: Gus got his chicken and mushrooms; Dorothy ordered the manicotti; Neil and Wayne both chose the crepes; and I asked for the croquets.

And then we turned back to the topic of Steve.

"Steve really cared about people with problems," Neil

went on. "His writing was top rate, but his underlying compassion was what made it really work."

"Yeah, Steve loved humanity. It was people he couldn't stand," Gus commented. For a moment, I let myself wonder how original Gus's own writing was. "The man was a do-gooder, and God help you if you got in the way of his do-gooding."

It was then that I realized I hadn't heard a word from Wayne, except for his order. I turned to look at him. How was he taking Gus's characterization of a man he'd cared for? Not well; Wayne's face had turned to granite, his eyebrows had lowered, and his breathing was almost still. Damn.

"Have you guys ever been to Mushrooms before?" I asked, hoping to lighten things up.

I *did* find out one thing during dinner: Gus's only complaint in life wasn't about Steve Summers. He could complain about anything. And did.

"Why isn't there any light in here?" he demanded. "And what's with the toadstools? Are they supposed to be cute or something?"

"Something," I answered.

Neil smiled. I wondered what his friendship with Gus did for him. But then, I'd seen many similar pairs of friends, lovers, and spouses before: One kind, one blunt; one saying nice things, the other saying the things the first one couldn't. Neil and Gus, as a pair, were a type.

By the time our dinners came, I was glad I didn't have to be Gus's friend. And then I lost myself in the food. The mushroom and almond croquets were so good, I wanted a private place to enjoy them. The avocado sauce was perfectly curried, and the side dishes of carrot salad, sesame rice, and mushroom pate were worth a few groans of delight just in themselves.

I glanced over at Wayne again. He was eating. And from the way he rolled the food around in his mouth, I knew he was savoring his crepes. High praise from a chef, even if it *was* non-verbal.

After eating for a while in silence, Dorothy got the conversational ball rolling again.

"Steve Summers was much admired by some in the journalism arena," she threw out.

Gus fielded the ball.

"He wrote some good stuff early on," he admitted. "But he barely wrote at all at the end. He was too much in his wife's shadow."

"Was he angry about that?" my aunt pressed.

Gus frowned. "It was hard to tell with Steve. I never saw him angry in real life. He got his jollies in his self-righteous articles—"

"Now, that's not fair," Neil protested.

"Sure it is," Gus argued, turning to his friend. "For all the do-gooding, didn't you notice how he always managed to stab some poor sucker in the back with his writing? Made me look God-damn friendly in comparison."

"He may have been occasionally cruel," Neil admitted. "But he didn't do it intentionally."

"Huh! Look at Dutton Cole," Gus insisted, bending over the table as if to shove his words down his friend's throat along with his food. "Steve Summers killed Dutton Cole with that God-damned article, and you can't tell me otherwise." Gus sat back now, arms crossed.

"What article was that?" I asked. We had been looking for someone who was angry with Steve, and if this Dutton Cole had a loved one in the group, we might have just hit pay dirt.

Gus leaned forward again, eager to tell us.

"Steve originally met Dutton through Laura," he began his story in a whisper that could probably be heard on the other side of the crowded restaurant. "Dutton was the CEO muckety-muck of one of the biggest Silicon Valley outfits, Mr. Charity, a do-gooder from the word 'go.' Everyone liked him. Everyone wanted their kids to grow up and be him. Then he made his big mistake: He and Steve were talking one day, all buddy-buddy, when Dutton admitted that he was secretly gay. Steve went into this big song and dance about how Dutton oughta tell the world he was gay, to support all the other closeted gays out there. Dutton said no way. But that didn't stop Steve. Steve wrote the story anyway. Some sort of rah-rah thing about how a gay man could make it to the top, even in Silicon Valley. Of course, very few people had known Dutton Cole was gay at all before the story."

"It was supposed to be inspirational," Neil tried.

"Oh, sure," Gus sneered. "Only if it was inspired by the fact that Steve really hated Dutton Cole."

"No," Neil insisted. "You've got it all wrong. Steve was trying to make a point. It was supposed to be a success story."

"Some success story!" Gus snorted. "Dutton killed himself."

"What?" I asked.

Neil just shook his head sadly. Gus finished the story.

"Dutton just couldn't take the publicity," he explained. "He wasn't ready. His parents didn't even know. When the article came out, he put a gun in his mouth and pulled the trigger."

Suddenly my croquets didn't taste so good anymore. Why hadn't Steve talked about the Dutton Cole story when the Heartlink members were all talking about their worst secrets? I wondered. And then I realized that Steve probably didn't think he'd done anything wrong. He probably just thought Dutton Cole hadn't appreciated a great story. I was beginning to adopt something close to Gus's view of the late Steve Summers. To Steve, I imagined, global good had probably been everything. If individuals were hurt for a greater cause, so be it. I'd known people with that attitude before. I didn't want to know any more of them.

"Did Dutton have any friends or family connected with the Heartlink group?" my Aunt Dorothy probed, bringing me back to earth from my high moral ground.

"Heartlink?" Neil asked.

"Steve's men's group," Wayne explained.

"I doubt it," Neil said. "This was years ago—five, six, seven, maybe. Dutton's parents are dead now. Most of his friends have probably drifted away."

"It's one thing to be the friend of a famous CEO, but it's another to be the friend of a dead gay guy," Gus summed up.

Aunt Dorothy enunciated the names of the suspects, one by one, asking if any of them had been connected with Dutton Cole.

Both Gus and Neil shook their heads at the mention of each name, except for Laura Summers. But that was just because she'd introduced Dutton to Steve. She hadn't really known him very well, outside of that initial encounter.

The rest of dinner seemed to take forever. No one was asking any more questions about Steve Summers, and no one was making small talk, either. When the bill came, Wayne grabbed it and slapped down his credit card in one motion.

Gus and Neil were still arguing as we left Mushrooms.

"He was a sanctimonious old maid," Gus insisted.

"He was a good writer," Neil insisted back.

"He—" Gus began, and we let the door slam on Mushrooms.

Back in the car, Aunt Dorothy asked, "Were those men really Steve Summers' friends?"

"I don't know," Wayne managed in reply.

I turned the key in the Toyota's ignition and asked my own question.

"Wayne, was he really that self-righteous?"

"Well, maybe," Wayne murmured. This, coming from Wayne, was a stinging condemnation. I was glad my eyes were on the car in front of me. I wouldn't want to see Wayne's face now.

"What about this story he was going to write?" I asked. "The one he never got to tell you about? Do you think it would have been cruel—"

"Steve had writer's block," Wayne broke in, his voice high-pitched.

"So?" I asked.

"Steve told me he would have done anything for a story," Wayne finished.

"Ruin someone's life?" Aunt Dorothy questioned softly.

Wayne shook his head so hard I could feel the movement rocking the car.

"Don't know," he mumbled. "Just don't know. Thought I knew Steve. Guess I didn't."

I reached over to pat his thigh. If there was only a way I could pat his aching conscience.

When I pulled up to Aunt Dorothy's hotel, the mood in the Toyota was somber.

"Katie?" Aunt Dorothy whispered.

"What?" I asked, turning quickly to look into the back seat. My aunt sounded guilty. She looked guilty, too, her eyes downcast, her shoulders slumped.

"I was just kidding about the cats," she finally told me.

"You were?" Wayne responded, an energy in his voice I hadn't heard since we'd entered Mushrooms.

"I'd just hoped to inspire you to a brilliant alternative," she admitted. "It wasn't very nice of me."

I parked the car and pulled my aunt out of the back seat to give her a good, long hug.

"You're a kick in the pants, Aunt Dorothy," I told her.

"Really?" She brightened.

"Really," I said and escorted her into the lobby.

When Wayne and I got home, it was still early evening. We plopped into the hanging chair. I had a feeling we were going to have a long talk.

"Kate," he began.

The doorbell rang.

I leapt from the chair and went to answer it. We all make mistakes, and this was one of mine. My ex-husband, Craig, was there on the doorstep, his big brown eyes pleading like a puppy's.

Then he began to speak.

"I don't wanna bother you," he uttered.

"That's all right," my mouth answered. Another mistake.

"I heard you and Wayne are going to get married formally."

"Where'd you hear that?" I demanded.

He stepped back on the deck like I'd punched him.

"From Felix. He's going on and on about how your Aunt Dorothy's some kind of big wedding consultant, and she's here to help you make it legitimate."

"My marriage is already legitimate, Craig." I didn't yell. How do you yell at a puppy?

"Felix said you're balking, though." Craig peeked out at me through his long eyelashes.

I shrugged my shoulders. Explaining why I was balking would have involved telling Craig that it was my formal marriage to *him* that had soured me on the institution. And as much as I was thankfully and gloriously happy to have shed Craig as a husband, I still liked him as a friend. I couldn't help it.

"It's me, isn't it, Kate?" he asked.

I could feel my eyes widen. Had Craig been granted psychic powers?

"You're still in love with me," he finished up.

"Still in . . . what?!" I screeched, blowing Craig back another step.

Then I remembered that I didn't want to hurt this man. I explained to him that I loved Wayne. His brown eyes blinked with hurt. I explained that we could always be friends. He looked down at the ground. I explained that he wasn't an appropriate wedding counselor for me.

"Sorry, Kate," Craig said, and turned and walked back down the front stairs without even telling me a single joke.

My heart was still hurting for him when I closed the door. And then I remembered Helen Herrick.

"Helen," I said to Wayne after I heard Craig's car drive off. "We were supposed to visit her this evening."

"Right," Wayne growled.

We got back in the Toyota with renewed energy. The steam might have gone out of our hunt for Steve Summers' murderer, but helping Helen Herrick find out who killed Isaac was another matter.

Helen met us at her door. Her house didn't smell like cinnamon anymore, and her bookshelves weren't as neatly arranged as they had been when we'd visited her before. Still, she led us into the living room, and we sat on her comfortable corduroy chairs.

I asked her if there was anything she needed to tell us.

"I was so afraid Isaac would drink himself to death. That's why I was leaving. If I'd stayed—"

No," I told her firmly. "Nothing would have been different

if you'd stayed. You couldn't have been with him night and day."

I saw understanding cross her gaunt face for a moment, and then it was gone just as quickly as it had come.

"I loved the old fool," she whispered.

"Then love yourself for his sake, Helen," I heard myself say. Maybe I was channeling my aunt.

Still, Helen's shoulders straightened. I allowed myself to hope that she'd really heard me.

We didn't stay long—just long enough to listen. On the way out, I noticed what she'd been reading, left face-down on the coffee table. It was a glossy auto magazine. I shivered.

Could Helen have run Steve Summers down?

I told Wayne about the auto magazine on the way out.

"Do you think it means anything?" I asked.

"Probably means she's looking for a new car," he answered gruffly.

When we got home, I went to the mail box. I knew it was Sunday, but I couldn't remember if I'd picked up the mail the day before. There was only one envelope in the box, and it contained no address. I opened it as I walked back to the house.

STOP OR BIE, it said in huge felt-tip pen letters. The "p" in "stop" had been originally turned backward, then scratched out and turned forward again.

TWENTY-ONE

STOP OR BIE. Huh?

I looked at the note again. What was that supposed to mean?

"Wayne!" I yelled and sprinted up the driveway, meeting him on the stairs. "We got another note."

"What does it say?" he asked as I panted.

" 'Stop or bie,' " I told him.

"Stop and buy?" he demanded. "Sure it isn't just an ad?"

I handed him the note impatiently.

"The 'p' in 'stop' was turned backward before," he pointed out.

"Ah," I said as the letters rearranged themselves in my mind. "So if the 'b' is turned backward, too, it's supposed to be a 'd'."

"Stop or die." Now *that* was a note.

It wasn't until I'd finished congratulating myself on the translation that I began to think about the message.

"Think someone wants us to stop investigating?" Wayne asked to the accompaniment of my bongo-drum heartbeat.

"Someone who tried to run you over?" I added.

"Maybe," he considered. "Kate, is this note really dyslexic?"

"We already went through this," I reminded him. "None of the suspects is dyslexic. They can't be, can they? And if someone wanted to disguise themselves as a dyslexic, it would've been Isaac—"

"Or Helen," Wayne finished softly.

"Oh, no," I murmured. "Do you think so?"

"Don't know," he answered. "Think it's time to call in Captain Wooster."

I nodded silently.

We took the stairs slowly, like prisoners on the way to our own hanging.

I handed Wayne the phone to call the captain once we were inside. I remembered only too well how badly I'd done when I'd tried to tell Captain Wooster about the Horquillo car incident. It was definitely Wayne's turn.

I stood next to Wayne as he dialed, a back-seat phoner.

"Captain Wooster, please," Wayne requested.

There was a long silence from Wayne.

"Is Sergeant Marge Abbott in?" he tried finally.

Cool, I thought. Sergeant Marge.

And then, I heard Wayne explaining about our most recent threatening note, and about the earlier one. He was just getting into his dyslexic theory when he suddenly stopped talking.

I leaned forward as his brows lowered.

"But why?" he asked.

His brows lowered further as he listened.

"Right," he said finally. "Thank you anyway." And then he hung up.

"What happened?" I demanded.

"I talked to Sergeant Marge," he began. "She said it probably wasn't a good idea to show the notes to the captain right now."

"But why?" I demanded, vaguely remembering hearing those same words from Wayne's lips a few moments earlier.

"She said that the captain would just think we were writing the notes to put him off track," he answered. "That he'd think we were the murderers—"

"But that's stupid!" I objected.

"Uh-huh." He nodded his head slowly.

"And you think she's right?" I asked.

He nodded again. "She called me 'sugar,' " he added irrelevantly. "She knows him a lot better than we do, Kate."

"But would he really think—" I started.

And the doorbell rang.

Wayne looked at the note he held in his hand, and then laid it carefully face-down on top of the answering machine. Then we approached the front door together.

Wayne cautiously opened the door.

Van Eisner stood in front of us, unshaven, sniffling, and jittery.

In less than a second, something told me not to let him into our house. But in that time, his foot had already crossed the threshold.

"Van," Wayne said quietly. "Can this wait?"

Had Wayne felt that same something I had?

"No, man," Van replied, thrusting his head forward belligerently. "It can't wait. For God's sake, I've got real problems. I thought you were supposed to support me. But suddenly, ol' Van is a leper or something."

Wayne closed his eyes for a few moments. I wondered how much control it took to speak to Van right now. But he did speak, finally.

"Come in," he growled. "Kate and I are in the middle of something, so we'll have to keep it short, okay?"

Van's other foot crossed the threshold.

"No, it's not okay!" he shouted.

"Van," Wayne warned, his hand in the air.

"Hey, I'm talking," Van declared, but his voice was back to normal. "And I'm asking questions too. The cops are real interested in my drug use. So I wanna know just who told them about my supposed drug use?"

"Van," Wayne answered, his voice low and controlled. "I don't know the answer to your question. If you're asking if I did, I didn't."

That should have ended it. I held my breath, hoping it would.

But Van turned toward me next.

"Okay, but what about wifey, here?" he snarled. "I've heard how nosey Kate is. Sniffing into everyone's business, making it hers. I'll bet she just loves talking to the cops."

"That's enough," Wayne informed Van coldly.

But I didn't want Wayne fighting my battles.

"Listen, Van," I put in. "I *have* been asking questions, questions about murder. I don't care about your drug use. I don't care unless it has to do with murder. And the way you're ranting, it looks like drugs aren't real good for your judgment—"

Van stepped toward me, but I stepped backward automatically. Fifteen years of tai chi can do that to a person. Still, I shut my mouth. Van was enraged, the skin tone of his pointy face not red, but paper white. I could even smell the rage on him, hot and acrid.

"You!" he yelled again, pointing a finger at me now. "You're the one that sicced them on me!"

"Listen, Van," I started.

But Van lunged for me before I could finish. His hands were up and moving toward me, maybe to grab my shoulders, maybe my neck. In raising his arms, he'd left his entire torso unprotected, but he didn't realize that. I thought of a knee to the groin and instantly vetoed it. Instead, I waited until he'd reached me and used my arms and body to receive his force and return it lightly. He backpedaled wildly, flailing against the door frame. My push hadn't caused his reaction directly; it was the reversal of his own momentum. But he didn't know that, either.

"Damn you!" he screamed, running toward me to swing a fist my way. I turned my body to the side and he sailed past me, propelled by the force of his own attempted blow.

"Van," I whispered. "Calm down. No one here is your enemy."

But Van whipped around, his eyes intent on me. I knew he wouldn't leave voluntarily until he'd landed a blow. Tai chi can be very frustrating to the uninitiated.

This time, though, Wayne grabbed Van and swung his arm behind him before he even got near me. Wayne probably didn't care about me fighting my own battles anymore. He wanted Van out of our house, and so did I.

As soon as Wayne had Van out on the deck, I tried one last call to reason.

"Van, why don't you just throw your drugs away if you're so worried about the police finding them?"

"Are you crazy?" he bellowed.

Maybe I was. Once Wayne had frog-marched Van back to his car, waited until Van drove away, and returned to the house, we locked all of our doors and windows before taking our places in the hanging chair.

Our world didn't seem safe anymore.

"Kate," Wayne announced. "I think we should stop."

"Stop investigating?"

He nodded.

"But—"

"This is my mess in the first place. I was the one who wanted to find out who killed Steve Summers—"

"And Isaac Herrick—"

"And Isaac Herrick," he continued. "But it's too dangerous, for both of us."

I thought about the car that had tried to run Wayne down. He was right. Still, if we found out who was responsible . . .

"What if we stick together from now on?" I countered. "Go everywhere together? We can back each other up—"

"Kate," Wayne pleaded. "I have to work. I need to go in tomorrow. Are you going to stay with me for eight hours?"

I shook my head. "But—"

"Ground rules," he insisted. "We need ground rules. We can still try to figure out who did it, but we can't let anyone know."

I tilted my head. I didn't want any more cars racing toward Wayne, or any more fists aiming at me, for that matter. I was willing to listen.

"Okay." Wayne took a big breath. "First of all, no more visiting suspects." Wayne put up his hand before I could object. "No more letting suspects in the house. And we tell everyone we've stopped investigating."

"But we don't stop?"

"We don't stop trying to figure it out," he clarified. "We probably know all we're going to know from outside sources now anyway, so we can work it through logically, in our own space."

I found myself nodding, and then wondering just whose pitiful head was bouncing up and down on my thin stalk of a neck. When had I become such a coward? When I saw the car bearing down on Wayne, that was when.

"Was it Van that tried to run you over?" I asked in the spirit of working it through logically.

"He drives a red Miata," Wayne argued.

"But he could have borrowed someone else's car," I argued back.

"Maybe, but I still don't think he'd do it."

"Even after tonight?"

"Even after tonight," Wayne muttered. "Kate, he's out of control. You saw him. Even if he didn't know you could defend yourself—"

"I can, you know," I threw in indignantly.

"Kate, I of all people know just how well you can defend yourself." He smiled. "I have the bruises to prove it."

I blushed. I'd forgotten about shoving Wayne, even if it had been for his own good. Now, I felt like Bluto.

"Point I was making," Wayne pressed on, "was that Van should have known I'd eventually stop him, even if he didn't know what *you're* capable of. He isn't thinking ahead; he isn't planning violence. His brain's so fried now, I'm surprised he can drive at all, much less aim a car at me."

"Okay, who then?" I asked.

Discussion of that question took us into the early morning hours. We made charts. We lined up black beans to represent the positions of all the suspects. We even tried hypnotizing each other. But nothing was working. By the time we rolled into bed that night, we hadn't reached any conclusions except that the world was a very scary place.

Monday morning, I woke out of a nightmare to the sound of my phone ringing. I looked for Wayne, didn't see him, and stumbled down the hallway into my office.

Ted Kimmochi was on the line. I picked up the phone

anyway. Maybe I could tell him we weren't investigating anyway.

"Kate, is Wayne there?"

I looked around the room.

"No," I answered, hearing Wayne's computer beeping from his office at the other end of the hallway. He may have been in the house, but he wasn't in *my* office.

"Kate," Ted sighed. "I'm wondering what this all means. Death, despair—"

"We're not investigating anymore," I interrupted him.

The silence that followed was so infinitesimal, I almost missed it. Then Ted started up again.

"I can't help but feel that Steve's and Isaac's deaths have a greater meaning."

"Greater than what?" I asked.

"All life is a charnel house," he replied.

Well, I guess that answered my question.

"Why am I caught in this terrible set of circumstances? Is it karma? Is it a punishment?"

"Do you feel you need to be punished, Ted?" I asked.

"Sometimes, Kate. Don't we all?"

Not me, I thought, but decided to ask something more practical.

"Ted, I heard that you and Janet were in some financial trouble a few years back. What was that all about, anyway?" As I asked, I hoped Wayne wouldn't consider my question investigatory. And I especially hoped Wayne wasn't close enough to be listening.

"Where'd you hear that?" Ted demanded, his voice hardening into crystalline clarity.

The hairs on the back of my neck stood up. Could Ted be a threat? He always seemed so vague, so tragic. I didn't like the new clarity in his voice.

"Oh, around," I lied. "So, what happened?"

"Nothing much," he mumbled. And then he mumbled some more. And finally, he hung up.

At least he was off the phone. But the phone wasn't through with me yet. It rang again before I'd made two steps away from it.

This time, Garrett was on the phone. But Garrett was experiencing guilt, not self-absorption.

"I keep asking myself," he confessed over the line, "Could I have prevented these deaths? I'm a psychiatrist. I should be able to tell what's going on. I should be more sensitive to the points of view of everyone in the group. If someone is troubled enough to murder, I should be able to spot their distress."

"What if they're a psychopath?" I asked.

"Even then, Kate. I'm trained. I'm the only member of the group who is. Anyway, there's no psychopath in our group, and none of the significant others is a psychopath either. I'm sure of it. I'd see it. I'd feel it."

Maybe he was right. You didn't have to be a psychopath to murder—I'd learned that the hard way. You just had to be pushed to your personal limit.

"Do you have any guesses yet?" I prompted.

"No!" he cried. Then he paused. "Excuse me, Kate. I shouldn't have raised my voice. But the answer is no. I don't have any guesses. Not one. I keep going over everyone in my mind and coming up blank."

"How about Van?" I asked.

"No, entirely the wrong type," he assured me. Maybe to him and Wayne, I thought. Van seemed exactly the right type to me.

"Garrett, it's not up to you. Or us," I added dutifully. "Wayne and I aren't investigating anymore."

"Oh, I'm sorry, Kate," he whispered, his voice as mournful as if someone had died. Then again, two people *had* died. "Of course, you have your reasons." His voice went into high gear. "It's really the murderer I'm worried about. Whoever it is, that individual is very sick. They need help. No matter what they've done, they are sick and crying for help. And I haven't provided it."

"Oh, Garrett," I sighed. How do you reason with a saint? "Have you talked to Jerry? He loves you. He'll tell you none of this is your fault. It isn't, you know."

"I'm a professional, Kate," he reminded me. "I have more responsibility than the other group members—"

"You're a professional psychiatrist, not a policeman. And when you're in the group, you're a peer. You don't have any more responsibility than anyone else—"

"But I *feel* I do, Kate," he cut in. "I can't help it."

I hate it when people use the word "feel." How can you argue with feelings?

I stopped trying, and within minutes I'd hung up the phone. Again. I was almost into the kitchen when it rang for the third time.

"Kate," Jerry Urban blurted when I picked it up. "Did you just talk to Garrett?"

"Um . . ." I faltered. Was my conversation with Garrett confidential? Garrett *was* a psychiatrist, after all.

"Never mind," Jerry muttered. "I just called because he's walking around like a sheepdog who's lost his flock or something. Garrett is not himself, Kate. It's like he's having a permanent bad hair day—"

"Have you ever thought of finding a psychiatrist for the psychiatrist?" I asked.

"He already has one," Jerry whispered loudly into the phone.

"He does?"

"Hard to believe, huh?"

"Maybe he needs an extra appointment," I suggested.

"Good idea," Jerry agreed, and I heard the scritch-scratch of him writing something down. "Do you and Wayne know who did it yet?" he asked a moment later.

"No, we don't know, and we've stopped investigating." Maybe I ought to just have little cards made up, announcing our resignation from further investigation. It would be easier than telling everyone.

"Oh," Jerry mumbled, and I could hear a volume of disappointment in his tone.

"Jerry, go cheer up Garrett," I ordered.

"Do you think a tutu would help?" he asked and giggled. Then he got serious again. "Believe me, Kate, I've tried. I even made this little robot that goes around bemoaning his existence like Ted. Garrett thought it was funny till I told him who it was supposed to be. Then he thought it was cruel."

"Bring it over here sometime," I suggested, laughing. Then I remembered the ground rules—no suspects in the house. Did that apply to their robots? I'd have to ask Wayne.

"Kate, he needs something from me," Jerry confided. "I just wish I knew what it was. I'd do anything for him."

"I know you would," I sympathized. "Maybe you could ask him what he needs. He's a psychiatrist. Ask *him* to figure it out."

There was a silence, and then Jerry thanked me. He was taking my suggestion seriously. He was going to ask Garrett to figure out what he needed.

I wished Jerry luck and hung up.

Jerry *would* do anything for Garrett, I thought. Would he kill for him?

The phone rang again before I even took one step away from it.

It was almost a relief to hear my warehousewoman, Jade, announcing that there'd been an "itty-bitty" fire at the Jest Gifts warehouse. Almost.

ℚWENTY-TWO

✷

An "itty-bitty" fire. It took a while for the meaning to sink in. Once it did, I clamped my teeth together to keep from screaming. Added to a couple of itty-bitty murders, not to mention an itty-bitty car and an itty-bitty Van Eisner, it was suddenly too much. And I hadn't even had breakfast yet.

"Kate?" Jade asked. "Are you still there?"

From the processing chip somewhere in my mind, a message was sent that I couldn't talk with my teeth clamped shut. I unclamped them slowly. A pain shot through my jaw as I did.

"How itty-bitty?" I finally managed.

"None of the merchandise," Jade assured me. "Whatever jackass set the fire last night just burned packing boxes—"

"Someone set it?"

"That's what the fire guy said. I called the fire station this morning when I saw the packing room. Yuck. What a mess—"

"Do you have any idea who set it?" I asked.

"Nah," Jade told me. "I dunno who. The fire guy said it coulda been anyone. Teenagers, maybe."

Or a murderer, I thought. *No.* I shook my head and refused that vista of paranoia.

"I'll call in an order for boxes—" I began.

"Hey, I'll do that, Kate," Jade insisted. "I'm just glad you're not, like, all hysterical or something. Don't worry, I'll take care of everything."

"Thanks, Jade," I whispered, and I meant it. Jade was a good warehousewoman. I'd have given her another raise if it weren't for the fact that she already made more money than I did. Maybe I'd give her another raise anyway.

Jade and I discussed the coming week's business, and then I calmly hung up the phone.

I stood, staring at the floor, wondering what it would take to stop whoever had started this fire from starting another one.

I felt a hand on my shoulder and rocketed into the air. The minute I did, my mind told me that the hand belonged to Wayne, and that I had to stop jumping every time he snuck up on me. Still, I turned as soon as my feet hit the ground again just to make sure I was right. I was.

"Sorry," he offered. "Maybe I should wear a bell around my neck."

"Maybe you should learn to walk like other people," I suggested impatiently. "*Clomp, clomp, clomp*, all right? Practice!"

Wayne stepped away from me, his bare feet slapping the carpet in a way that had to be painful to the soles of his feet.

"Is that any—" he began.

The phone rang, interrupting whatever he had to say. I was already smiling—until I picked up the phone.

Janet McKinnon-Kimmochi was on the other end of the line. And she was angry. I plopped down in my comfy chair, ready to have Janet eat a good portion of my morning. C. C. plopped down in my lap as if she'd just materialized on the planet. Luckily, her claws were sheathed for the moment. Then she began to purr. Unfortunately, Janet wasn't purring.

"I am too a good mother!" she screamed at me.

"I'm sure you are," I replied, wondering if I'd ever have time to change out of my pajamas.

"Shower?" Wayne whispered, pointing at himself.

I nodded. I'd miss being in it with him, but I had other matters to tend to.

"I don't care what your Aunt Dorothy says—"

"Aunt Dorothy?"

"Yes, your deranged aunt has some kind of idea that Steve Summers was molesting my girls. She called me five minutes ago."

I closed my eyes and listened to my stomach practice knotting itself—internal macrame.

"What kind of mother would I be to let anyone molest my children?" Janet bulldozed on. "Do you think I wouldn't notice? Just because I work hard doesn't mean that I'm not watching them. Working mothers are the brunt of the worst kind of sexist nonsense. I'm used to that. But molestation!" Her voice raised an octave on the last word.

"Did my aunt actually say you did anything wrong?" I demanded.

"No, but that's not the point. That she could even believe such a thing at all is enough of an insult."

"Janet, I doubt that she believes it. It was probably just a theory." I hoped I wasn't lying. "I'll talk to her," I promised.

"You do that!" Janet ordered and hung up.

"We aren't investigating anymore," I said to the dial tone.

And then, I just sat in my comfy chair, thinking of pleasant places. It's never too late to try astral projection.

Wayne showed up minutes later, showered, shaved, and smelling good. His step was good and heavy, too.

"Breakfast?" he offered.

I didn't need any arm-twisting. He pulled a homemade coffee cake from the freezer and stuck it in the microwave, apologizing for of its lack of freshness. I just sat at the kitchen table and smiled as he threw a thousand and one ingredients in the blender for a vegan smoothie and then bent down to feed C. C. her Fancy Feast. Finally, he made me a pot of peach tea. I had just drunk the last of my smoothie and was reaching for the rest of my coffee cake when the doorbell rang. I looked down. Yup, I was still in my pajamas.

And suddenly, I remembered our second ground rule: No suspects in the house. Wayne snuck to my office window and peeked out.

"Helen Herrick," he whispered.

"Oh Wayne, we can't just leave Helen standing there," I insisted.

"She's a suspect," he insisted back, crossing his arms.

"How about the deck?" I tried.

He opened his mouth to object, then seemed to think better of it.

"Okay, the deck, but only because there are two of us," he conceded.

Wayne and I walked out on the deck to greet Helen. I just hoped none of the neighbors were seeing me in my pajamas, cute as they were, with their large, turquoise cat paw prints. The pajamas were a gift. I swear.

"I've been to see Wooster," Helen started out. As far as I could tell she hadn't even noticed my pajamas or our use of the deck as the venue for our discussion. "Wooster is off his rocker."

Wayne and I both just nodded.

"I want justice,"

"Helen, you'll get justice," Wayne said soothingly. "Remember, Wooster isn't the entire Cortadura Police Department.

"There's Sergeant Marge," I threw in.

"I don't care!" she cried out. "I want justice *now*."

"Helen, we're not investigating anymore," Wayne announced.

I shrank beside him. I wished he hadn't said it. I wanted to take Helen in my arms and promise that we'd find her husband's murderer. But I didn't.

Helen gave us each a look that could have fried tofu . . . and burned it to ash. Then she turned and stomped down the stairs without another word.

"Oh, dear," was all I could say.

Wayne escorted me back inside and locked the door behind us. The phone started ringing the minute the door was locked. I picked it up automatically.

"Ms. Jasper, this is Mike Russo," a hesitant voice announced.

"Hi there, Mike," I tried.

"It's my dad. He's crying. I don't know why. Do you think Wayne could, like, talk to him?"

I turned to Wayne and pointed at the phone.

"This one's yours," I informed him and handed him the receiver.

I listened for a few moments as Wayne talked to Mike. Then there was a short silence, and his voice tone changed. He was talking to Carl.

Finally, I headed down the hallway to take *my* shower. I made it quick, no matter how good the hot water felt on my tense muscles. Then I brushed my teeth, fussed with my hair, and changed into a T-shirt and Chi-Pants. I was back in my office within fifteen minutes.

Wayne was standing by the phone, a scowl on his face.

"Bad?" I asked.

"Worse," he replied. "Carl's a good man. But he's a rigid man. These deaths have really thrown him. He can't understand how it could happen. He's flailing, worried about his kid, worried about himself, worried about the group."

"You can't blame him," I said.

Wayne nodded. "Told him we weren't investigating anymore. That really upset him."

Wayne looked me in the eye.

"Kate, we've done all we can, right?"

"I think so."

"If there was something else we could do, I'd try. But it's useless. I'm out of ideas. You got any?"

I shook my head slowly. But even as I did, a picture of Barbara formed in my mind. I wondered what it was I thought Barbara could do for me. Maybe I just needed to talk to a friend. I promised myself that I would give her a call.

Wayne sighed. "Going to work," he told me. "Have to do menus for the week, and see what's been going on while I was gone."

I nodded, then remembered our transportation dilemma.

"Wait a minute," I stopped him. "You don't even have a car, and I've got tai chi practice tonight."

"Not to worry," he assured me. "My manager is on his

way to pick me up." He paused, and his scowl deepened. "But I don't want you here alone, Kate."

"Me, neither," I agreed, feeling cold already at the thought of Wayne's departure. This time, I wasn't arguing. Wayne wasn't speaking from male arrogance; he was just being practical under the circumstances. I would be a sitting duck without him.

"Dorothy," I said. "I'll call my Aunt Dorothy."

And I wasn't kidding. I was on the phone to my aunt before Wayne and his manager had stuffed themselves into his manager's car and driven off at a sedate speed.

"Of course, Katie," my aunt told me. "I'll be over as soon as I call Helen back. Just leave a key under the mat for me if you're busy, or leave the door unlocked. And I'll ring the doorbell to let you know I'm there." She paused. "Helen says you've stopped investigating."

Guiltily, I explained about Van's attack and the threatening letters.

"Oh, Katie," she murmured. "Of course, you must stop."

When I hung up the phone, I had the feeling that everything would be all right. Aunt Dorothy was coming. I reminisced about how she'd let me make cookies and eat the cookie dough as a child, and my rigid body relaxed. Then I remembered that I had one trick left up my sleeve: I'd never called the DRUGLAW people to find out just how much trouble Van Eisner would be in if the cops *did* find his drugs. There was still research that I could do without talking to suspects. I smacked my fist into my palm and picked up the Yellow Pages.

I knew a lot more about 1-900-DRUGLAW after scouring their ad. For a set fee per minute, a caller could not only speak to a lawyer, but also to a psychologist or a general counselor about their drug problems. It was a lot cheaper than finding a lawyer, driving there, and asking about Van Eisner, especially since I was under house arrest. I shut the phone book, went outside and stuck a house key under the doormat, and dialed 1-900-DRUGLAW.

I got their law division and gave them my credit card number, and then the meter was running.

"Um," I began, wishing I'd written out my questions beforehand. It would have been a lot cheaper. "I have a friend with a drug problem."

"Right, a friend," the voice on the other end of the line replied, a sneer evident in its tone. Jeez, you'd think a professional wouldn't be so judgmental.

"He has a former conviction for drug use, and he's afraid the police will find the drugs he's currently using in his house. What kind of trouble would he be in then?"

"Depends on the nature of his prior conviction."

"Um," I said again.

"Never mind," the voice told me. "Whatever the nature of his prior conviction, your *friend* could be in big trouble."

"Oh."

"So, if I were you, I would call counseling and get a recommendation for a rehabilitation center."

"He won't do that—" I began.

"Let's forget your *friend* for a moment. *You* have a problem. You need help. Let us help you."

"No, really—" I objected.

"We hear it all the time, lady. Now, listen . . ."

Me, Kate Jasper, with a drug problem? I don't even drink coffee! Huh! I smashed the receiver into its cradle. Then I hoped I hadn't just goofed up my new telephone system. So much for my last investigative ace in the hole.

I sat down at my desk to do some work for Jest Gifts, trying not to think of murder or burning warehouses. But I couldn't concentrate. It was time to call Barbara.

I went to my bedroom. For this phone call, I wanted to lie down. I only wished I'd been lying down for the last one. I pulled the extension as far as it would reach and lay down backward on the mattress that served as our bed.

I punched in the first digit of Barbara's phone number. But a mechanical voice stopped me before I could go any further.

"Someone is on the other line," my new phone system told me.

TWENTY-THREE

꙳

I dropped the phone and got up off the bed, my heart racing. Who was on the other phone receiver?

I opened the bedroom door and looked out into the hallway, wondering if Wayne had come home already. Maybe he'd forgotten something. Maybe—

"Wayne?" I whispered and walked down the hall toward his home office.

There was no answer. I told myself to calm down and wriggled my shoulders as if to pull back the hair that was rising on my neck.

There were only three phones on that line in the house: one in my office, one in Wayne's office, and one in the bedroom. It had to be Wayne on the line. Or maybe Aunt Dorothy? Could she have walked in and borrowed the phone in my office? No. I shook my head, my aunt wouldn't be that rude. It had to be Wayne.

"Wayne?" I tried again, louder than a whisper this time. What if he just hadn't heard me before?

But all I heard was silence. No, not silence, I realized suddenly. Somewhere behind me, something moved. I heard a footstep—a soft one, but a footstep nonetheless. I stopped my forward movement and listened. Someone was breathing behind me.

I centered myself and turned around slowly, raising my arms in a tai chi ward-off position.

My senses hadn't deceived me. That someone who had stepped and breathed was down the hall, only a few yards from me. Someone in chinos, a loose sweater, dark glasses, and with a scarf wrapped around their face. Someone with a gun in their hand, pointed in my direction.

So much for tai chi. Even with a kick, I couldn't reach that gun. I considered running toward it, then dismissed the idea. This wasn't a movie; I didn't want to feel what that gun could do to me.

Slowly, the hand that wasn't holding the gun unwrapped the scarf and shoved it in a pocket. Laura Summers' face emerged.

Laura Summers? My mind refused to believe it. Logic told me the only reason Laura Summers would be pointing a gun at me was if she was the murderer. And—

"But you loved Steve," I mumbled, dazed.

"Maybe," Laura replied, her deep, quiet voice as soothing as usual. She removed her glasses and tucked them in another pocket. She had come well-equipped. "You shouldn't have left your key under your doormat," she informed me. "You aren't careful enough with your keys."

I stood, gazing at Laura. She was so tall and broad; I could imagine how she could disguise herself so no one could be sure if they'd seen a man or a woman. I saw her pert, earnest face with shimmering clarity now. No wonder she'd had to wear dark glasses and a scarf—evil didn't show on that face. It wasn't even showing now. But I could smell the evil, acrid and angry, burning. All my senses seemed heightened. I felt something that might have been exhilaration, all the while knowing I should be afraid. But I was talking to the murderer. She might tell me everything. And maybe, just maybe, she wouldn't kill me.

"Why?" I asked, not stalling for time but genuinely curious.

"You know!" Laura hissed, her face almost the same as usual, except that now her eyes were bright with hatred.

"No," I told her in all sincerity. "I don't know."

"Don't try to fool me," she articulated slowly. "You and Wayne. You couldn't give it up. You must have put together all the pieces by now. Steve was going to write an article about me."

"And?" I prodded. I had to know.

"I'm dyslexic," she rapped out, her gun hand dancing in frustration. "How do you think a dyslexic person can take the state bar exam to become an attorney?"

It was interesting puzzle; I ran it through my brain. The answer had to be that a dyslexic person *couldn't* take the bar exam. But Laura had been a lawyer before she became a politician.

Laura took a step closer to me. My pulse took a step, too, but she still wasn't close enough for me to disable her gun hand.

"I took your phone off the hook," Laura whispered, and then she smiled, a smile that would have bought my vote under other circumstances, but that chilled me to the bone under these. I was no longer exhilarated by the prospect of knowing why. I just wanted to live.

"No one can call," she told me. The smile left her face. "You paid no attention to my notes. You didn't care when I tried to run Wayne over, or when I burned your warehouse. What did you think I would do next?"

I didn't want to answer that question because the answer was obvious: Kill. Kill me. Kill Wayne.

"We stopped investigating," I said.

"You what?" she demanded, her head rearing back.

"Wayne and I decided to stop investigating. I guess we didn't tell you that."

"Well, you'll both have your chance," she said. She looked around suddenly, as if remembering something. "Where is Wayne?" she asked abruptly.

"Wayne isn't here. He's at work."

She hesitated for a moment. "Of course you'd say that, to protect him."

"No," I insisted. "He really isn't here. You can search the house if you want to."

JAQUELINE GIRDNER

"It doesn't matter," she snapped impatiently. "I'll just take care of him later."

"You don't have to," I told her, working to keep my voice steady. "He doesn't know any more than I did. Neither of us suspected you—"

"Ha!" she cut in. At least she wasn't pointing the gun at me now. She held it at her side as she spoke. "When our son was conceived, I told Steve I was dyslexic. I was worried about the genetic factor. Steve was, of course, thrilled. He marvelled that I had overcome such odds, done so much despite my disability, blah-blah-blahdee-blah, ad nauseam. He wanted to write his story then, as an inspirational piece. He never did think about the implications. How did he think I took the state bar exam? I talked him out of the story, then, for my baby's sake. I didn't want my child worrying that he might be dyslexic. And he wasn't. My son never realized that *I* was, either."

"But at the funeral—" I began, suddenly remembering.

Laura shook her head. "I know, I know. 'Invisible disabilities.' I don't know if Steve Junior figured it out unconsciously, or if I left some sort of clue. But he's always known something was wrong with me. He just didn't know what."

"Oh."

Laura looked at me as if she'd forgotten I was there for a moment, or forgotten the circumstances that had brought us here. Finally, she straightened her shoulders and went on.

"So, Steve forgot about writing the story until the men's group meeting when everyone talked about the worst thing they'd done. Then Steve remembered the fabulous story he'd left unwritten. He told me he needed to write it, that it would help others who suffered from dyslexia. He said that it would get him over his writers' block. Steve . . ." Her hand searched her pocket, and she used her scarf to blot her eyes. Were those tears? Yes, they were. Steve had hurt Laura. Had he ever realized what a big mistake it was to have hurt this woman?

"Steve," Laura went on. "Never a clear thought in his head. Did he think dyslexics were actually going to *read* his article? He was the same way about my growing up wealthy—he thought it must have been so great. Well, it wasn't. I was raised by a series of nannies. Some of them liked me, some didn't. One dropped me on my head all the time. Another one hit me. I got everything . . . except love. He never understood." Her voice dropped to a low pitch. "I asked him to hold off for a month on the article. Then I made my big mistake: I told him he couldn't write the article, that if he did, people would figure out I'd hired someone to take the bar exam for me. That's fraud. Do you think I could stay in office if anyone found out? And Steve was offended! *Offended!* After I'd spent more than half my life married to him, he said he couldn't believe I had done something so unethical. He told me he wasn't sure he could remain married to me. He acted like I was slime. It wasn't good enough for him that I've done all the right things, taken the right stands, helped the state, raised our son. One mistake, and he hated me."

Yes, Steve had hurt her. Laura blotted her eyes again. "And I knew that if he left me, he'd write the article, that he'd probably include the part about the bar exam. What did he care if he ruined my career, ruined his son's life? He'd be over his oh-so-important writers' block. But he said he'd keep his promise, that he'd give me a month to think about 'helping' him with his article. The s.o.b. was going to leave me and then destroy me. I couldn't let him do that, so I planned his murder. I'm good at planning—"

"But why Wayne's car?" I asked. The words seemed to tumble out of my mouth without thought.

"To discredit Wayne. I thought Steve might have told Wayne he was going to write an article about me. I figured no one would listen to Wayne if he was the prime suspect . . . but then you had to show up to alibi him! Because of you, Wayne was never the main suspect." Laura's face actually looked angry now, her brows low and her lips thin. "And then you two had to keep sticking your noses in. I know you talked to Steve's so-called friends. I know you know he caused one suicide. You *had* to see the parallel. You *knew* it was me!"

"No," I insisted. "We didn't—"

"And Isaac, with his goddamn dyslexia obsession. He once told me he knew I was dyslexic. He thought it was a great joke. I knew he would eventually figure out why I killed Steve—"

I opened my mouth to tell her once more that Wayne and I hadn't known, but the doorbell rang before any words came out.

The doorbell?

Laura lifted the gun and pointed it my way. She took a couple of steps toward me. She was only a few feet away from me now. I heard the front door open. Then I realized that Laura had left the door unlocked when she'd come in.

"Yoohoo!" Dorothy called out. Laura looked behind her. I took one long step, shortening the distance between us. I lifted my knee. Then I circled my foot in a lotus kick, meant to disable an assailant's kidney, this time modifying it so that I knocked the gun from Laura's hand. Laura's mouth stretched and she let out a piercing scream.

I jumped in place. I hadn't expected her to scream. But I also hadn't expected C. C., who wobbled precariously on Laura's shoulder, her claws embedded in Laura's sweater and the flesh beneath it.

I kicked the gun behind Laura, taking a second to watch it skid down the carpet of the hallway. I would thank C. C. later.

Laura turned, looking for the gun even as C. C. leapt from her shoulder and slunk away. I grabbed her wrist from the side and tried to force it up behind her back, but Laura squirmed away from my awkward grip. Laura advanced on me, and I shoved her, much as I had shoved Van the night before. Laura flew backward . . . toward the gun. Damn. I ran after her and shoved again, losing my balance. My tai chi teacher hadn't taught me to fight someone who wasn't attacking me first. Now I saw why—it didn't work. Laura hadn't thrown any momentum my way, so I had nothing to use against her. Still, I regained my balance in time to kick the gun further down the hallway.

I had to keep Laura Summers from that gun. *Talk*, I thought; if only I could get her talking.

"But how could you kill your own husband?" I demanded. It worked.

"A widow is just as electable as a wife; maybe more so," she told me. But then she turned her head, her eyes searching for the gun. "All that sympathy helps. Divorcees don't get sympathy." She could talk and attack at the same time. I should have known.

She turned away from me, toward the gun. We don't get much practice shoving people from behind in tai chi, either, but I did it anyway. She swung around so that she was facing me once more.

"Forget it," she declared, her voice low. "You're dead."

Then I saw my Aunt Dorothy over Laura's shoulder.

"You're as bad as Steve—"

My aunt trotted toward the gun, picked it up, and pointed it at Laura Summers' head. Dorothy moved her gun hand, and something clicked. I didn't care what. Maybe Dorothy had cocked the gun. I didn't know. All that mattered to me was that the gun was no longer in Laura's hand.

Laura must have heard the click, too. She whipped around to face Dorothy. But my aunt's grip on the gun didn't waver; she kept it pointed at Assemblywoman Summers' head.

"You!" Laura screamed.

"Go ahead," Dorothy told Laura, her voice no longer sounding like my sweet aunt's. She spoke each word with ugly menace. "Make . . . my . . . day."

TWENTY-FOUR

❧

It was Wednesday, and the members of the Heartlink Men's Support Group, their significant others, and a couple of my significant others were having their last meeting in Carl Russo's garden, mingling in the sun and shade. The smell of barbecue floated over from the yard next door, as did the sound of rap music. Carl looked good in his Hawaiian shirt, better than he looked in a suit. And he was proudly showing his roses to Garrett, Ted, and Helen. Garrett bent over to smell a crimson rose and sighed with pleasure. Jerry and I looked at each other and joined Garrett in the sigh. But our sighs were of relief because Garrett actually looked happy.

Ted Kimmochi, however, still looked moody, his eyes turned to the clouds instead of the roses. But somehow, he managed to look content in his moodiness. Helen Herrick didn't look entirely happy, but she looked satisfied and peaceful as she fingered the petal of a lavender bloom.

"Closure," Jerry mouthed.

I nodded.

This was the good life, rap music, barbecue smells, and all. I grabbed Wayne's hand and squeezed as the sun beat down on the tops of our heads.

Meanwhile, Janet McKinnon-Kimmochi stood a few feet

away, attempting to instruct Mike, Niki, and Zora in the finer elements of language.

"You don't call anyone a wiener-head . . ." she tried, shaking her finger.

Felix and Aunt Dorothy guffawed along with the kids. For some reason, they'd become great friends once Laura Summers was behind bars. I shivered in the sun, rememberering again why we were all gathered—to speak of Laura Summers.

"So," Jerry asked, as if he'd caught my thought. "What happened after your aunt got the gun?"

Aunt Dorothy turned our way. "It wasn't just any gun," she told him. "It was a Colt .38 special. Splendid, sturdy—"

"Aunt Dorothy!" I yelped.

"Well, aren't you glad I know about guns, Katie?" my aunt teased. She tilted her face, the curlicues on her head looking like little goat horns. And I'd thought this woman was old.

She strode my way and wrapped me in a hug, only letting me go so that I could continue telling the story of her bravery.

"Laura jumped at my aunt—" I began.

"So I shot in the direction of her feet," Dorothy tossed off nonchalantly. "My, you should have seen her face change then—"

"Especially when you said, 'Next time, I go higher.' " I giggled. I couldn't help it. It seemed funny now, though it certainly hadn't at the time. And I wondered if we'd ever be able to replace the carpet where the police had pulled it up to find the bullet lodged in the wood below.

"And then my Katie got Laura in some kind of choke hold, and we tied her to a chair," my aunt went on.

"Finally, we called the police," I ended.

I could feel Wayne squirming beside me, feeling guilty for having left me alone. I thought maybe it was time to change the subject, but Dorothy wasn't finished.

"Even tied up, Laura kept talking," my aunt remembered. "It was as if her mouth couldn't stop her thoughts from flowing out, even when the police came." She shook her head.

Dorothy probably would have just kept silent and asked for an attorney. Of course, my aunt wasn't capable of murder . . . I hoped.

"Did she confess?" Garrett asked from his position near the roses.

"Boy, did she—" I began, but Felix had to have his say.

"Not only did she tell every friggin' thing she'd done from age one," he interrupted, "but that potato-brain Wooster got corroborating evidence. Laura's sister's mouth couldn't stop, either. Blathered all about Laura's big-deal dyslexia, the schools with the greasy palms, the whole enchilada—"

" 'Told you it was the wife. Hell's bells, just look at her,' " my aunt mimicked the captain all too accurately.

I shook my head, putting my hand over my grinning mouth because this was serious. One look at Helen Herrick was all it took to remind me.

"I hadn't told Laura yet that we'd stopped investigating," I admitted.

Wayne put his arm around me and kissed my cheek, and the garden was beautiful again. I didn't want to talk any more. Of course, Felix was more than happy to take over.

"Ms. Bigshot Laura Summers has been dyslexic since day uno," he began. "Like it was a friggin' life-stopper or something." I wanted to say that it was a life-stopper for her, but I kept my mouth shut. "Mummy and Daddy had big bucks, so no one ever had a clue. She went to hoity toity 'experimental schools' from kindergarten through law school, with the experiment being verbal exams, at least for lucky Laura. And Big Daddy slipped all the educational institutions major money for endowments. But then Laura got to the state bar, and even Big Daddy didn't know whose palm to grease there. So, he bought his daughter a proxy to take the bar for her." Felix paused, making sure he had his audience. Then he went on.

"From the moment Laura passed the bar, she was Ms. Bigshot Attorney. She didn't have to read. She didn't have to write. She owned a stable of geeks to do her work for her. She dictated everything that she signed." He shook his head. "Un-friggin'-believable."

"She really was a good person . . . as an assemblywoman," I murmured. I shrugged my shoulders, wondering why I'd felt the need to defend her. "She and Steve believed in the same causes. And as humans, she and Steve were a matched set—good with causes, but they didn't care much about people. She asked Steve for a month to think about writing the article, but she was sure he would just leave her and write it anyway."

"And he hurt her," my aunt sighed, no longer smiling.

Yes, he hurt her. I remembered Laura's tears for the husband she had killed.

"Do you think he would have?" Jerry asked.

"Would have what?" I said, shaken from my reverie.

"Written the article? Left her?"

"We'll never know. But Laura was so paranoid about it, so ashamed of her dyslexia, that *she* was sure he would."

"I don't think Steve would have," Wayne declared, loyal to the end.

"I hope not," I told him, turning and looking into his vulnerable eyes. "But she thought *we* knew." I turned back, facing the others. "She tried to run Wayne over, and when she failed, she came back to kill us both. And she was smart; when my aunt whisked her out of the house in disguise to avoid the reporters that day, I should have noticed how good she was. Laura had already used someone else's car to come to our house. It never occurred to me it might be a habit."

"She thought Isaac knew she killed Steve," Helen put in.

I nodded, my heart nodding in tandem with my head for Helen's loss, a loss none of us were speaking of directly.

"I'm sure Isaac didn't know," Helen whispered.

For a moment, I glimpsed Isaac's weathered face nodding, too, from behind black-rimmed glasses, but then his ghost was gone. I just wished it could have been as easy for Helen to let him go.

"Laura thought she had a month to kill Steve," Wayne took over the narrative. "She stole Kate's spare key to the Jaguar at the potluck, then waited for the group meeting and walked from the beach to where the car was parked. She wore a scarf wrapped around her hips, and a wig and dark glasses. Then she took the scarf, wrapped it around her head, and drove my car into Steve—"

"Oh, my God," Janet muttered, shaking her head.

"And now she's got some nutso defense," Felix said, jumping back into the act. "Some diddly-doo about an abusive nanny who dumped her on her friggin' head when she was a baby. Hey, dyslexia, murder, all little neurological problems—"

"Is it true?" Carl Russo asked seriously.

"No one knows but Oz, man," Felix replied.

"After she'd hit Steve, she dumped the car, dropped the scarf back around her hips, and jogged down the beach in her wig and dark glasses, looking like any other jogger," Wayne finished up. "Got in her own car, pulled off the wig and dark glasses, and drove away."

"She was very proud of her planning," I said, remembering.

"Her logic was convoluted by fear," Helen Herrick objected. "She should have been more worried about getting caught killing two men than about using a proxy for the bar."

I nodded. That logic would work for any of us. Still, were Laura's neurological wires really so crossed that her logic was different? Or was the hurt just too great to bear?

"Made sense to her," Wayne growled. "Wondered why she kept sidling up to me, hugging me all the time." His face flushed. "Steve and I were close. She was afraid Steve might have given me a clue."

"And then she tried to run you over when the hugs didn't work," Aunt Dorothy chirped. "My, she *was* confused."

"But why was it such a big deal that she didn't take the bar?" Mike Russo asked.

"Might be criminal fraud," Wayne answered. "Could have gone to jail."

"She certainly couldn't have practiced law," Garrett pointed out.

"Much less stayed in office," Ted added.

"She friggin' panicked—" Felix began.

Something clicked behind me in the yard. I spun around, irrationally expecting to see Laura Summers cocking a gun.

But the click was only the latch to the garden gate opening, and the only person coming our way was Van Eisner.

He slunk in, his eyes downcast.

"Hey, man," he muttered to Wayne. "Sorry."

Wayne shrugged, his face granite.

"I'm going into rehab," Van whispered.

Wayne's features softened into flesh again. He smiled and shook Van's hand. Someone started clapping—maybe it was Garrett—and then everyone was clapping.

"I have an announcement, too," Ted broke in, once the clapping had died down. "Thanks to Felix, I've finally found meaning in my life."

"Brother Ingenio?" I demanded.

He nodded eagerly. "Jim Morrison has . . . talked to me."

Janet stopped lecturing her kids and walked over to stand by Ted, her face proud. *Couples*, I thought. You never know.

Felix looked at me and laughed. I shut my hanging-wide-open mouth.

"How about a friggin' spiritual candidate for Summers' assembly seat?" he suggested, standing straighter.

"Brother Ingenio?" I demanded again.

"Nah, forget him," Felix shot back. "How about me?"

This time, it was Ted who started the clapping. People clapping for Felix? This worried me. I opened my mouth to object, but someone else was shouting over the clapping. It was my Aunt Dorothy.

"You're all invited to Kate and Wayne's formal wedding ceremony!" she sang out. "Will you all come?"

Now they were seriously clapping—and whooping and hollering. And I was seriously worried.

Wayne grabbed my hand and tugged.

"We have to wash our hair that day!" he roared.

Dorothy put her head back, frowned for a moment, and then grinned.

As we ran through Carl Russo's back gate to my Toyota, I could hear the clapping give way to laughter. And then I heard the clatter of high heels on the sidewalk.

"Hitch a ride?" my aunt asked flirtatiously.

Wayne and I looked at each other. He lifted his eyebrows mischievously and nodded toward the back seat. Whatever he wanted to do, it was fine with me. I winked my consent and opened the back door of the car for my aunt.

Wayne grabbed Aunt Dorothy's hand and kissed it long and passionately, then swept her up into his arms, lifting her into the air. Then he folded her into the back seat and finished up with a deep bow.

"Oh, my," my aunt breathed, goggle-eyed. My unflappable aunt was finally flapped.

Wayne and I climbed into the front seats, giggling, and I drove us all home.

FOR WHOM THE BELL PEPPER TOLLS

(With Ernest apologies to Mr. Hemingway)

Yield: Massacre for 4 . . . and final triumph.

INGREDIENTS:
1 tablespoon innocent sesame oil
2 teaspoons crushed garlic
¼ teaspoon chopped ginger
1 handful sundered fresh basil
1 bunch amputated green onions
½ cup broken red bell pepper bits
2 tablespoons suspiciously sweet maple syrup
1 tablespoon silent soy sauce
¼ cup wet sherry (or apple juice)
½ cup hewed eggplant
1 cup flayed and slashed mushrooms
½ cup hacked zucchini
1 pound dismembered, marinated tofu
1 tablespoon hot and sweet mustard

DIRECTIONS:

1. Stalk your ingredients in local markets. Carry a stun gun. You never know when veggies will get wise to you.

2. Use revolver to blow away the ends of the zucchini and eggplant, then hack them into desired state of submission.

3. Drown the mushrooms and scrub them till they hurt before slashing them to bits.

4. Place tofu in your favorite marinade. Then dismember the soy body.

5. Place unsuspecting sesame oil in frying pan, then scald. Add garlic, ginger, basil, green onions, bell pepper, maple syrup, soy sauce, and sherry. Keep the heat on until they squeak for mercy.

6. Add eggplant, mushrooms, zucchini, and tofu. They deserve it!

7. Continue cooking until the vegetables become limp.

8. Stir in the mustard, hot and sweet—the ultimate irony.

9. Serve over seething soba noodles or rice. It won't do them any good. You may now eat and celebrate your single-minded mastery.

10. Hide the remains.

---

*The preceding recipe has been added to increase the violence quotient of this book in order to meet community standards.